Still Falling for You

Still Falling for You

Nina Wynter

First published in Great Britain in 2025 by
The Book Guild Ltd
Unit E2 Airfield Business Park,
Harrison Road, Market Harborough,
Leicestershire. LE16 7UL
Tel: 0116 2792299
www.bookguild.co.uk
Email: info@bookguild.co.uk
X: @bookguild

Copyright © 2025 Nina Wynter

The right of Nina Wynter to be identified as the author of this
work has been asserted by them in accordance with the
Copyright, Design and Patents Act 1988.

All rights reserved. No part of this publication may be
reproduced, transmitted, or stored in a retrieval system, in any form or by any means,
without permission in writing from the publisher, nor be otherwise circulated in
any form of binding or cover other than that in which it is published and without
a similar condition being imposed on the subsequent purchaser.

The manufacturer's authorised representative in the EU for product safety is Authorised Rep
Compliance Ltd,
71 Lower Baggot Street, Dublin D02 P593 Ireland (www.arccompliance.com)

This work is entirely fictitious and bears no resemblance to any persons living or dead.

Typeset in 11pt Minion Pro

Printed and bound in the UK by 4edge Limited

ISBN 978 1835741 450

British Library Cataloguing in Publication Data.
A catalogue record for this book is available from the British Library.

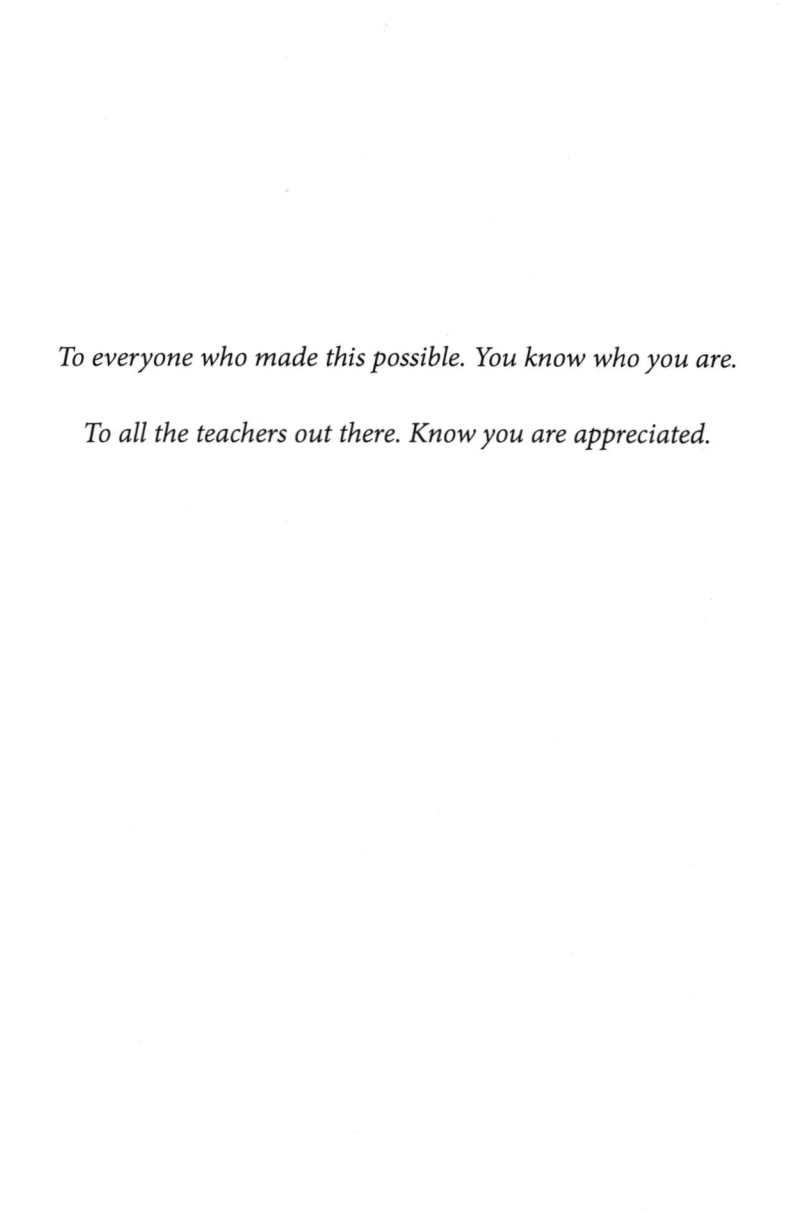

To everyone who made this possible. You know who you are.

To all the teachers out there. Know you are appreciated.

Disclaimer

Education is a dynamic sector that always evolves and, as such, it can be challenging to capture it accurately in a fictional setting. The intent of this book is not to mirror the education sector, but to create a fictional version of it. As a result, there are differences.

This book references Ofsted's single word judgments, which were removed in Autumn 2024. Despite this, Ofsted continues inspecting schools against the same standards.

While this story revolves around a newly qualified teacher and references the Early Career Teacher Framework, certain aspects of the program have been adapted for narrative purposes and may not accurately represent actual teaching programs or procedures.

1

'Always have an umbrella and a spare pair of knickers in your bag. You never know when you might need them.'

While I find the second part of my mother's advice disturbing, I wish I'd listened to the first part. My mother has always had a way of creeping into my thoughts when disaster strikes. I try to quieten her voice in my head, but like old Blu Tack, she sticks.

I keep wondering how I've got here. I don't mean King George's Academy's car park but at this junction of life.

Instead of rushing inside the grey building, I'm sitting in my old Fiat, dissecting all my past life choices, while the rain is pounding insistently against the window. The sheets of rain are so dense I can only see the blurry outlines of the imposing building. Hands clammy, I'm clutching the steering wheel in a death grip, and my breath is coming out in short puffs like I'm practising breathing techniques for labour. Finally, when I snap out of self-pity and the start of a panic attack, I check the glove compartment again to confirm what I already know and one of the reasons why I'm stuck in the car. After checking the weather forecast twice and being assured by Carol Kirkwood that there was no chance of rain, I left my umbrella at home. If the decrepit place can be called that.

Clenching my teeth, I gather my bag, scarf and the almost empty standards portfolio and tuck my DBS form in it so it doesn't get wet. I'm reconciled to the fact that there's zero chance of me staying dry.

I get out of the car and immediately my brogues fill with water because I've stepped into a puddle the size of Lake Titicaca. My shoes squelch as I rush towards the looming colossus. The neat blonde bob that I only had done yesterday is now plastered to my cheeks in the vague shape of sideburns. Hair gets in my mouth, and I try to spit it out, but it sticks to my upper lip instead. I catch a glimpse of myself in the glass panes of the entrance door and flinch in shock. All reedy and with hair in all the wrong places, I've never resembled my Uncle Anthony more than now.

The vintage yellow jumper is glued to my arms and clings to the outlines of my lanky body, making me look vacuum-packed. Professional. Bah. I missed my chance of looking professional by being late on the first day of my ECT – Early Career Teacher – year. Schools like this with a great reputation and Outstanding Ofsted rating don't let things like this slide.

Nobody would believe me if I said that the power socket I plugged my phone into to charge last night wasn't working, alongside half of the stuff in the blasted studio I've occupied for the past three weeks. But due to Aaron, my ex-boyfriend, deciding to test the new sofa with his acupuncturist, I couldn't stay another minute in our bungalow. I moved out with only two grand in my bank account while waiting for Aaron, the cheating piece of human faeces, to arrange repayment of my share. Life has been a beach.

I enter the building, sliding doors snapping behind me and immediately cutting off the storm's audio. I walk to the glass door that separates the reception from the school's corridor, but the prim-looking, middle-aged receptionist stops me before I even reach for the handle.

'I'm sorry, but the school is closed to parents and pupils.' Her left eyebrow lifts at the state of me. She doesn't look sorry but thoroughly unpleasant. She has dark and expressively judgy eyebrows for somebody whose hair is the colour of lemon sorbet.

'I'm the new teacher,' I mumble because I've lost the last scraps of courage I had on the way to that glass door. I push the standards folder in my arms up, but it immediately slides down under my elbow again.

Mrs Receptionist scans me up and down before she pauses on the thin jumper plastered to my chest. I peek down, and to my embarrassment, the green bra I'm wearing underneath is showing through. The offending underwear has turned into a beacon of light, my hardened nipples beam headlights. I should have done my laundry and opted for a safe black bra, but, apparently, a furnished studio doesn't always come with a washing machine.

I try to cross my arms, but that's impossible while carrying a folder, a bag and a wool scarf. She grimaces with distaste.

'Name?' The receptionist gazes at one of the screens of her fancy-pants dual monitor.

'Collins. Holly Collins.' I'm doing the whole James Bond thing without planning to. I barely stop myself before I say *vodka martini, shaken, not stirred* because I don't think Mrs Receptionist would appreciate my joke. I get hysterical under duress. My best friend, Lydia, would find this situation hilarious. The corner of my lip twitches, and my belly starts bubbling vinegar-mixed-with-baking-soda style. I need an outlet.

Without offering me a smile or a blink of an eye that would confirm she's human and not an evil anthropoid robot vowed to destroy all humanity, she gestures to the door. 'Our online register is currently down. Please use the staff register book on the table round the corner.' That's when she stops paying me attention.

Palms slick, I push against the glass barrier, but nothing happens, and I have a sudden urge to either cry or laugh. My lip wobbles. I've never been a crier, but who knows today? At last, she must press a button because the door beeps and I walk through to the other side.

I lean over the register and sign my name as neatly as I can while my sleeve is dripping water onto it, obscuring the names of the other staff. Once it's done, I realise I have no idea where to go, having been in the school only once for my interview.

I know where the principal's office is, but just the thought of Jane Trainer, the school principal, and her impenetrable face makes me think I'd rather volunteer for a dental extraction than ask for help when I'm already running late. When she interviewed me during the last week of the term, I couldn't stop squirming when her dark eyes behind purple-framed glasses bored into me with unusual intensity. After thirty minutes in her office, I felt like I'd undergone an X-ray scan. I was gobsmacked when she offered me the job the same day. I doubt she would appreciate me coming into her office now and dripping on her carpet.

For about half a second, I consider asking the prim receptionist, tuning into the swift, almost aggressive tapping of her fingers on the keys of her ergonomic keyboard. I think better of it.

I think longingly back to my old school, but they're the reason I'm here. After working as a teaching assistant for two years, completing my PGCE – Postgraduate Certificate of Education – while teaching full-time, all I got back was 'Sorry we can't extend your contract due to funding issues' at the end of June. Only two weeks before the end of term and before the most important milestone of my career, my ECT period. I try not to think of the possibility of not passing my ECT and having to redo the entire teaching degree. I shudder as panic zaps down my spine.

'You look lost.'

I flinch as a male voice sounds behind me.

I school my features into a neutral expression because the last thing I want is for a new colleague to witness my discomposure. When I'm ready, I turn around and gawk. I didn't expect a tall, brown-haired and exceptionally good-looking specimen of manhood standing in front of me. With my five-foot-nine height, men are usually shorter than me, but this guy is at least six feet tall. He's wearing a tight-fitting navy T-shirt and tracksuit bottoms that do fantastic things to his thigh muscles.

'Is it raining outside?' He feigns confusion. His lightly stubbled jaw spreads into a lazy grin.

'No. What makes you say that?' I quip.

He cackles appreciatively and then scans me head to toe in a very different way from the receptionist. Eyes as wide as charger plates, he ends up staring at my chest. I twist so I'm standing at an angle, and he tears his look away.

'Are you the new teacher by any chance?'

My credibility is saved. 'Yep.' I straighten up. 'Holly,' I say more firmly, my words carrying newly found confidence scraped from the almost empty barrel labelled *self-esteem*.

He extends his toned arm. 'John Fitzwilliam. The PE teacher.' His grip is firm and confident, and he's giving me a wide-toothed smile that probably causes all women to swoon or melt into a puddle. 'This way.' He points down the long corridor. 'I can see you've already met Mary, King George's efficient receptionist. She brings constant joy to this place.' I make a face, which makes him chuckle.

A little bit of warmth pours back into my body. Maybe it won't be so bad here.

'So where did you teach before?' John makes small talk as he leads me down the narrow corridor and up the stairs to the upper level.

'Nigel Longfleet Academy,' I say and strategically arrange the scarf so it hides my chest.

'I've heard of that place. Weren't they marked *requires*

improvement by Ofsted?' He scratches his chin and the muscles in his arm press against the fabric of his T-shirt.

'That was the Ofsted inspection before last. They got a *good* a few months before I left.' It's a sore spot for me because I worked hard during my teacher training year and was praised by the Ofsted inspectors only to be dismissed two months later. But I'm not going to divulge all that to a virtual stranger even though he seems nice. Aaron used to be nice to me before he was repeatedly nice to the acupuncturist on our John Lewis sofa.

'My car's broken down. What's your excuse?' he asks.

We steer left and start walking along another long corridor whose walls are covered in examples of pupils' independent writing and art projects. A number of internal windows to my right show the classrooms on the other side.

All the classrooms are spacious and light, fitted with interactive boards the size of my studio flat's wall. I could get used to that. Some of the doors have tinfoil-covered robots made out of cardboard boxes standing guard. The air smells of glue and paper, making me feel at home straight away.

John is still staring at me, and I remember he asked me a question. 'Pardon?'

'The reason why I'm late? My car broke down.'

He winks at me, and I feel a little aggravated. I don't want him to think I'm one of those constant latecomers, no pun intended.

'Road maintenance.' I check my watch nervously; we're fifteen minutes late.

We pass the inclusion team's office, and I wish we had already reached our destination, but John is strolling down the corridor like he's taking a walk in a park.

'Just wait for Alex. He'll flip his lid.' John exclaims with mirth.

My heart kicks up as it always does whenever the name is uttered despite ten years passing by.

Then the weirdest thing happens. John grips the bridge of his nose with his thumb and index finger, plasters a pained expression onto his face and then huffs with exaggeration. It makes me think of somebody I used to know, minus the huff and dramatics.

'Who's Alex?' I barely make myself say the name, mentally scanning my memory of the school's limited website currently under construction. I don't remember any Alexes there.

'Don't worry about the old fart. He always gets his knickers in a twist over something. He's just got promoted to assistant head, and now he thinks he's been elected prime minister and can boss everyone around.'

He pats my shoulder in camaraderie and somehow the gesture, despite his sexist pun, reassures me.

The tightly knotted bundle of nerves inside me eases. Alex is my age so it can't be my Alex. Not mine, I correct myself inwardly. Painful memories of Alex Bennet, my first love, flash through my mind. Alex was the first person whoever said he loved me. There's only one other person who said those words to me and I wish that person nothing but gangrene, rat torture or life entombment.

But despite the zero chance that this Alex is the same person, John's action brings back memories that heat my cheeks. Alex used to pinch his nose whenever his mum forgot to pay the internet bill, spilt a glass of milk on the floor without wiping it properly or when she left her hair-curling iron on and it burnt a patch into the towel underneath it before Alex switched it off. Alex was a fixer. He made you think that everything would be OK, even if the world was literally going to rack and ruin around you. He definitely didn't 'boss people around' and think he was important. Quite the opposite.

My mind wanders towards the happiest year of my life when I was seventeen and madly in love. But guilt and hurt chase away the warmth building in my chest and muddy the memories.

John stops in front of a classroom door, truncating my self-pitying thoughts. I pull myself together. Through the internal windows, I can see twenty-odd people sitting on child-size chairs. The desks interrupting the small pockets of people are littered with empty chocolate wrappers, half-eaten packets of biscuits and unfinished mugs of tea and coffee. They're all listening to somebody speaking in front of the whiteboard half obscured by the door.

John walks in without knocking, beaming, winking and waving like he's a celebrity on *The One Show*. I'm a ghost in his wake, a sodden shadow. The room is crowded, but I don't have any strength left to carve my way through. Thankfully, John does that for me with his big personality and wide shoulders.

He heads towards the only two empty chairs in the far-right corner of the classroom, right under the literacy working wall decorated with rainbow-coloured streamers.

I stop and start a few times as people's crossed and stretched-out legs, bags and chair legs get in my way. It feels like hours before I'm even halfway to my seat. A couple of people smile at me encouragingly, but the majority ignore me and a few even scowl as if my late arrival spoils their day. I finally slump down next to John and school my features to neutral. The back of my jumper drips onto the lino floor in the silence that has reigned over our arrival.

I look apologetically at Jane, the school principal, who's standing by the teacher's desk with a PowerPoint presentation running in the background. It says *safeguarding update* in shouty capitals and it's still on the main page. Maybe they were just starting. Good.

'Now we're all here, we can start,' Jane announces not unkindly, but there's something wary about the way she says it that makes me stiffen. For some reason, Jane's eyes flick to the opposite side of the classroom before they return to the front.

The realisation hits me like a punch in the gut. They've been waiting for us. I slouch in my chair and pull out a notebook, wishing the ground would swallow me whole and spit me out in a different dimension.

Jane discusses the day's agenda. All of us will first sit through a safeguarding update and then we will set off on our own, completing an online safeguarding training before the first tea break. Then the whole afternoon is devoted to classroom prep and another tea break. Jane even includes a teaching assistant rotation to help out with classroom displays. I'm impressed with how organised this school is.

John's knee knocks into my notebook. Looking like he's ready to take a nap, he's manspreading with one of his ankles crossed over his knee, his foot hovering dangerously close to the nearest cup on the desk. When he catches me staring, he winks at me. Not wanting to seem unapproachable, I smile despite feeling like shaking him like maracas. If he was any more laid-back, he'd be horizontal.

It happens then. I peruse the classroom to familiarise myself with all the faces in the room when I meet with a pair of the greenest eyes I've ever seen. My stomach plunges while my heart claws up my throat. The one and only Alex Bennet stares back at me from across the classroom like I'm a stranger.

He looks different. His wild red hair is short, and he's dressed in a grey suit with a waistcoat. His features are harsh and unsmiling. The temperature between us drops to Arctic in the dead of winter, but nobody else notices.

At that precise moment, Jane says, 'Alex, the floor is yours.'

But he's still staring at me like he hasn't heard her, and a few people turn their heads our way. Finally realising that people are gawking at him, he focuses on Jane and his face relaxes, resembling, a little, the Alex I knew. My chest twists.

When he passes by, a black-haired woman to John's left titters while openly assessing Alex's backside. Then she whispers something to John who leans toward her a little too eagerly.

Alex stands in front of the room with confidence, and it hits me once again. This is really happening. I've never been more grateful to have mastered the art of a poker face. But despite my best efforts, I can't stop cataloguing the changes that the last ten years have made to Alex's body. The boy's gone, and instead, there's this intimidating grown man. He's filled out around his arms and shoulders while still retaining some of his boyish leanness. He's also taller, but maybe it's the effect of the power suit and the confidence he holds himself with. Immediately, his demeanour puts me on the defensive.

'Morning, everyone. It's nice to see you back. I hope you had a restful summer and are ready for the new term. Let's get to work.' His voice is deeper, more clipped, and it makes my insides twist into figure-eight knots.

This version of Alex is alien. The eighteen-year-old Alex never spoke in front of more than three people and avoided crowded spaces. That Alex detested power suits and authoritarian figures. He's become everything my version of Alex hated.

Alex starts speaking. I vaguely catch the words *safeguarding* and *law*, but my head isn't really in it. I'm still utterly stunned, a feeling similar to local anaesthesia before minor surgery.

I watch him as he leans to retrieve a stack of handouts and passes it to a woman in the front who distributes them. A smattering of freckles shines golden across his nose and cheeks under the spotlight above the teacher's desk.

He points towards various people in the room who are directly involved with safeguarding procedures. Ellie, the SENCO and designated safeguarding lead, who is a woman in her forties and beams at everyone perhaps too enthusiastically for the start of a new academic term, her assistant Becky, and Tom, the pastoral lead, who is my dad's age and has a wild mop of greying hair.

By the time I recover, Alex wraps up the update and directs people to complete the safeguarding online training in their respective classrooms.

Most people immediately vacate their seats and a few grumble that this whole meeting was pointless, eventually trickling out of the classroom. Nothing new here. A few people hover, chatting with their colleague friends. I pretend to be gathering my things when in truth, I'm inconspicuously checking Alex out. He sits down by the computer and starts tapping on the keyboard like I'm not here at all.

'Morning, Holly.'

I find Jane towering over me. I wonder how long she's been standing there. Her brown eyes behind the purple glasses have sparks of amusement in them that I haven't seen before. I think she's trying not to laugh at the state of me.

'I see you've had a bit of a disaster this morning.' Her eyes drift to my sodden jumper. 'Sorry I didn't respond to your email.'

I emailed Jane to tell her I was going to be late due to road maintenance before I left my flat.

'I'm so sorry. I'm never late, but I guess today has been...' I trail off, but she stops me from finishing the sentence anyway.

'Don't worry about it. I know you're always punctual. Your previous school spoke highly of your commitment.' My eyebrows rise in surprise. 'Some days everything goes wrong.' She hits the proverbial nail on the head. 'Do you have anything to change into?'

'I didn't think I would be struck by a tsunami, so I didn't pack a change of clothes. I'm sure it'll dry soon.'

She shakes her head. 'That's not acceptable. Come with me and I'll find you something.' She throws a quick look Alex's way, but he doesn't even lift his head.

When we get to her office, Jane rummages through lost items and finds me a green T-shirt that fits snuggly around my torso. It's embarrassing because I'm ninety-nine per cent sure that it belonged to a child.

After, she leaves me in my new classroom and tells me

my ECT mentor will be with me shortly. Before she leaves, a puckered v appears between her neatly plucked eyebrows.

My new classroom feels empty, a clean slate. The windows running along the entire outside wall let in the morning sunshine. A solitary beam reaches my desk and sets the surface alight, a silver lining.

I get an overwhelming sense that everything is going to be OK. It'll be the new start I so desperately need and not even the unexpected appearance of Alex is going to spoil it. It's a big school and the chances of seeing Alex often are minimal.

The door swings inwards, and my ECT mentor enters the room. I train a pleasant smile on my face, but it drops immediately when I home in on a neat grey suit.

Bollocks.

2

Teenage Alex wasn't your typical bad boy. He always smelt of cigarettes, but I never saw him smoke. His clothes were always crumpled but meticulously clean. His fire-red hair was constantly messy like he never bothered to comb it, and he opted for scuffed Converse shoes with obscure band names Sharpied onto the sun-bleached fabric. To add to any mother's distress, his freckled nose was pierced with a silver ring. But he was also intelligent and funny in a sardonic way. His smile melted my insides.

Most of the girls in my year had a secret crush on him, and I wasn't an exception. My stomach always did strange twists and turns whenever he was in the same room.

I remember every Tuesday we had French followed by science together, and I always equally dreaded and looked forward to Tuesdays. I remember the day Alex spoke to me for the first time like it was yesterday.

*

The class sighs in resignation when Mr Samson strides in and announces himself as our cover teacher. Immediately, he launches into French history and soon the details of the Battle of Poitiers fill the board in chicken scratches that we're all supposed to be able to follow and record.

At some point, Mr Samson gets so consumed by Edward, the Black Prince, and his defensive manoeuvres, he doesn't notice a late straggler slipping into the classroom. My heart vaults into my throat as Alex weaves his way to the back of the class and seats himself in the only available space, which is next to me. He doesn't acknowledge me, so I carry on pretending I'm listening to the teacher.

My heart slows from a gallop to a canter when Alex starts scribbling notes into a battered notebook. When I eventually start tuning into Mr Samson's words again, it becomes clear that he really likes saying the word *Poitiers*. There's more of a chance of me becoming proficient in Cantonese by the end of the lesson than being able to write anything meaningful down sitting next to Alex, so I start tallying instead.

From the corner of my eye, I catch Alex leaning in and scanning my page. The smell of Lynx and cigarettes hits my nostrils, and I try not to lean in and inhale because that would be weird.

His whole face lights up when he whispers, 'You've missed four. When Samson covered in my maths lesson last term, he got to twenty-two. The Battle of Poitiers is his all-time jam. I reckon he's taught it at least two hundred times by now.'

'Maybe he only knows that one battle in the entire French history,' I whisper back, mock-appalled but add the missed tallies anyway. I ignore my pulse picking up again.

'Or worse. What if he's forever stuck in the Battle of Poitiers? What if the Hundred Years' War never ended for him?' Alex's tone turns haunting.

'What if Cortés never encountered cocoa?' I quip, pretending to be horrified.

'Or Kevin Systrom never co-founded Instagram?' Alex joins my game.

'There're worse things in life than Instagram never existing,' I say dryly.

'I agree. Objectively, being stuck in 1356 somewhere south of France with a raging army of French and Anglo-Gascons trying to kick each other's arse is worse.'

'You've got a good memory. I was convinced we were somewhere around the Napoleonic Wars,' I admit, and he chuckles, his nose piercing gleaming in the artificial light.

'No, I don't. I've just heard the lesson four times since last year. In fact, it's hard to push it out of my memory. I'm scarred for life.'

I can't stop the laugh that escapes my mouth, and Mr Samson gives me a warning frown. For the rest of the lesson, I pretend to note down Mr Samson's words, but secretly I keep staring at Alex.

After the lesson, we walk to the science lab, and Alex automatically sits next to me. When I open my science book, my fingers tremble, but I force myself not to react. In between the sheets, there's an unfamiliar page torn hastily from someone's notebook.

At first, I mistake it for a bookmark except the writing is alien. There are no flourishes, just bold letters with sharp angles and no-nonsense descenders burdened by loops or curls. On the page it says, *I like it when you laugh.*

*

I force a mental reboot because I don't think either of us would appreciate my reminiscing right now. While I was spaced out, Alex had crossed the room and stopped behind the safety of the closest student desk.

My entire body stiffens, and I wait for him to acknowledge he knows me, but he doesn't. He sits down smoothly, tucking his athletic legs underneath the tiny desk. He takes out a plastic wallet from a thick green folder. Before he closes it, I catch subsections filled with more wallets. Alex's level of neatness makes me itch.

'Let's start,' he finally announces. His gaze wanders in my general direction before it settles back on a form in front of him. His golden-red head lowers over the sheet; he's actively ignoring me. He carries on without any inflection, 'Just let me fill this out, and we'll start going through some of your ECT responsibilities.'

'So, you're my ECT mentor?' I think I'm in denial.

His hand stills over the form. I get why they say you could hear a pin drop when tension rises because I think I hear my stomach drop to what feels like my feet and shoot back up all the way to my throat like a puck struck by a mallet at a high striker. His pink lips purse, and a strange expression flashes across his features before it disappears.

'Is there a problem?' he asks casually like he doesn't care whether he's my mentor or not. Annoyance bubbles in my chest. I can't deal with this level of disregard from somebody who will decide my entire teaching future.

A part of me wonders if I should tell Jane there's a conflict of interest. Or lack thereof. Then, I wonder whether Jane knows we were romantically involved in the first place. I wonder whether he was forced to be my mentor. I bet he hates it.

I consider telling him that, obviously, neither of us wants this foisted on us but decide against it at the last minute.

'No. I just didn't know,' I say stupidly because I can't think of anything else to say.

'Good.' He studies my ridiculous outfit before he returns his attention to the paperwork.

I try not to watch his throat as it bobs up and down, but it's impossible because somehow over the last ten years, he's become even more attractive, and it makes me angry all over again. He looks like a sexy headmaster while my haircut makes me look like a sodden mushroom. If he wasn't behaving like a colossal arsehat, I would find it difficult to focus on anything else but the way his physicality fills the room. Instead, I want to wipe that noncommittal expression off his face or skew his tie out of line. I have an inkling it would really vex this new Alex.

'I have a few questions.'

'I expected you would,' I retort before I manage to stop myself.

He frowns but continues, 'I need to ensure that the information on the ECT portal is up to date and correct. A hard copy of your ECT details will also be filed in the admin office together with all your original induction documents and a signed copy of your contract. I hope that is agreeable,' he says flatly without looking up for my approval. 'All my feedback will go directly onto the portal where you will be able to read my comments on your progress but also have access to official reports. On top of that, we'll schedule weekly meetings where we'll set targets during your teaching experience at King George's Academy.' He says this like it's a given I will leave the school once my ECT time is done.

He takes his laptop out of his bag and fires it up. In an onslaught of monotone questions, he asks me to confirm my date of birth, teacher number and national insurance number. The entire time, his eyes are glued to the screen.

He makes a note. Even from this angle, I can see that his handwriting has changed, and the memory of his letters makes an ice cube drop into the pit of my stomach. How is he so composed and detached?

Involuntarily, I notice his bare hand and wonder whether he's married. Some men don't wear their wedding rings. Does he have any children? A lot of people my age do. My best friend Catherine has a girl of three and has been happily married for the last six years.

'The finance office asked me to confirm your address because the one on the system is different to the one you submitted with your signed contract.' Alex reads out my old address.

His golden eyebrows knit together when he looks up, waiting for me to answer.

I want to bang my head against the table. I had been about to sign the contract for the studio flat when I got the job, and that was the only available address at the time.

'I no longer live there. I submitted my new address with the contract.' My answer turns steely because something about his manner puts me on the defensive.

'Are you likely to move again?' He doesn't let the topic go and his expression turns prim. His attitude is giving me chilblains.

'Did the finance office ask you to ask me that as well?' I sit up in my chair to make myself taller, trying to communicate the message *you don't intimidate me*. Instead, I probably look like I need a wee badly.

'No,' he snaps, finally putting some emotion into his tone. When he speaks again, he sounds like he's reciting from a book. 'The school needs to know whether your permanent address is likely to change again so they know where to send your P40.' I feel a little embarrassed until he adds pettily, 'I wouldn't be asking that question if I didn't need an answer.'

I refuse to huff, but his presence brings the worst out in me. With a chilly calmness, I state, 'I don't expect my *current residence* to be changing any time soon.' I glare at him. I've had enough of his hostility. Maybe I should ask him whether he wants me to also send him what I had for breakfast and what socks I'm going to wear tomorrow so he can inform the finance office about that too.

'I see.' He scribbles again.

He asks more questions, jotting a few notes down. It doesn't escape me he subtly leans away when he passes the sheet to me to sign.

After I push the signed form back to him, I can't stop the shivers that travel down my body that have potentially something to do with the aftermath of getting soaked and spending the last ten minutes in one room with the coldest person I've ever met. Goosebumps spread up my arms, and I grit my teeth to stop them from rattling.

'You should put the air con on to warm up the room,' Alex says dismissively, giving my arms a sidelong glance.

There's no way I'm going to admit that I didn't know until this point I had an air con unit, nor the fact I don't have the vaguest idea how to operate it. He's probably dying for me to ask, but I don't give him the satisfaction.

'I'm fine.' I don't think *fine* has ever escaped my mouth this passive-aggressively. I could cut slabs of meat with that *fine*.

He nods and smoothly moves to the topic of my ECT year. 'Apart from snapshot visits, I will also formally observe you twice a term. After each term, I will write a report based on your performance and progress against teachers' standards.'

My teeth make a loud chattering sound halfway through his speech. I snap my mouth shut, but he catches it. His eyes flit towards the air con unit on the ceiling before he continues frostily, 'You are welcome to read and comment on your progress prior to the official submission. I'll take your comments into consideration.' He gives me his iciest look yet, which confirms my suspicions that there's zero chance of me taking any part in the report writing.

Worry squeezes my insides, and the truth hits me hard. Alex holds my future in his freckled, neatly manicured hands.

'You are also expected to file evidence of teachers' standards in your ECT folder. I trust you have one?'

'I have. I've collected and filed some of my evidence from last year. I was told that I can reuse some evidence as long as it doesn't amount to more than ten per cent.' I want to show Alex I'm diligent.

'I'm afraid that won't do. All evidence needs to be collected this year. The trust's policy,' he states in a tone that brooks no opposition. I'm pretty sure that that's bullshit, but I guess I'll have to play by Alex's rules now.

'Pardon?' he barks. I must have shared my thoughts out loud.

'I said not a problem.'

He tugs at his waistcoat and nods even though it's obvious he knows that's not what I said. The atmosphere between us grows chillier.

'I want to address one final point before I go,' he adds haughtily. I wait for the other shoe to drop and brace myself for the impact. You could attempt to cut the tension in the room with a person-sized machete and still not hack through it. 'I don't have to remind you that you now represent not only me but also King George's Academy. As a teacher, you are a role model. As such, tardiness or idleness is not going to be excused.'

That's the final nail in my proverbial coffin. Even Jane, who is the bloody principal, let it slide on my first day, but Alex can't. I guess we're at the point of open hostility. From now on, it's guns blazing, tripwires in corridors and sneaky laxatives in drinks.

Anyway, who uses the word *idleness* these days? Who does he think he is? Jane Austen?

'There was road maintenance,' I force through my tense lips because I'm so livid I'm beyond making up semi-believable excuses.

'How unfortunate,' he whispers under his breath, but there's no trace of emotion in his voice.

I grip the edge of the desk and accidentally bump into the coffee Jane made me in her office. The black liquid, still surprisingly hot, spills over the rim and scalds my hand. I ignore the burning pain in favour of the lava-hot anger that engulfs my insides. My mouth opens, teeth bared. The wild animal in me is ready to pounce, scratch his eyeballs out and feast on his entrails.

With satisfaction, I realise that for the first time today, Alex is anything but in control. His lips set into a thin, bloodless line. His eyes narrow with a challenge and he leans forward like he wants a front-row seat to whatever comes next.

I wait for something to spontaneously combust with the friction between us. Either I'll become a human torch or the display behind me will catch fire like a sacrifice in a satanic ritual. I open my mouth, but before any words come out, someone knocks on the door.

A moment later, Jane walks in smiling, totally oblivious to the tension in the room. Immediately, my mood cools off like a switch was flicked. Inwardly, I shake my head at myself. Had I almost told my ECT mentor to *eff off* on my first day? I can't afford to lose this job, no matter how much I can't stand Alex Bennet.

'How is our new ECT doing? I hope you don't feel overwhelmed with all this new information. I bet Alex has been thorough,' Jane says almost jovially. At the word *thorough*, I cough. After an awkward pause, I nod. She looks between me and Alex before her gaze snags on the spilt coffee.

I notice Alex's shoulders easing despite the awkwardness of the situation. Even being a complete stranger, it's obvious he trusts her. I can't quite decipher how it makes me feel as a bubble of mixed emotions lodges in my ribcage.

'Am I needed elsewhere?' His suddenly casual tone breaks the tense atmosphere with a single question like cracking the top of a crème brûlée.

'I wondered whether you could join me for coffee so we could discuss budgets.' Her smile stiffens fractionally as some wordless communication passes between them. I catch Alex's frown of confusion before his face clears.

'Of course. Budgets.' He pushes to stand. Adjusting his grey trousers, he collects his things. He checks the time on his expensive-looking watch, his attention landing on me as an afterthought. 'Make sure you test all your logins, and if there is anything you can't access, let me know. The safeguarding link should be on your staff email.'

Jane leaves the classroom, and Alex makes to follow, but at the last second, his fingers freeze on the handle. My pulse starts racing when he turns around and heads back to me. I'm certain he's about to tell me he's never going to let me pass my ECT, but to my utter astonishment, he veers right at my desk and grabs a small controller from the top of the whiteboard. He taps it a few times and hot air starts blasting out of the air con unit attached to the ceiling.

I feel too stunned to react. He passes me the controller and our hands meet for the briefest moment. A bolt of electricity shoots up my arm. His lips pucker in distaste, and my ears turn hot at his expression. Without a word, he strides out of the classroom, leaving me aggravated, embarrassed and bothered.

3

When my body unfreezes, I slump in my chair. I didn't realise how tense I was until now. I don't have time to process what has just happened because the door opens again. Apparently, it's turned into a revolving door at Currys during black Friday sales. This time it's John and the black-haired woman who sat next to us. Before the door closes behind them, they're trailed by Becky, the assistant SENCO.

'Hey, we thought you might need some cheering up after spending half an hour with Mr Boss,' John says over-familiarly, like we've known each other for years, swapped friendship bracelets and braided each other's hair.

I immediately reach the conclusion that Alex doesn't behave like he's got a massive interactive board stuck up his arse only when with me, which is almost comforting. I get the feeling he's not exactly popular here, which is in jarring contrast to the teenage Alex I knew. Despite keeping to himself in sixth form, he always managed to make the people around him like him.

'We've brought refreshments.' The black-haired woman shakes a packet of Tunnock's teacakes in the air.

'I say choose a seat,' I answer with pretended joviality, but my hands are shaking from leftover adrenaline, so I clasp them together.

Five minutes later, I learn that the black-haired woman

is called Danielle, that she's a year-four teacher and we'll be planning together with Alex.

They're a lively bunch, and they gossip about people at school, dropping names that bear no meaning to me while they're trying to explain who's who. I've never been popular at school, so this sudden influx of friendly people wanting to talk to me makes me wary and suspicious, but I choose not to look a gift horse in the mouth.

'He could occasionally stop being such a stuck-up pain-in-the-arse,' Danielle drops in between two bites of her teacake, reverting to the topic of Alex.

Not for the first time, Becky defends him weakly. 'He means well. He's just goal-oriented.'

'I think he's a robot on the inside,' Danielle says meanly. She gets crumbs everywhere, and the neat-freak person in me cringes at the mess on the desk.

'Ignore her. Becky's got a thing for Mr Boss.' John nudges Becky, and she blushes to the roots of her chestnut hair.

'I don't,' she says unconvincingly.

'You know he's taken,' Danielle interrupts.

My eyebrows furrow, and John elaborates. 'He's been hitting it off with Jane. I bet that's why he got his new role. So he can *assist* her all the time.' His eyebrows wiggle suggestively.

I feel a bit awkward with the conversation reaching an unprofessional and uncomfortable depth. I carry on listening politely because I don't know how to change the topic without looking like a hopeless killjoy.

Becky interjects, 'They're just friends.'

'Friends with benefits more like it.' John throws me a meaningful look.

'The old minx.' Turning into a nine-year-old, Danielle titters.

Jane must be in her early thirties which makes her only a few years older than Alex and I. I'd hardly call it cradle-robbing. But a knife twists in my side at the idea, nevertheless.

After they leave, I spend the entire afternoon trying to sort out my logins, scraping a disconcertingly resistant brown substance from the bottom of the teacher cupboard and completing the safeguarding training. Compared to my morning, the rest of my day is almost boring in its uneventfulness.

Six hours later, I'm sitting in a café with my best friend, still mulling over my bad luck.

'When did we stop going to the Slug & Lettuce for margaritas and start to meet in Coffee & Crayons for a spot of soft play?' Lydia truncates my thoughts. Her gaze sardonically roams around the small café, homing in on the number of snotty toddlers crawling over brightly coloured padded obstructions in a designated soft play area only two tables away. Somehow, she still manages to make *soft play* sound dirty. I refrain from telling her so because she'd take that as a compliment.

She's got a point though. I wish, not for the first time, that the tall glass filled with a frothy latte in my hand was Irish coffee. I've never been an afternoon drinker, but after the day I've had, I might reconsider.

As soon as I processed the news of Alex being my mentor, I messaged my two best friends to meet for an emergency coffee. They both responded within a minute with *on my way*.

At that precise moment, my other best friend, Catherine, arrives at our table, half dragging a sour-looking three-year-old with slightly lopsided pigtails. 'Since we found out they don't allow three-year-olds into bars,' she exclaims as a way of hello. Lydia nods in a sombre gesture that can be only interpreted as *fair enough*.

Catherine's black corkscrew curls bounce around her cheeks as she unceremoniously unhooks her multiple bags. She takes an exaggerated leap over them like they're contagious, dragging her slightly grumpy bundle of joy with her. She looks rushed off her feet, but as soon as she joins us, her expression turns into one of pure delight at being reunited with us. 'Sorry, ladies.'

She apologises in a dignified way. 'We're late because we had an emergency poop.' She pauses for effect before she finishes with, 'In the car.'

Lydia makes a face before she takes a sip from her Virgin Bloody Mary.

'Hi, Gabby.' I simper at the mini version of Catherine. Immediately, a goofy grin follows. 'I like your pigtails. I bet the piggies you've taken those tails off are really upset now.' She giggles and almost topples over to give me a sloppy kiss on the cheek. Catherine mouths *thank you* and slumps down next to me with a huff.

Then Gabby hugs Lydia, who smooches her little cheek when she thinks we're not paying attention. Lydia is hard on the surface but a big softie on the inside. Like a walnut, minus the wrinkly shell and potential of one out of three people being allergic to her.

'Off you trot, sprite.' Catherine shoos Gabby towards the soft play area and wastes no time unpacking and placing a jar of pumpkin and sweet potato puree, apple and beet pouch, banana Frube and Babybel in a line on the table like she's stacking dominoes.

Gabby rushes clumsily over a soft padding barrier with her purple boots still on. Like her mum, Gabby doesn't dawdle and joins a little boy wearing cute dinosaur overalls. She gives him a mega-watt smile and without hesitation he surrenders all his toys and gawks at her like she's invented Kinder Surprise.

'That girl has some moves.' Lydia echoes my thoughts.

I feel more depressed with every passing minute. Three-year-old Gabby only smiles at a boy and gets what she wants.

'Yep. She does that to Richard, and he gives in every single time,' Catherine complains in mock annoyance. But I know she loves her geek husband.

'So, what's the emergency?' Catherine asks after she orders a double espresso with an extra shot on the side. It must be one of those days. She scans my face with her laser eyes. Even when Catherine and I went to school together, she always sensed when something was seriously wrong. She's now staring at me with her signature worried look. She should have it trademarked; it's that good.

I brief them on the Alex situation and finish with him turning the air con on just to gain the upper hand.

'I was always convinced Alex was a wanker,' Lydia exclaims without an ounce of surprise, and her sharp eyebrows knit together as she starts scrolling on her phone.

'You've never met him,' I point out. Lydia and I met at uni, post-Alex. I was still heartbroken when Lydia took me under her wing. I introduced her to Catherine, my best friend since we were five, and we immediately hit it off and became an inseparable trio.

Lydia shrugs, her sleek brown hair falling over her shoulder, still perusing her phone. 'He was a penis to you ten years ago, Hols. He should have grovelled after what he did.'

'I split up with him, you know,' I interject, ignoring the anatomical descriptor of Alex. 'We're not in an episode of *EastEnders*. We dated. We broke up. He fancied somebody else. We stopped talking to each other. We went our separate ways. The end.'

'So, you're telling me that there are no feelings and that you're only shaken because you didn't think you would meet him ever again, and not because you still think he's seriously hot and you want to get into his pants because you didn't get a chance the first time?' She says this all in one breath.

Then, she practically rams her phone up my nose, Alex wearing a navy version of a power suit illuminating the phone screen. My stomach coils like a swarm of slippery eels, and I avert my eyes because there's a risk they will burn holes into the screen if I don't. It's nice to know the website is working again.

Lydia pretends to fan herself with a napkin. 'Is it suddenly boiling in here? Why are the biggest, most evil gits always so hot?' To my embarrassment, she starts making slinky moves in her chair while singing *Hot in Here* by Nelly. I have half a mind to remind her that she should keep it PG, but I've run out of steam.

'Except for Voldemort, I guess,' I add in a semi-pathetic attempt to distract her. Lydia makes a confused face, so I elaborate, 'Voldemort. Definitely not hot.'

'A matter of opinion.' Lydia shrugs.

'Have you told Vicky?' Concern softens Catherine's words.

Vicky and I lived on the same road when we were children. It was one of those unlikely, whirlwind friendships where Vicky was uber-popular and pretty, and I was a mousy nerd with a taste for vintage dresses that nobody understood at that time. Vicky was loud and confident and encouraged me to *take up space*, but she also never approved of Alex and had some pretty strong opinions about him. I shake my head to answer Catherine's question.

'Can he really make you fail your ECT period?' Catherine changes the topic. She's the voice of reason that finally stops Lydia's pretended fornication dance.

'If he does, you don't go down without a fight. You take him down with you,' the public relations Lydia announces.

I'm usually level-headed, so I refuse to lose my composure over this. 'I'll complain if he does. There are procedures in place for a reason. I won't let him ruin the only good thing I have going for me right now.' That wasn't so bad. It sounded almost convincing to my ears.

'Thanks. You've just dismissed our nine-year-long friendship in one sentence.' Lydia pretends to be deeply hurt, clutching her breast like she's seconds away from cardiac arrest. 'But I have to admit that your life has been a shit-tip.' She shrugs when I look at her sternly.

'What about the dog? Have you heard from him lately?' Lydia asks, referring to Aaron.

'I'm going to meet him at our bungalow on Saturday.' I wince. 'His bungalow,' I immediately correct myself.

'You're sure it's a good idea to meet him there?' Catherine glances in Gabby's direction. She has now recruited two more boys to build a tower out of foam blocks. She's got them wrapped around her tiny finger.

'We need to go through the furniture costs and agree on a repayment plan. I'm hoping that my presence will unnerve him and he'll agree to everything I want.' My statement is frosted with ice, but on the inside, I'm hurting.

'You don't have to pretend to be strong with us, Holly.' Catherine touches my elbow. 'He betrayed your trust in the most cowardly way.'

Avoiding the weight of her stare, I start fiddling with the abandoned sugar sachet on the table. Catherine always knows what to say, but I won't let myself go. I haven't cried over a guy for ten years, no matter how dire things have been, so I'm not going to start now.

I clear my throat. 'I just want to start my life again. To rewind. If I admit how hard this is and that my heart is broken, I'll fall apart,' I say matter-of-factly.

'He's broken your pride, not your heart, Hols. You just have to glue the pieces back together and do something you can be proud of,' Lydia says with a steadiness customary for my best friend.

'Next, you're going to say feel all the feels.' I laugh flatly, but my mood has slightly improved.

'I've been reading *Eat, Pray, Love*, so now I'm full of wisdom and deep proverbs, but it might potentially be the tequila I had for lunch.' Lydia shrugs again, and Catherine shakes her head but laughs.

You have to love those two.

After two more coffees and a slice of coffee and walnut cake, the sugar and caffeine finally hit my body. After spending a few hours with my best friends and discussing anything from Catherine's PhD and her immediate chapter submission deadline while trying to tame her little dragon and Lydia finally finding a good Chinese takeaway near her flat, my head is almost clear, and I feel less sorry for myself.

I'm almost composed by the time I get home. That is until the lightbulb in the shower dies unexpectedly while I'm washing myself. I end up groping in the dark while second-guessing which one of the bottles on the side is shampoo. I end up washing my hair with a body scrub, but who cares at this point?

I come out shivering and dripping wet to find that the showerhead somehow ended up spraying water onto the floor and half of the bathroom is now damp. I spend the next hour drying the disgusting, geometric lino, and when I eventually manage to peel it off to let it air, I discover another layer of much older toothpaste-blue lino decorated with five squashed spiders and a bruise-coloured stain outlining the shower corner. If I carried on uncovering the layers, I wouldn't be surprised to find a dead body or a dinosaur fossil. The seedy studio is exactly a place where I would hide a cadaver if I were a murderer.

The rest of the evening is mundane enough until I get a call from my mother.

'Darling. How did your first day go?' Her high-pitched, overly enunciated voice screeches through the receiver. I push the phone away and turn on the speaker.

'Fantastic, Mother.' I instil some cheer into my tone.

'You don't sound particularly thrilled. I didn't think that school would suit you.' After I got the post, my mother didn't waste a minute to google the hell out of the school, as Lydia would put it, and tell me that it was too prescriptive for my nature, whatever that means.

'I'm fine,' I repeat.

'Maybe you should contact your old principal and ask whether they have any vacancies.' I'm waiting for the other shoe to drop. She doesn't disappoint. 'I had a little peek at the website, and they're looking for a pastoral support assistant.'

'Mother, I'm a teacher, not a pastoral support assistant.' I try not to roll my eyes because my mother has a sixth sense for those sorts of things.

'If you say so,' she says briskly. She's on a mission. 'Anyway. This reminds me, have you spoken to Aaron?'

I don't understand how my work situation reminds her of Aaron, but I can't find the will to question it. My mother's thoughts work in mysterious ways.

'I can't sleep or eat from all the stress. I don't think I've closed an eye or had a proper bite of food since you two broke up.'

My mind is immediately transported to two weekends ago when she dozed off in an armchair after polishing a slice of Victoria sponge the size of my head. I ended up watching *Salvage Hunters* to the noise of her snoring.

'Your father and I are devastated, aren't we, George?' she continues shamelessly.

My dad grumbles noncommittally in the background. At the sound of his voice, a frown works its way onto my face, furrowing my brows.

I check the time; it's seven o'clock. He's probably annoyed with Mother because she's interrupting *Pointless*. After a prolonged pause, he eventually *yeahs*. She must have given him one of her exasperated looks.

'How did your pottery class go?' I hurriedly enquire, steering the topic from me because I know my mother lives for four things in her life.

Number one is two-for-one bargains in Haskins Garden Centre. Number two, dissecting all the life choices I've made since I was a teenager. Number three, annoying my father with rhetorical questions when he's watching the TV while simultaneously discussing number one or two. Number four, always the most rewarding because it can't be combined with any of the above and on which I'm now relying, talking about herself and her hobbies.

She takes the bait. 'Thank you for asking. The pottery class was so invigorating, makes your mind run away with it. Very mind-filling. The pottery teacher was very handsome too. Before I forget, I gave him your number.'

I wonder whether she's referring to mindfulness until her words bring me back to reality and I choke on the crisp I'm chewing.

'Your personality might clash less with an artistic type. Somebody who is a bit more fluid and understanding of your unusual taste in fashion and decor.'

I ignore her insult and zone in on her giving out my personal information to a complete stranger slash potential serial killer.

'You did what?' I squeak, sounding like Gadget Hackwrench from *Rescue Rangers*. I try not to panic and bite my lip before I swear on the phone. Despite my mother's frequent proclivities with my personal life, I've never sworn in front of my parents. Maybe it's time I started. I abandon the bag of crisps on the table.

'He was very nice. Very good teeth. Mind you, not as nice as Aaron's. You can always tell a lot about a man by their teeth.' I purse my lips together. 'Maybe you can invite Aaron over for dinner on Sunday,' she carries on without a pause.

One has to admire my mother's attention span of a mayfly. I'm so bereft of words by her constant one-eighty turns that I can't quite decide what to comment on first and whether there's any point at all. I decide to tackle one issue at a time.

'I'm not inviting my ex-boyfriend to Sunday lunch.' My patience is waning thin, and an edge is creeping into my voice.

'I still don't understand why you broke up with him. He was such a nice boy.'

I don't deem it prudent to tell my mother that Aaron is many things but definitely not *nice*. If only things were as simple as they are in my mother's world.

Something about the way she says *boy* makes me think of teenage Alex. I never invited Alex to meet my parents. After I saw Alex's cramped studio he lived in with his mum, my stuck-up, upper-middle-class family with a big house and a perfectly mown lawn, a professor dad and a stay-at-home mum, sat uncomfortably with me. I understood that my lifestyle was a privilege.

Where Alex pretended not to notice that my parents were well off, Aaron always made me feel bad for my parents' money and never understood why I didn't ask them for any.

My dad's grumbling in the background pulls me out of my thoughts. 'Leave her alone, Cassie.'

'I have to go, Mother. I'll see you on Sunday, OK?' I finish the conversation before my mother starts dissecting any more of my life failures.

'OK, darling.' She makes a disconcerting noise that sounds like she's sending me a kiss over the phone or chewing on an extremely tough sweet. I hang up before she gets a chance to go on another tirade.

Becoming every teacher's cliché, I end up drinking a big glass of red wine and scrolling through my and Aaron's pictures from last year's holiday to Italy. I have a sudden urge to print the pictures off so I can draw horns, a monobrow, a split tongue, a wart or a pig's nose on his stupid face. Instead, I end up reading through the King George's Academy's website until I land on the photo of Alex that Lydia found earlier. I study him for a long moment, his impenetrable green eyes boring into me unapologetically. I close the website as a decision crystalises in my head.

Alex belongs in the past, and I intend to keep him there.

4

The next day is much less eventful. I get to school on time and even manage to look presentable. I had put on my lucky outfit, a maroon peplum dress fastened by black buttons sweeping in a line from the neck to the shoulder. It's my power suit equivalent, my armour. I stroll into the school with my head high, coolly saying 'good morning' to Mary, the receptionist.

When John catches me in the corridor, he whistles.

'I dig your '50s secretary look.' He offers me a cookie from a paper bag he's holding, which I accept because I'm a sucker for refined sugar.

John's comment unnerves me because my fashion choices had always been a sore point between me and Aaron, who stated once that I dressed like a French schoolgirl mixed with Lolita. I was astonished he managed to come up with a literary reference of any sort because Aaron has always been a bibliophobe. As a result of our opposing opinions on fashion, he constantly treated me to overpriced black dresses that I detested and he couldn't afford.

I take a bite of the cookie, and it dissolves on my tongue like spun sugar. I must moan out loud because John chuckles. 'That good?' I nod with embarrassment. 'Oh man, I wish I still enjoyed eating crap like this.' He checks the corridor when he swears, but the school seems abandoned. 'Ever since I did a nutrition course a few years back and learnt what this does to your arteries, I can't enjoy the simple pleasures of life. Luckily, there are other pleasures to enjoy.' He winks at me, and I laugh out loud at his attempt to be seductive.

I don't take his suggestive tone personally because I'm starting to gather that that's his way of communication. Despite this, Lydia's words creep into my head. *Would it be so bad to have a quick romp with Mr PE Teacher to do a bit of unnecessary exorcism to rid you of Aaron?* I shake my head to clear the invasive thought. I'm done with men. Plus, John doesn't really do it for me.

I'm still grinning at John's goofiness when I hear a cough. In sync, we turn our heads around to witness Alex exiting his office. A deep scowl working onto his face, he nods in acknowledgement as he breezes past us. My nose registers the woody fragrance of his expensive aftershave, and all of a sudden, my heart has swelled to twice its original size and feels too big for my ribcage. How long has he been listening?

'Yikes. That was chilly even for Mr Boss.' John eyes me with uncomfortable intensity.

I swiftly change the topic. 'Whose cookies am I eating anyway?' We start walking towards the upper floor where my classroom is.

'Becky and Danielle's. Do you want to join us for a tea break at ten?'

At least someone seems to like me here.

I reluctantly make vague plans of finding them later because I was planning on holing up in the classroom, working through my lunch and not leaving until I had everything ready for next week. I wasn't planning on including any time for social interactions, tea breaks or even toilet breaks. I've learnt that one can achieve double the amount of work when equipped with finger food and thermos flasks.

By the time I'm left in peace for a few hours, I start falling into a false sense of security. That is until Alex stops by my classroom mid-morning. He even goes to the great lengths of knocking on the door before he enters, as opposed to John and Danielle who barged in without a second thought an hour ago and had left a mess of finished cups and half-empty plates of biscuits.

When Alex knocks on the door, I'm studying the last year's planning template. I lift my head as he walks in and immediately freeze.

His face is wearing a customary unapproachable expression so unlike the Alex I knew. But I promised myself to stop making connections between the person in front of me and the Alex I knew ten years ago.

I try not to study him, but it's hard not to notice the muscles forming under his crisp white shirt. He's abandoned his jacket and waistcoat today and opted for charcoal trousers and a white shirt. The outfit makes him look much younger and less severe, that is until my attention draws back to his face.

He uses that cool, we've-never-met tone that unnerved me so much yesterday. 'I trust you have had a productive day so far.' He silently judges the empty, shrivelled-up packets of biscuits.

I just incline my head because, apparently, I can't be trusted to be professional around him as a number of inappropriate and unprintable words automatically spring to my mind.

'I've already spoken to Danielle. I won't be able to join you planning because I have an emergency meeting with Jane and the board of governors this afternoon,' he stiffly informs me. A part of me feels relieved that our imminent planning session is postponed, but a minuscule part tucked at the back of my mind deflates.

I nod. I'm so proud of my polite detachment that I could pat myself on the shoulder and pin a golden rosette to my chest. I almost don't notice how his shoulder muscles press against the shirt when he folds his arms in front of him in a gesture that says he wants to say more but thinks better of it.

An errant memory of what his body felt like on top of me when we were teenagers lances through my conscious mind. Sometimes even now, I can't stop imagining what sex would have been like with him. Through rose-tinted glasses of teenagerhood, the chemistry between me and Alex was all-encompassing. We were frantic, all hands and hungry mouths. I've never felt such energy with anyone who came after Alex. I tell myself that all first physical experiences are like that. Despite trying hard not to relive the past, I'm transported to ten years ago when it all started.

*

The coach is full, except for two seats. One next to me in the front of the coach, the seat of honour for the cursed people who suffer from travel sickness like me, and the doomed seat by the toilets that is affectionately known among our classmates as the *shit seat*.

My nerves are jangling, pleading wordlessly with myself to not vomit on the coach. I don't mind a sneaky vomit in whatever services we stop at, but puking here would be social suicide. I can't even get excited about the fact that I'm going to France for the first time because of the torturous eight-hour journey ahead of us that I can't share with Vicky because she flat out refused to sit by the teachers and instead flopped down next to Jade at the back. And Catherine got a terrible bout of flu two days before the trip. At least I've got the seat next to me to myself because nobody wants to be next to a person who might decorate their outfit with projectile vomit. To save my middling reputation, I haven't eaten since yesterday's lunch and doped myself with enough motion-sickness tablets this morning that would sedate a horse. My head is drowsy and my belly won't stop growling like a starving bear cub.

I vaguely listen to Mr Browne calling out people's names and ticking them off his list as my classmates holler back. He reminds everyone to check their passports one more time because, quote, 'whoever fails to present one at the passport control, will be abandoned on the spot with no remorse and left to their devices, meaning they will have to find their way back home, be it hitchhiking or walking'. Mr Browne thinks he's funny sometimes.

The driver, Ms Serrurier, the French teacher, is setting the satnav for Paris past Calais. Everyone is strapped in and ready to go, but last minute somebody bangs on the closed door of the coach. Mr Browne remarks dryly, 'This must be your lucky day. One minute and we would have been off to France.'

'How timely of me,' a familiar voice says as a head with messy ginger waves appears on the steps of the coach. A few girls closest to me titter.

'Find yourself a space, Mr Bennet,' Mr Browne says flatly, not impressed by Alex's comment.

My body clenches as his attention lands on me, eyes unblinking. He doesn't check whether there are any more seats available and immediately swings his backpack over my head, stuffing it into the compartment above. He proceeds to seat himself next to me. Apart from a subtle nod, he doesn't acknowledge me after that. On top of worrying I'm going to purge my stomach of the last vestiges of food all over the seats, I'm now terrified of spending the next eight hours with Alex Bennet because as much as we've spent the last month swapping notes, I have no idea what to say to him.

For twenty minutes, there is deafening silence between us. I can hear Vicky, as always a little loud, retelling a story about how her mother found a condom in her underwear drawer and went ballistic. I think I see Alex roll his eyes, but maybe I've imagined it.

'Late or travel nausea?' Alex asks without preamble like he's unable to listen to any more of Vicky's far-fetched stories despite half the coach being entertained by them.

'Pardon?' I startle and knock my elbow into his abdomen. I mumble *sorry*, unnerved by his closeness. I'm a frayed rope about to snap.

'Why are you sitting in the second-worst seat in the entire coach?' He nods towards the teachers two meters away. As if to reinforce his question, Jessica starts sneaking small sips from a metal flask at the back and passing it to others. Vicky throws me a strange look, but I have no energy left to decipher it.

'Motion sickness, I'm afraid.' I shrug, narrowly avoiding his torso. Despite his wide shoulders, he's lean and boyish in shape, his pale arms in a grey T-shirt covered in golden freckles. 'But don't worry, I won't cover you in vomit. There would have to be something in my stomach, and I can tell you that it's even more barren than the Sahara at this point,' I blurt and as if planned, my belly growls loudly in proof of my statement. Alex chokes out a surprised laugh.

His laugh gives me an ounce of confidence. 'Why were you late?' I pin my gaze to his pierced nose as he speaks because it's easier than losing myself in the green abysses. The proximity to his face makes me want to kiss him, and the realisation colours my cheeks.

'I helped my mum wash her hair,' he offers simply. I wonder why his mum needed help, but I don't ask.

He rifles through the pockets of his sweatshirt resting over his long legs until he pulls out a small tin. He opens it with a pop, and the smell of fresh mint and ginger burns my nostrils. He offers me the tin that is full of neatly cut ginger slices and a handful of mint leaves.

'Helps with nausea,' he explains as he places a leaf in his mouth. When he sees the realisation on my face, he smirks. 'Don't worry. I won't cover you in vomit.'

Grinning, I stuff a ginger slice in my mouth and chew. Immediately, my eyes start streaming and my nose feels tingly.

He puts his hands up while laughing quietly. 'I didn't say it would be pleasant or pretty, but it does help. Tried and tested by *moi*.'

I take a mint leaf from the tin.

After that, the conversation flows, and we spend the next four hours chatting about everything and anything. The outside sky slowly darkens to a charcoal grey, and a few people have closed their eyes to rest and perhaps stall the starting hangover. In the last hour, Alex has leaned towards me, and eventually, we end up with our heads drawn together, our elbows and thighs resting against each other. My skin prickling at the closeness, I watch distractedly as the landscape changes on the other side of the window. Soon we pass the sign that welcomes us to Maidstone, the county town of Kent, the Garden of England.

'You know what gets me really vexed?' I whisper, ignoring the electrical current running through my skin where it touches his. I don't wait for his response. His eyes are shut, his golden lashes fluttering, but I know he's listening. 'The way signs describe towns with positive superlatives. Why don't the signs ever describe the things that aren't great or totally awful about the place, to make people's expectations a bit more realistic? Like, Bournemouth, known for mediocre deep-fried mini doughnuts and food-stealing seagulls.'

His lips quirk in the semi-dark. He joins my game. 'Poole, known for chewing-gum-laden pavements and ancient pawn shops.' His face moves even closer to mine and when he opens his eyes, they contain a spark of amusement laced with something darker.

'Exactly,' I beam at him despite the nervous energy that spreads through my limbs at the intimate nearness. Copying his move and twisting towards him fully, I add, 'Christchurch, priding itself on the loudest gaggle of swans and mobility scooter central.'

He pauses on my mouth. I have an urge to lick my lips

because they're suddenly dry, but I resist. 'Isn't a collective noun for swans a bevy?' he wonders out loud. He's so smart, it's almost annoying. 'Plus, don't forget Christchurch's county-famous traffic jams. They should be celebrated. Christchurch, known for the loudest bevy of swans and mobility scooter central, where it takes you at least an hour to get anywhere from anywhere. The distance doesn't matter. Be glad that you've reached the destination.'

We both start laughing at the same time, our hands between us tangling into a motley of fingers. He smells of laundry detergent and mint, and the combination is headier than my mother's Christmas punch. My attention is yanked to where we're entwined. He lifts one of his hands and pushes a strand of hair behind my ear, but instead of letting go, he rests his palm against my cheek, cupping my face. My breathing picks up, and I'm utterly terrified of what might or might not happen next. He focuses on something behind him for a second and when I follow his look, I see Mr Browne sleeping with his mouth open, drool covering his chin. I turn back smirking but when I catch Alex's serious expression, my smile freezes. Finally, he closes the distance between us, but just before his lips touch mine, he hovers. I realise he's waiting for my permission, and as soon as I nod, his lips cover mine.

It's soft, electrifying and dizzying at the same time. My lungs cannot get enough air in them. He glides his lips against mine in a graceful dance, and I copy his moves, unsure whether I'm doing it correctly. I'm utterly mortified that my first-ever kiss is on a coach in front of at least twenty-five unaware classmates. I slide my hand up his arm and end up clutching onto his shoulder because I have a sudden need to steady myself. When he pulls away, his pupils are wide, and he looks anything but composed. I know in that moment that I'll never forget that expression. It burns into my retinas.

*

Eventually, Alex's voice snaps me back to reality, his look very different to that day in my memory.

'Danielle will show you how to fill in the template on the system. Please refer to my email about planning expectations.' He carries on without a pause or an inflection. He's about to turn around, ready to go without any input from me, but I stop him.

'Hold on. I have some paperwork for you.' I cover the length of the classroom to reach my bag tucked in the corner in a few brisk strides. I bend to pick it up, my dress moulding around my backside tightly for the briefest of moments. As I straighten up, a throat clears loudly behind me.

Alex is rooted to the spot wearing his coldest expression yet. I cannot fathom what I've done this time to deserve that look. But when he halts on the lacquered buttons on my shoulder, I catch his lips twitching before they flatten into a firm line in what I gather is distaste. I shove the folder in his direction with perhaps too much force, but I'm past caring.

Unexpectedly, Becky walks into the classroom and almost backs right out. 'Oh, sorry, Alex. I didn't mean to interrupt,' she mumbles, and her cheeks colour deep maroon. She starts stammering, 'We've left a mess here, so I wanted to help. With the mess, that is.' Even I can tell she's got it bad. I don't understand why because even the iceberg that sank the *Titanic* seems more approachable.

To my surprise, his face morphs into something akin to affability. 'That's OK, Becky. We're done here.' A lump forms in my throat when I detect a softness in his tone I didn't know he was capable of.

He glances my way, and the fingers of his right hand start drumming rapidly on his upper thigh. The next second, he rushes out of the classroom like someone has clamped a time bomb to his ankle. Embarrassment the intensity of a flash flood washes over me.

The classroom is oddly silent after his departure. 'I've never seen him this put out before.' Becky blanches. 'Sorry. That was inappropriate and unsolicited.' I know she doesn't mean it unkindly, but something in me freezes, nevertheless.

If Becky has noticed the tension between me and Alex after being in the same room for less than a minute, how long is it going to take everyone else? The problem is that I can't even pick him up on his behaviour because technically he hasn't done anything wrong.

After helping me tidy up in awkward silence, Becky leaves me to my troubled thoughts. I try to regain my lost momentum, but I can't push Alex's face out of my mind.

I end up planning with Danielle. After a mere twenty minutes, I make a full assessment of Danielle's character and decide I'd rather have my nasal hair waxed than spend any more time with the black-haired woman. Despite her helpfulness and patience when I ask a gazillion questions about the planning document, she's a little too eager to share gossip with a virtual stranger. It doesn't matter whether they're friend or foe, if she has something on them, she'll spill it to anyone who's willing to listen.

After less than half an hour, I learn that Rob, the year three teacher, has a child with a married woman; Ellie, the SENCO, has been divorced twice; at a Christmas do, Becky got so drunk on Jägerbombs that she puked in Alison's *CELINE* bag and lied about it, and that John once went on a date with Jane. The first, second and third titbits of gossip don't cause a reaction whatsoever because I don't remember which one of the two male teaching staff is Rob or who Alison is. However, I must admit that the last comment shocks me to the bone even though I don't give Danielle the pleasure of reacting.

There's a cutting nastiness to her remarks that puts me on

edge and makes me grateful that the gossip isn't about me. I keep steering the conversation back to work, but she keeps reverting it to personal matters like we're playing a game of Swingball, the cord constantly moving up and down the post, never quite reaching the top or bottom.

We order a pizza, but it only gives her more fuel to keep trying to suck any personal information out of me. I've never been much of a sharer. I prefer to keep private things private. Some might say I have trust issues, but who doesn't? Unwillingly, my thoughts steer to my dad, Aaron and eventually Alex.

I only half-listen as Danielle happily alternates between backstabbing Becky and her – what she calls – *pathetic* obsession with Alex and instructing me on how to write steps to success to match my learning objectives in the planning document. One has to admire her multifocal mind.

After she steers the conversation forcefully towards Alex for the fifth time, I get an uncomfortable feeling she knows something is amiss between him and me and is fishing. When I don't show any interest in her gossipmongering, she gives up and goes for a direct hit.

'I've got a bit of goss that I've been dying to share and thought you might be interested in.' Despite her small frame, her ample bosom rises and falls as she inhales dramatically. I have no idea what she's going to say, but I try not to clench my jaw, my nervous tell. 'John overheard Mr Boss and Jane earlier.' Dread constricts my chest, but I force myself to stay silent.

'Apparently, John heard Jane and Alex talk about you. He made it sound like he knew you before yesterday.' Her big red lips smack loudly against each other like she's ready to eat a juicy chunk of meat.

I consider negating her statement, but then I decide that coming out with a half-truth and pretending it's not a big deal is a better tactic. 'We went to sixth form together. We weren't in the same study group so I didn't recognise him at first,' I say as breezily as I can and physically make myself shut up before I say too much. Questions multiply in Danielle's eyes like comments on Instagram Live.

Before she has a chance to ask, I dash her hopes. 'I didn't really know him that much.' I shrug in what I hope looks like a carefree dismissal. Despite my outward composure, everything inside me tenses until Danielle nods, repeating my noncommittal gesture. I don't think she bought it, but I guess I'll only have to wait to hear the gossip to see whether she did.

'Well, he seemed to remember you. When Jane asked him what he thought of you, he said you looked nothing like what you looked like back then.'

I force a laugh. Alex's rude comment is a prompt reminder he's never been what I painted him to be and that back then he'd deceived me into thinking he was a decent human being. I'm not going to make the same mistake now.

'I guess that's a good thing.' I attempt a weak joke. 'Nobody should stick with the fashion choices they made at seventeen. Even though I still stand by flared jeans and rainbow crop tops.'

'He's not very friendly towards you, is he, though?' When I don't say anything, she stops fishing. 'But that's Alex through and through.'

After that, our conversation dwindles, and the silence becomes oppressive once again. Eventually, we manage to complete planning for the whole week, but I stay long after she's gone.

From my classroom window, I see all cars but two have left the car park by half five. Both are much fancier than mine. It's good to know that I'm not the only person staying late. No matter how long I stay, I never feel I'm on top of things. I guess it comes with the territory of being a teacher.

Finally, I'm ready to leave at six. Last minute, I manage to reshuffle the desks to match my seating plan, check all stationery supplies are in place and all books are ready for Monday. My back is aching from hefting a cumbersome bookcase from one corner of the classroom to another to get some semblance of feng shui, but despite that, I feel something akin to happy.

I'm ready for my new life to start.

5

I wake up bright and early on Saturday. Despite a shattering headache caused by one glass of cheap Sauvignon, I'm surprisingly composed. I dress on autopilot, putting on a polka dot dress with a jabot collar until I remember that Aaron used to tell me he fancied me in it. I almost rip it off my body and instead put on a grey knitted dress that I bought post-Aaron. I appeal to my reasonable self and convince her that incinerating every item of clothing I ever wore around Aaron is not feasible unless I'm happy to resolve to walk around in underwear.

Before I overthink it, I grab the keys and head out. The day has turned mild, and for early September, the air is unseasonably warm and muggy. Despite that, my skin feels chilly. By the time I park on a street across from the familiar bungalow, I have full-on goosebumps.

I sit in the car for long minutes, despondently staring at the compact bungalow that once embodied everything I used to want. A distant future full of potential. A life with Aaron. A start to my teaching career. For the first time buying something with my own money without help from my parents. All destroyed by one spineless bastard.

I square my shoulders and step out of the car. Some of the tension leaves my body at the sight of only one car in the driveway. The familiar convertible Porsche sums up Aaron pretty well. It's pretentious, over-polished, and there's something littlish about it after a close perusal. Not to mention the occasional dodgy gear stick. Think what you will about that one.

An old habit has me reaching into my bag for a key that's no longer there before I stop myself and instead knock on the door. I feel I'm trespassing, and it doesn't sit well with me. I school my features just as the door creeps open, and Aaron steps out in all his five-foot-eight height. Perfectly groomed stubble and longish brown hair decorate his chiselled face in an achingly familiar way. Dressed in sweatpants and a T-shirt with sweaty circles around his armpits, I guess he's just returned from the gym. He couldn't even be bothered to clean up for our meeting. I wonder how I could have ever found him anything but *lacking*.

He looks unfazed. 'Hi, Hols.' He steps out of my way to let me in. I hate that he calls me by my nickname. He robbed himself of the privilege by repeatedly drilling his acupuncturist while we were still together.

I nod because I refuse to be petty and because the fewer words I say, the less of a chance they come out as a shout. I step into a meticulous lounge-slash-diner-slash-kitchen open-plan space. It's the complete opposite of my messy studio flat, and I try not to lose it again. Instead, I quickly scan the place, making a mental inventory of all the new items on display. There is a very distasteful, and frankly disturbing, painting of two swans, their glittering purple, pink and green necks bending towards each other and forming a heart-shaped gap. I itch to take a quick picture and send it to Lydia because she would appreciate the irony. There's only a carved wooden *home is where the heart is* sign missing to complete the cooked-up idyll. I feel like vomiting. Maybe Lydia and Catherine were right; I shouldn't have met him here.

There's an ugly hand-knitted throw that smothers the beautiful grey sofa I got as a gift from my parents. But it's the lack of my items that's disturbing, not the additions made over what seems like five minutes. All my quaint touches and potted plants are gone. Aaron used to say he liked my quirkiness when it came to home decor. That was until a year or so back when he told me he would have preferred I had a more mature taste. I'm not sure what he meant by that because a cack animal print canvas doesn't precisely shout sophisticated or mature to me.

'Tea?' he asks, but sits down straight away, expecting me to say no. No change there. He was always a goldbrick when we lived together. When I think of it now, he's the most selfish and laziest person I've ever met.

'No, thanks,' I answer sardonically.

I look around the place again. He follows my sweeping perusal, waving his hands around like he's a traffic warden taming a particularly messy gridlock. 'Eva wanted to make it cosier.'

'I've brought the copies of my bank statements and the mortgage contract.' I try not to dissect what he means by his comment, not deigning to lower myself by acknowledging the existence of that woman or the poorly disguised insult.

The next half hour is spent arguing. He thinks there's no rush to be changing the situation while I'm renting. I, on the other hand, think it's an urgent matter as I'm currently living in something akin to a large four-walled rubbish bin.

'What is the point when you don't have any intention of buying a place?' he questions without any filter or consideration. What's the most puzzling is that I can see he genuinely looks like he can't fathom any possible reason why I'd want my money back. I can't believe I ended up spending four years with this emotional troll.

'What I do or don't do is none of your business. As I no longer live here, either your acupuncturist pays me rent or you pay me back the money I've put into the bungalow. It's up to you,' I say with detachment that even impresses me. But I've always been able to keep my cool on the outside. That is unless I'm in a certain ginger-haired man's vicinity, it seems.

'We're a bit tight at the moment. Couldn't we discuss this next year when we're settled a bit more?' He glances to the corner of the room over my shoulder. I hate how 'I' has so effortlessly been replaced by 'we'. He never used 'we' when we were together. 'You can always ask your parents for money if you need to.' He lands the final blow. He knows I hated every penny my parents paid for my undergrad and that I haven't asked them for any money since. As soon as I got a job, I started paying them back. He knows it's a matter of pride; he must be desperate.

'Honestly, Aaron.' I barely make his name pass my lips without gagging. I take a deep breath and channel my inner Lydia. 'I don't care whether you're a bit tight or not. I'm entitled to my money, and I need it now. Based on my calculations, you owe me my share of the deposit and the repayments for the first ten months, which makes twenty-nine thousand three hundred and two pounds.' I can't help feeling a bit petty.

He swallows loudly and looks towards the corner of the room again. I can't help it this time and my head follows. My mind bottoms out when I realise what I'm seeing.

A modern, pink-painted crib is shoved behind the dining table. After further inspection, there are a few items that should have clued me in earlier. There are milk bottles on the kitchen counter that I previously mistook for water bottles and a few blankets with the design of pink balloons flung over the sofa. My head fills with sand. It whooshes out of my ears, clogs up my throat and makes my eyes itch. I search his familiar face, but I don't recognise the person staring back at me. His cheeks turn blotchy and then I know. Has he agreed to meet here thinking I would be more sympathetic, knowing what I know now?

It takes almost everything in me to swallow down the growing emotion and calm my trembling hands. 'I'm entitled to my money. I expect you to work it out and get back to me about how and when you repay me.'

'Are you not going to say anything?' He waves vaguely in the direction of the incriminating piece of furniture. In my head, I'm chopping the crib with an axe until only a pile of pink kindling is left.

'What do you want me to say?' My forehead puckers in genuine confusion. Does he expect me to say *congratulations* or *fuck off*? I forbid myself to give him the satisfaction of making a scene. I've never made one and I'm refusing to make one now.

He does something that I would have never expected. He snorts.

'I'm surprised you're finding this situation funny.' My foot starts tapping anxiously on the floor, and I press my palm against my knee to stop it. My entire body is hijacked by an alien force, no longer in control. There's this strange tension that vibrates through me, like electricity through a steel rod.

The sharp jaw I used to find so sexy tightens. 'Typical you. You never give me anything, do you? You're like an ice queen. That's why it would have never worked between us.' This is the last thing I expected him to say. I gawk at him for a moment. Has he always read me so wrong?

My head tilts in a 'Are you serious?' expression.

'You were never that into me. You never showed me any affection even when we were together.'

'I bought a bungalow with you. I made plans that involved the next twenty years of my life with you. Wasn't that enough for your reassurance?' I'm so stunned that my voice comes out a little high.

'You never seemed to have time for me.' Is that self-pity I detect in his tone? I feel repulsed.

'I was doing my training while working full-time.' His comment rings in my head, and I start questioning everything. Am I an ice queen? Have I been emotionally unavailable?

'Even before that, you weren't really fully committed, you've always been holding back like you were waiting for someone better to come. I always felt like I wasn't your priority. Eva makes me feel I matter and like she wants me in her life.'

I stand up abruptly and collect my stuff; I can't stay here a moment longer even though we haven't quite finished discussing the repayment of my money. I'm a coward, leaving before I make my point, but my sanity is hanging by a thread that is about to snap.

He doesn't stop me, not that I expected him to. I pause by the door, hand hovering above the handle, but I'm too raw to do anything to take back control of the narrative. I refuse to let him see me like this, so instead, I keep my last scrap of dignity and leave without glancing back.

I just about make it to the car before I lose it. When I've put my seat belt on, I hit the steering wheel so hard my hand stings. I can't seem to breathe, my ribs a tightly laced corset. I ram the key into the ignition and stall it, then try again and stall it again. That's just so typical of my life. To be done before I've even started.

My phone beeps with a text message from my mother that obliterates my murderous thoughts for a second.

Wear something nice on Sunday. That pink dress I bought you would do xx

I know that only means one thing; Mother is matchmaking.

6

I stop counting after the second packet of Hobnobs. What difference does it make whether I eat twenty or forty biscuits? In the grand scheme of things, it means fuck all.

It's four o'clock now, and I've been holed up in the flat since returning from the ghastly visit to Aaron at ten. As soon as my feet landed on the stained '80s lino, I slipped out of my dress and straight into my favourite silk pyjamas. A tent made of threadbare blankets and propped-up sofa cushions over me, Häagen-Dazs Pralines & Cream ice cream tub in one hand and Hobnobs in the other, I feel almost OK. Almost. Except there's a spring popping into my left bum cheek, but my legs have gone dead, and I don't think I can move.

My only companion is Elizabeth Bennet passionately vowing from the small fourteen-inch screen of my laptop she'd never marry Darcy even if he were the last man on earth. At some point, I call *Huzzah* so loud that a neighbour bangs on the wall to shut me up.

By five o'clock, with Anne Elliot on the screen for a change and a beige stain in the shape of the Isle of Wight on my pyjama top, I am truly turning into a recluse. I shouldn't stink so badly after only one day of being holed up, but I do. I need a shower, but that would require me to turn Netflix off and find my way out of the den, which is both unacceptable and potentially impossible at this point.

Who needs men? They're an inconvenience, a liability. I even go to the lengths of taking out two boxes of tissues to mourn all those what-ifs I could have had with Aaron, but the tears just don't come. They never do. I try to force them, but I freak out that the grimace will only make my forehead prematurely wrinkly and stop.

I'm suddenly reminded of the famous scene in *Bridget Jones* with Jamie O'Neal blaring out she doesn't want to be all by herself while Bridget is drowning herself in cheap alcohol. I refuse to be a Bridget, so I give up and text Lydia and Catherine for moral support.

After checking our WhatsApp group, I realise they've been constantly messaging me for the last three hours. The last two messages sent by Lydia say, *'What did the arsehole do?'* and *'Should I get a Russian mafia on him with specific instructions to dismember him into at least ten pieces?'* Catherine's last message is of a very different vibe. *'I hope you are OK. You are stronger than you think.'*

I ignore Vicky's message from earlier today, asking how's the new job and whether it's as boring as the old one. I don't feel like talking to her or telling her about Alex. At least not yet. For now, I leave her messages unread.

My mind keeps snagging on Aaron's words, and no matter how much ice cream I shovel in my mouth and how many Jane Austen adaptations I binge-watch, they keep playing in my head until it's unbearable. After some deliberation and retyping the message three times, I send Lydia and Catherine the undiluted view of my current state of mind.

Am I an emotionally unavailable ice queen?

They both start typing, but before I get any responses, I type another message to give them some context.

I can't even cry at the fact that Aaron's having a baby with his acupuncturist.

WTF?! Lydia replies within seconds. Three dots follow like she's typing an essay.

Unable to let it rest, I add,

I wonder how long he'd been sleeping with her before we broke up. Surely, people don't buy a crib if they are less than halfway into their pregnancy.

The notion unsettles me. I shove a mental stop sign in front of my mind to prevent it from heading in that direction, but it ignores all warnings and zebra crossings and sets straight for the busy road of destructive thoughts, ready to be bulldozered. I do the worst thing possible in this situation and open the photo gallery on my phone, flicking through pictures that I took six months ago. I land on photos of Aaron and me in Vienna. I send a particularly happy-looking selfie of the both of us at the top of the Giant Ferris Wheel to the WhatsApp group.

Lydia's message lights up my phone mere seconds later.

OK, Hols. Enough moping over someone who doesn't deserve it. I'm calling an emergency cocktail pyjama party. Get some sexy pyjamas ready for me. No Snoopy or Me to You shit this time.

Lydia calls, but I don't pick up. Instead, I reply.

I'm fine. Honestly. You're at work. I know you have an important meeting.

The meeting's done. Sod them all. They'll survive the last hour without me. I'm stopping by Tesco to stock up. Do I need to buy Hobnobs or have you restrained yourself this time?

Because she knows me so well, laughter forces itself out of my mouth as I confirm that I need a packet of Hobnobs. I've always admired Lydia's brusqueness and no-bullshit attitude. Catherine messages a moment later.

Oh, Holly. I'm so sorry. He's not worth it. I'm stuck with the sprite at home, but I'll call Richard. He's at a golf course pretending to play while what he's really doing is catching up on office gossip. I'll see what I can do. Hold on in there. Sending love.

Forty minutes later, there's a knock on the door, and when I open it, Lydia drops two massively overpacked Tesco bags on the threadbare doormat and sweeps me into an embrace that almost cracks my ribs. I lean into it and squeeze back. At the familiar smell of Lydia's Chanel perfume and coffee beans, my throat thickens. I love this woman.

Ten minutes later, she's wearing my classiest nightwear, a pair of men's soft, stripy pyjamas in green and blue, and we're mixing Bloody Marys. Not long after, we're joined by Catherine swathed in an overlarge nightdress that says *My people skills are just fine. It's my tolerance to idiots that needs work*, which is not only fitting but also brings much-needed comic relief to this gathering. For somebody so sweet, Catherine is a mama bear, and thankfully for me, I'm one of her cubs.

'I still can't believe he said all the shit he said.' Lydia spits the words. All she needs is a spark to hurl fire. 'You know none of it is true?'

I stop hacking the thick sticks of celery with a knife that should have been sharpened at least a decade ago. 'What if it is? Who doesn't cry when they lose a job, a boyfriend and a house in a single week?'

'You're strong. Isn't she, Cat?' Lydia raises her fist when she says this and Catherine nods. I vaguely wonder whether she wants me to fist-bump her, but she carries on before I make a decision. 'I've never seen you crumble, and you've had some god-awful luck in the last ten years.'

'Everybody processes grief and pain differently. Just because you're not a crier, doesn't mean that you don't feel anything. He shouldn't have judged you just because you're not like him,' Catherine chimes in. 'And thank god for that,' she adds a very un-Catherine-like comment that almost makes me smile.

'He's a selfish bastard. I can't believe he asked you to wait for him to get his shit together to pay you back *your money*.' Lydia picks up where Catherine has dropped off. Their double act is really boosting my confidence.

'He must have been really desperate to have invited me to the bungalow and to witness all the incriminating stuff. But I guess it worked because I did leave without really resolving the money situation.' I think out loud, unable to say the word *baby*.

Catherine steals a celery stick and chews it pensively. 'Or insensitive.'

'Either he's desperate for money or a reaction from you. After all, he does sound like he needs mollycoddling.' Lydia's lip curls in disgust. 'I've had enough of men who are looking for mothers instead of girlfriends.'

I nod as she passes me and Catherine a glass of the red concoction. I put a slightly anaemic-looking celery stick in mine and pretend this is one of my five a day. I take a deep gulp and make a face at the amount of vodka in my drink. 'He said I could always ask my parents for money.'

Catherine stops drinking and Lydia grabs the counter, the piece of plywood groaning under her grip.

'What a fuckwit,' Lydia swears and splashes half a bottle of Tabasco in her drink. 'Sorry, babe, but I'm going to say something I never dared to say before.' She scrunches up her face like her drink is unbearably hot, and then her lips shape in satisfaction. 'I'll never understand what you saw in that cock. The fact he needed somebody to make him feel important is so fucked up. The fact that he had to stick *his needle* into his acupuncturist to feel special is so pathetic.'

Maybe they're right. Maybe I'm not emotionally unavailable; I just bottle up my feelings in order to keep going. When I really think about it, I used to cry. Then, the day Alex and I broke up, everything changed. I didn't let myself go even though I felt like howling. I promised myself I would never ever be weak or be played for a fool. How ironic considering my status quo.

Soon all my thoughts of Aaron and Alex are obliterated with the rhythm of '90s music pumping through the studio. During our absolutely awful rendition of No Doubt's *Don't Speak,* we stop dancing and start jumping from the coffee table to the sofa and the armchair. Lydia and I end up shouting out all the words to the song while Catherine does her heavy metal head toss.

Around eleven they both head out, Catherine going home and Lydia to visit a *friend*. When the oppressive silence hits once again, I un-pause Anne Elliot. Together, we mourn our what-ifs.

7

My parents' house is a classic example of an upper-middle-class semi with a decent-sized garden. The neighbourhood is known for its great school catchment, a low crime rate and a garden centre that sells above-average custard slices and always boasts two-for-one bargains. Basically, nothing ever happens here unless you count Mrs Baxter's cat going missing every second week and the Doyle kids occasionally drawing a cock and balls with their finger on the dusty window of Mr Cox's van.

I've always been aware of how lucky I was to grow up in an area where you didn't have to dial 999 when walking around after dark. But it only occurred to me how very fortunate I was when I met Alex. His mum rented a studio flat in the East Town where streets were unkept and half of the shops were littered with uncollected bins. I always remember feeling being watched.

I could only remember a handful of times Alex invited me over to his. Most of the time, we were tucked in the recesses of a local greasy spoon, sipping the same coffee for hours, sharing a plate of chips and stealing kisses in between the aforementioned.

Thinking about those times still makes me raw. Perhaps it's because I never expected to see him again. Yet, a part of me so small it's almost non-existent always hoped to see him again and demand why things ended the way they did. In that faraway future, I always pictured myself much braver, more mature and sophisticated.

Now standing in front of the white-washed house, it reminds me of everything I hated about myself when I went out with Alex. This place used to be a haven until it wasn't. My chest feels tight, but my legs don't slow down, and my hand doesn't hesitate when it presses the bell.

The door opens, and the sight of my dolled-up mother breaks the vicious cycle of looping thoughts. She's had her blonde hair freshly permed, her stiff updo making her resemble a poodle competing at Crufts. She's wearing a floral garment that I can only describe as *a frilly-apron-dress-thing*. I'm all into vintage clothing, but my mother takes it to the next level. Today she's playing the fifties hostess. She opens the door holding a tray full of canapés that look like something that has been regurgitated by an animal and garnished with rocket and watercress to hide the sickly purple colour. There's much to be said about my mother and her obsession with micro herbs, but nobody wants to be that bored.

When she sees it's only me, her round-with-age body sags in disappointment, and the pleasant smile that embellished her face vanishes. Any minute, I'm waiting for a female voice from behind my mother's back to shout out, 'Doilies, Pam?' and my mother to respond in a clipped tone, 'Third drawer from the top, Una. Under the mini gherkins.'

Instead of greeting me with warmth and affection accustomed to other mothers, she gazes disapprovingly from my green patent shoes, past the orange corduroy skirt and fixes on the satin shirt. Her nose crinkles. 'Couldn't you have put on something more…'

I don't let her finish. 'Hello to you too, Mother.' I inject some cheer into my compliment. 'You look fantastic.' She gives me a mock, self-deprecating wave, swatting her hand like it's nothing, but it somehow ends up in her hair, plumping it absentmindedly like she's shaping a ball of candy floss. I will be doomed the day that compliments don't redirect my mother's attention.

I follow her into the kitchen, trailing in the wake of her sugary perfume. She deposits the tray of appetisers on the faux marble breakfast island with a dramatic huff and immediately checks her rose gold watch. She mumbles the word *late* and shakes her head.

I can guess that whoever is late isn't scoring well so far. I can even go as far as to guess that someone is not Carol the next-door neighbour or the old university friend of my dad's, Martin, who often frequents our Sunday lunches. No, my mother keeps a score for only one type of visitor, which means that she is matchmaking. Again. My suspicions are confirmed when I make to pick one of the strange-looking appetisers just to see her reaction and she slaps my hand with the words, 'They're not for you!' making me feel like an errant five-year-old raiding the sweets cupboard.

Her face crinkles up, her foundation creating orange lines on her forehead and under her eyes, reminding me of the leftover rind bits you get at the bottom of a marmalade jar.

'Mother,' I start and decide there's no point beating about the bush. 'Who have you invited over?'

She ruffles her hair all innocently, but her words are rushed. 'Nobody. Just a friend from my pottery class.'

'Does this friend happen to be male?' I ask in disbelief.

'Don't be sexist. Can't I have friends who are men?' Her voice is suffused with defensiveness. 'Just for your information, it's a female friend.' She starts twisting her engagement ring. I sigh. That's her guilty tell. When I count the number of plates set out on the table and encounter an extra one, my mouth opens.

Before anything comes out, she interrupts, finished with this conversation. 'Go say hello to your father and tell him the dinner is almost done. I bet he's fallen asleep in that ridiculous sun lounger of his. I should have gotten rid of that old, tatty thing years ago.' For a moment, my eyebrows draw together in confusion. I'm unsure whether she's referring to my dad or the sun lounger.

The garden is a spacious lime-green rectangle wrapped

around by perfectly manicured hedges from all sides. The space is penned up by two metal, arty-farty bird baths whose phallic shapes have always reminded me of the male anatomy and a double-apex wooden shed whose floor plan is probably bigger than my entire studio flat.

Together with the timber casement window and a mini porch, the shed looks like a micro pool house minus the pool because we're in England and the chances of swimming in a pool are somewhere between never and don't-hold-your-breath-forget-it-once-in-a lunar-eclipse never. But my dad always says that no respectable gardener would go without a decent shed. Apparently, neighbours judge other neighbours based on the size of their shed. Euphemism? Perhaps.

I pause. My throat tightens at the sight of a mop of greying hair peeking from above the infamous sun lounger.

At my approaching steps, my dad stirs and the lounger creaks. First, the sharp nose adorned with old-fashioned rimmed glasses and then the rest of my father's profile appears. The glasses and his solemn stoic look mark my dad as the scholar he is. His lined face pulls into a smile.

'The prodigal daughter returns to the nest.' He stands up with a heavy groan. Before I have a chance to say a word or decide what to do, he envelops me in a second-long hug like he's worried I'll pull away if he makes it any longer.

'Hi, Dad,' I say stiffly. 'Mother says the dinner is almost ready.' At this, he rests his hand on my shoulder, steering us towards the house.

'Let's not make her wait because otherwise she'll turn into a *roastzilla* and god knows what she'll do.'

Despite myself, amusement lifts the corners of my lips because talking about my mother's shortcomings behind her back used to be our thing. My half-grin turns grim.

To fill the awkward silence that follows, I hastily ask, 'What's all the hoo-ha about?'

'You mean the vomit-looking appetisers and the...?' He motions with his hand around his head in the vague shape of my mother's soufflé hair. But I hear the affection in his voice that has always been a mystery to me. I love my mother, but sometimes she can be hard to like.

'She found the recipe in *Good Housekeeping* magazine. They're supposed to be vol-au-vent spinoffs. I did tell her there was nothing wrong with the old-fashioned vol-au-vents, that nobody would eat purple food and that there was a reason why purple carrots didn't go down well in history. That's when she booted me out of the kitchen. I've been exposed to the elements since eleven. Don't ask me about the hair because I have no clue.'

The grinding sound of a car parking on the gravel in front of the house travels to my ears. I strain to hear the bell and then the door opening and closing. My mother's over-polished and suddenly very posh voice greets two guests. Judging by the deep quality, one of them is positively masculine. Colour me genius.

I clasp my hands in front of me in nervous anticipation. Let the show begin.

As soon as I stroll into the kitchen, I think I'm suffering double vision. Unbeknown to me, I've walked into a *Stepford Wives* revisited set. I'm greeted by an older woman dressed in cigarette trousers and a puff-sleeve blouse. Her resemblance to my mother is uncanny; she could be my mother's twin except her beehive hair is light brown and she's not wearing floral wallpaper.

I'm surprised when Penelope is followed by a tall brown-haired man with ocean-blue eyes and a perfect five o'clock shadow that one could grate Grana Padano on. Involuntarily, my insides tighten at the perfection, but otherwise, I'm unaffected. I've always preferred Domhnall Gleeson to Liam Hemsworth.

'Nickolas, this is my daughter, Holly-Anne.' My mother doesn't give up on her posh accent. Until this very moment, I didn't realise I had a middle name nor that it was hyphenated like we're in an episode of *Downton Abbey*.

'Holly,' I correct my mother and grab his strong hand. He smirks, obviously entertained.

'Nick,' he quips, and I smirk back. I think I like him. Not in an I-want-to-jump-your-bones kind of way, even though he's easy to look at.

The dinner proceeds from there onwards in a similar fashion. My dad is quiet and detached but polite as he usually is with anyone who isn't me, Mother or his limited number of university friends. Nick's mother answers all my mother's relentless questions about their house and garden like it's the pinnacle of modern life while Nick's glazed eyes follow the conversation from left to right like it's a mediocre game of tennis. I stifle a few yawns when their conversation naturally turns to curtains and how difficult it is to arrange fittings with John Lewis these days. I should have been more grateful for the topic because a moment later the conversation switches to me. Correction, my mother forcefully steers the conversation towards me.

'Nickolas, did you know that Holly-Anne is a teacher?' she asks in between two bird-like bites. One would think she's been eating air the entire time.

I slide an extra roast potato onto my plate from a green ramekin and shove it in my mouth to avoid speaking. Immediately, a foot kicks my shin, and I barely suppress a yelp. I don't think Mother is impressed with my third helping of potatoes and general lack of conversational input. But the payday is far, and my fridge is stripped bare minus skanky-looking ketchup and a three-week-old Saint Agur rind.

To make matters worse, the potato gets stuck in my throat, and I end up guzzling a glass of water in one go. I know I'm behaving like a neanderthal but better to send a clear message now and avoid embarrassment later.

'No, I didn't. What do you teach?' he asks politely.

'Primary,' I answer when I can speak but don't elaborate.

'I'm sure Nickolas would like to hear more about that. One can't really get a feel from one-word answers,' my mother adds icily, her eyes boring into me with the intensity of a nuclear reactor about to explode.

Up till now, every lunch where my mother's tried to set me up with yet another single man between twenty-five and thirty-five, I've been polite and detached. But after the week I've had, I've had enough. I barely contain the vexation I feel.

'I don't want to bore you, Nickolas.' I imitate my mother's posh voice. My father gives me a warning tap of the foot under the table that I choose to ignore. 'You spend around forty-odd hours per week at work. Who wants to talk about it in their spare time? Nobody wants to hear about a year four peeing in his chair because he couldn't be bothered to go to the toilet or two year fives sending messages to each other during a literacy lesson with a stick person who looked suspiciously like me. Except for the fact it was fishing in its overlarge nose for bogies with a speech bubble saying, "*At last, I've found ya.*" Truth be told, I was impressed that they used an adverbial of time followed by a comma despite the unconventional spelling of *you*.'

Nickolas coughs into his drink but recovers quickly, however, Nick's mother is turning distinctly appalled.

Before I have a chance to really give them a proper description of what being a teacher is like, my mother interjects resolutely. 'That's enough.' I don't know what has gotten into me. She carries on smoothly like I've never spoken. 'Before that, Holly-Anne worked at Nigel Longfleet Academy and singlehandedly improved their school's Ofsted rating from *requires improvement* to *good*,' she boasts.

'Mother,' I warn her. The rebuke comes out sterner than I meant to. 'That's not true. It was a shared effort.'

She ignores my protests. 'Instead of being grateful, they told her they no longer needed her.' She huffs on my behalf. I've never been this embarrassed.

I interrupt her before she goes on a tirade about Aaron because I wouldn't put it past her. 'What do you do for a living, Nickolas?'

'I'm glad you asked, Holly-Ann,' he responds with a similar cheer. No doubt he's having a whale of a time. If not a pod of whales. 'I'm a vet.'

He's just scored triple points in my mother's eyes. She's probably planning our kids' names and where they're going to go to college.

'Nice,' I say dumbly because I have nothing to contribute to this conversation.

'I rather like it myself.' His grin is wide. I bet I will be an anecdote at his next pub meeting with friends, but I'm at such a low point in my life, I actually don't care. However, he surprises me by adding, 'But I won't bore you about how a five-year-old Staffy once puked in my face, or an old Yorkshire Terrier pooped all over my new watch because who really wants to be having conversations about work on their day off.'

This time I can't help it and burst out laughing. His mother hisses, '*Nickolas*', but he only shrugs and grins at me.

After that, both mother hens revert to discussing home decor and the last pottery class.

I endure another half an hour of my mother's chitchat, silently grinding my teeth; at this speed, I will need a mouth guard soon. My easy-going, always-ready-to-avoid-conflict dad seems more interested in his cabbage than the conversation. I grip the fork with perhaps a little too much pressure.

Later, I help my mother load the dishwasher in the kitchen. It gives me an excuse to talk to her while our guests are drinking coffee and enjoying a slice of my mother's famous Victoria sponge that is actually bought from the local bakery. Only I know, and I've been threatened on numerous occasions that if I ever have the desire to divulge that secret in front of any guests, I might not be invited to Sunday lunches for the rest of my life.

The clinking of mugs and plates being loaded interspersed by the clock ticking loudly in the lounge as the conversation stalls are the only sounds between us.

Silently, I pass my mother a prewashed plate because, of course, she prewashes all the crockery.

'Nickolas seems nice, doesn't he?' Her look is positively dreamy. 'A vet. A steady profession. Despite your ogre ways back there, I can tell he likes you.' She puts a tablet in the dishwasher and closes it with a firm click. 'I could ask for his number if you wanted.'

The now-familiar annoyance burns down my throat like I've swallowed a whole tub of Toxic Waste sweets without chewing. 'He was feeling sorry for me.' He's probably thinking I'm a desperate woman who needs her mother to set her up like cattle at an auction. 'If you invite another man to Sunday lunch, I'll stop coming,' I threaten. Because my tone is as mild as the curry in Wetherspoons, she confuses it for disinterest.

'Don't be silly. I didn't invite him for you. Penny just happened to have a son who was visiting today.'

When I speak next, my voice comes out more of a hiss. 'You can't have it both ways. Either you're still upset over Aaron, or you want me to meet another man.' She pales, unused to this assertive version of me. That makes two of us. I inhale before she has a chance to say another word. 'I'm more than capable of finding a man myself.' She's about to dispute that. 'And I'm not looking right now.'

'It wouldn't harm you to keep your options open.' She concedes her intentions, undeterred by my flinty stare.

My dad marches stiffly into the room with a pile of dessert plates decorated with crumbs and whispers in annoyance, 'Can either of you please return to your guests? I didn't ask for this nonsense and I'm the one stuck with them in the lounge talking about cricket finals. I have no blimming clue about cricket.' His words vex me because he makes it sound like inviting all the available bachelors of Mountbatten Road was my idea and Mother only helped to orchestrate it.

I take a deep breath, about to argue, but the air whooshes out of me together with my confidence. I'm saved by my phone buzzing. When I see the number on it, my stomach clenches.

'I need to take this.' I head to the garden, grateful for the distraction.

I force a smile into my voice. 'Hey, Vick. How are you?' I'm not fooling anyone with my overdone cheer.

'Hey back at you. I'm in town for a while. I wanted to get in touch so we could catch up on all the exciting things happening in your life.' She sounds high-pitched and manicured like her persona, but I've always admired that quality about her. We've known each other since kindergarten. We grew up on the same street and were shaped by the same high-maintenance-mother upbringing. For some time during sixth form, we were joined at the hip until we were seventeen and drifted apart. We've still kept in touch, but because she travels for work a lot, we only see each other sporadically. Nevertheless, it always makes me feel like I'm seventeen again, playing at being an adult all these years.

'Not much,' I mutter reluctantly.

'How's the loser?'

'Everything is alright.' I sigh because I have yet to update her on the latest happenings with Aaron. She *oh-ohs*. My mind drifts to Alex, and I know I have to tell her about him as well. I'm reluctant because Alex has been a taboo between us for the last ten years.

'That's what you always say and then Armageddon is unleashed. Your life is a series of unfortunate events sometimes.' Despite any spite on her side, her words spear me in the chest, nevertheless. She's never minced her words and maybe that's what I've always liked about her. 'Put me on your calendar next Friday. We're going out.'

The cheek of Vicky to always expect people to drop everything and do whatever she wants. But I can't resist being pulled by the charm of her personality because, where Vicky is concerned, I'm a shrimp lured by the anglerfish's luminescent fin ray before being eaten. I can hear Catherine's disapproving tone in my head, but I shove it in a mental cupboard, lock it and throw away the key.

An unwelcome thought stops me in my tracks. 'Vick, I've had a few additional expenses this month with moving and starting a new job. Should we meet after the next payday?' I don't really want to divulge this, but I'm totally skint.

'Don't worry about that. There's a new cool bar on Christchurch Road called Loungers. I know the manager, so drinks are on me. Or rather on him,' she adds coquettishly. We make plans, chat for ten more minutes, and when I hang up, I feel better until I turn around and almost bump into Nick.

'Hey.' He thrusts his hands deep into the pockets of his dark jeans, eyes riveted to the bag resting in the crook of my arm. A bag that I retreated on my way to the garden in the hope that I'd be able to escape straight after the call. 'Ready to run?'

'A bit of an emergency,' I lie unconvincingly.

He sweeps his head in the direction of the lounge where our mothers are chatting away.

'No hard feelings. I can see what our mothers did there. She started doing it when I turned twenty-seven.' He continues. 'I have really enjoyed myself.' I give him a withering look and he laughs. 'Even you must admit that your mother and my mother's double act has been quite something.'

'I bet your favourite part was straight after the dessert. I have to admit my mother's rendition of me breaking up with my ex-boyfriend *at the ripe age of twenty-seven* was the best.'

I repeat her words with a haunting quality that makes his eyes crinkle at the edges.

'Your mother has got a bit of a dramatic streak. Has she ever tried am-dram?' he jokes, but when he sees my deadpan expression, he howls with laughter.

He passes me a napkin with his number. 'If you ever fancy going out with me and my boyfriend, give me a shout.' He winks at the word *boyfriend*, making me cough. Then he shrugs and leaves me to my musings.

8

The following week, I attempt to avoid Alex like the plague, but the universe thinks otherwise. I see Alex everywhere I turn; it's relentless. I see him rounding the bend when I'm leaving my classroom. I back into the learning mentor office before he spots me only to find out that he was heading to that exact office. I bump into him in the staffroom reheating soup. We exchange a few painfully awkward words before I make a hasty retreat. By Thursday, my nerves are so frayed I decide to hole up in my classroom during lunches because there's no respite from Alex. It seems like cosmic coincidence is trying to catch up on all those years of long time no see.

It doesn't help that Alex is a Duracell Bunny with endless reserves of energy and rarely takes a break. He's monitoring the corridors, covering break duties and supervising the lunch hall. By Friday, I'm jumping out of my skin at the mere sight of a grey suit. There's no surprise that when the first week is over, I'm ready to meet Vicky, get a few cocktails in me and unburden myself.

When I arrive at the agreed bar, Loungers has Vicky written all over. It's not exactly disappointing but very par for the course. The walls are lined with exposed copper piping that gives the spacious place a deep bronze hue, and the air smells of craft beer and perfume. The barmen's lips are adorned with a range of flashy moustaches and impressive beards, and they're all clad in variations of lumberjack shirts, leather belts and boots that are probably vegan. The clientele is somewhere between twenty-five and thirty with a mixture of trendy trainers, silk dresses and tucked-in shirts. All of the above makes me feel totally out of place. I've always been more of a vintage tearoom, country pub or nostalgia bar kind of person. Small places with old, quirky details.

I don't spot Vicky immediately because she's a chameleon, able to assimilate to all environments like the Royal Marines. I've always thought she's wasted in hospitality. She was the same at school. She went out with the right crowd and was always a bit too loud and self-assured, but being with Vicky felt empowering, especially for an introverted person like myself. It still feels good. In return, Vicky revels in the retellings of my misadventures. It's a symbiosis of sorts; I'm the clownfish to her sea anemone.

Finally, I spot her sitting by the bar on one of the repurposed cracked-leather bar stools that I know will be painfully uncomfortable. She's chatting up one of the strawberry blond specimens of the bar workforce, probably the bar manager himself. Enviously, I notice that her slinky black dress makes her into a sexy business associate. Like the fashionista she is, she's paired it with funky red-and-blue Nike shoes. Her silver blonde hair is shaped in loose waves, and her flawless make-up looks so natural she appears she's not wearing any. God, one has to love and hate Vicky in equal measure. Despite the conflicting emotions, a spike of excitement warms my insides at seeing her.

For the shortest of moments, I'm transported to sixth form, but I shake my head before any uncomfortable memories resurface and sour my mood. I force a pleasant expression onto my face, I've always been good at those. I try to push away the guilt that has budded in my stomach at feeling resentful when Vicky has been nothing but a good friend to me.

When she swivels on her stool towards me, her face splits into a wide grin, looking all dazzling like a falling star. I return a slightly damper smile, inconspicuously checking the high-waisted black skirt and white blouse with mother-of-pearl buttons I put on for the occasion. I realise too late that my outfit is screaming *librarian*. I almost touch the purple lipstick I dabbed onto my lips last minute before leaving to check it's still there, but no matter what, I feel inadequate.

'How is my favourite primary teacher?' she starts, and all the bad thoughts evaporate. I almost simper despite being twenty-seven.

'Not bad.' I downplay it as always. I mumble a hello to the broad-shouldered barman who winks at me with his grey eyes framed by expressive coppery eyebrows and leaves us to our conversation. I try to ignore the fact that he's totally my type. Then, I push the memory of another ginger man in my life deep into the recesses of my brain.

She immediately reads my expression. 'You're such a liar, Holly. But never mind, if you don't want to share your drama, I'll share mine. I've got tonnes to tell you because so much has happened since the last time I saw you.'

Before I even have a chance to order myself a drink, she launches into an elaborate retelling of the last three months of her life like it's an episode of *Dynasty*. Her story is full of glamorous places and even more glamorous people. My life seems a little lacklustre next to hers. The truth is, I used to love my contained life because I was never one to enjoy being in the spotlight anyway. I always used to love listening to Vicky and her wild stories.

The hot bar manager, whose name is Dave, treats us to two cosmopolitans and occasionally joins us for a minute or two to chat while very conspicuously ogling my limited cleavage. I'm starting to think that I'm a magnet for idiots.

The stool's back support digs into my lower back, but I

don't say anything because Vicky is in her element by the bar where she can freely flirt with whichever barman serves us the next drink. Their reactions are fairly predictable, flirting back, frequently ogling our way and some even offering us more free drinks which she doesn't refuse. They'll be disappointed to find out at the end of the evening that she has zero intention of furthering their acquaintance. It's sort of fascinating to watch. Vicky's world has always been a great window into the unimaginable. She talks about her job as a quality assurance manager for Mercury Hotels, and the places she's been, but eventually our conversation comes to a natural pause.

She sips her fourth cosmopolitan while I'm on my second. The alcohol creeps into my head, opening doors that should stay closed. My belly is warm and tingly.

'I've blathered on for ages. It's your turn. What's happening in the world of Holly?' She's clever because her stories and booze have softened me up.

'I went to see Aaron.' I'm very succinct with my recount compared to her flamboyant descriptions. Reluctantly, I tell her about his further treachery at which she swears like an old sailor and shows more anger than I have since I've learnt the truth. I find it somehow soothing.

I shrug when she calls him *a spineless slug of the human variety* for the third time. I don't tell her that using the word *spineless* is a little obsolete as slugs are shell-less terrestrial gastropod molluscs and don't have spines because she's gotten right into it and there's no slowing her down.

'In a sense, he did me a favour.' I force the words through my tight lips. Deep down, I know it's true because it's obvious from his actions he's never really understood me or cared for me enough to have the decency to split up with me before he started sleeping with another woman.

'How's your mother taking it now her favourite golden boy turned into a nasty douchebag?' I squeeze my eyes shut for a moment. 'You still haven't told her, have you?' Her voice drips with disbelief.

I shrug dismissively. 'You know how she gets, Vick. She doesn't know the meaning of the word *private*. It would be passed on at her weekly book club meetings, pottery classes and no doubt Friday dinners at Bentley's like it was some meaningless anecdote.'

Vicky's mother, Jane, and mine are practically inseparable. When I don't get updates on Vicky's life from Vicky herself, I get them from my mother.

'True. Sometimes, it's better to avoid poking the bear,' she agrees.

'The only problem is she's now reverted to the pre-Aaron matchmaking phase.' I show her Nick's number on my phone. I don't know why I saved it. Instead of looking exasperated to match how I'm feeling, she cracks up.

'She did not,' she bursts out, gulping her cosmopolitan.

'I guess next time she should check whether the person she's setting me up with is interested in women and single.' Vicky splutters her drink all over the bar. 'I did, however, get an invitation to dinner with Nick and his boyfriend,' I say as a punchline and can't stop the cackle that comes out of my mouth. I'm reminded of the other set of news that I need to share, and my face pulls into a serious expression. I brace myself. There's no time like now.

'It gets worse,' I say in between two sips.

She abandons her drink on the side when she senses the sudden change of atmosphere.

'Guess who's my mentor at the new school?' Her eyes get that faraway look of somebody who's thinking of the most unthinkable options, sifting through them and trying to decide which one is the most unlikely. With a nod, I silently encourage her to dig deeper, but she comes up blank and shakes her head in defeat.

'Alex Bennet.' My words are a rasp, and the sharp sting of pain in my chest that follows takes me by surprise. She necks the rest of her drink.

'Fuck me. What's he like?'

'A total penis,' I respond. I startle at how much I sound like Lydia at that moment.

'That guy never deserved you.' She echoes her words of years back. She was never keen on Alex when I was going out with him. My mind returns to a memory of ten years ago.

*

The party at Aiden's house is in full swing when Alex and I arrive. A few people greet Alex as soon as he walks through the door, but he sticks to me like glue, and I'm grateful for it because parties have always made me uncomfortable.

Barely visible through the crowds of people I only vaguely remember from school, Vicky is dancing on the makeshift dancefloor in the lounge. She's wearing one of her short sequined dresses, and it's tight as a snakeskin on her, exposing her tanned legs strapped into high-heeled sandals. She's glamorous, and involuntarily I scan my Audrey Hepburn-esque green dress, unable to suppress disappointment.

Alex looks in her direction and his face turns unreadable. It's been only two weeks since France where we hung out every day of the trip, ate a lot of croissants together, drank litres of black coffee and even exchanged a few chaste kisses, but when he's like this, I find him difficult to understand. Is he embarrassed by me? Has he changed his mind?

As soon as Vicky spots us, she waves exaggeratedly and makes her way towards us.

'I'll get us some lemonade and lime,' Alex mumbles into my ear and disappears before Vicky gets to us. I'm a little pleased that he remembers my favourite drink but feel mixed emotions at his vanishing act. He's been doing that a lot whenever Vicky's around, probably sensing Vicky doesn't exactly approve of him.

'Do my eyes deceive me or have you arrived with the one and only Alex Bennet?' I can smell booze wafting off her. I shrug dumbly, nervous all of a sudden. 'What's up?' She senses my mood.

When I don't say anything, she tugs me to follow her down to the toilet and locks the door behind us before I can protest.

'Spill it.'

The confined space and Vicky's insistence have me pouring out all my insecurities, ending with how he hasn't kissed me since Paris. When I finish, she laughs. Vicky's never been the emotional type so I didn't expect her to be passing me tissues to cry into, but her blatant dismissal stings.

'That's weird.' She gets a little distracted halfway through with her reflection in the mirror and starts smoothing her hair with her hand. 'All the guys our age want to do is snog and you know.' Giggling, she meaningfully raises her eyebrows.

Noticing my reaction, she shifts her weight from one foot to the other. 'I'm sorry, Holly. Maybe he's not that into you. Don't waste your time with somebody who isn't a hundred per cent in it. You could do so much better than him.' At her words, I want to laugh. Alex is it. I know it. I've never felt like that about anyone, and if he doesn't want me the way I want him, it will crush me.

'Any advice?' I feel faint, but I wait patiently for her guidance.

'Play difficult to get so he tastes his own medicine. Guys like that. If he doesn't take the bait, sod him.'

I don't argue with her logic, but I've never been up for playing games.

After that, Vicky carries on partying, and I get a little lost in the crowd. Twenty minutes later, I'm ready to leave because Alex has disappeared to god-knows-where. I feel utterly stupid and pathetic. I'm ready to call Catherine and pour my heart out. She'd let me cry on the phone and listen to all my worries without a complaint.

Unshed tears brimming in my eyes, I head for the door only to be stopped by a dishevelled-looking Alex. His golden hair is mussed like he's run his hand through it numerous times in frustration or like somebody's hand combed through it in passion. I wince at the thought. His expression stops me in my tracks; he looks almost worried.

'There you are. I've been trying to find you.' His words come out gruff.

I think of Vicky's words, but if Alex doesn't like me, I'd rather know now.

'It's OK if you want to just…' I vaguely gesture towards the crowd, encouraging him to do whatever he's been doing the last twenty minutes.

'What?' His expression is startled. 'I came with you because I want to be with you. I don't really care for parties, to be honest. I just thought you wanted to go.' He's playing with the button on his shirt, and Catherine's words resurface in my head. Maybe he's shy. People don't ever think that guys can be shy.

My heart pounds as I grab hold of his sleeve, drag us to the utility room and close the door safely behind us. The music immediately seems miles away. Because there's nobody around us, I feel almost brave. 'Why haven't you kissed me since France?' It comes out a bit breathless because his face is only a few inches away from mine. We're the same height, and I like him like that. It's like we fit, like we're made for each other.

Instead of answering, he grabs me by the waist and presses his lips to mine with unexpected eagerness. It's not the gentle exploring of each other's lips like the last time; this kiss sends heat pooling to the pit of my stomach. My lips part and soon our tongues are touching and it's beyond description. I can't help exploring his body through the thin fabric of his T-shirt, my fingers tracing his back, his sides and his long arms.

He leans into me, and I can feel every part of his body against mine. Where he is lean and solid, I am soft. It's perfect. He lets his hands travel down my waist to my bum, squeezing and pushing me against him. A strange breathy moan comes out of my mouth that I'm vaguely embarrassed by. At the sound of that noise, Alex growls. I think he likes that.

Eventually, we slow down, and when we pull apart, I feel bereft. His eyes are anything but unreadable, and what I see in them makes my cheeks flush.

'Should we get out of here?' His voice comes out hoarse.

Later when we sit in a small square nearby, sharing fish and chips, Alex is looking contemplative and torn.

'I feel I should get some things straight.' He rubs his hands against his jeans.

I stop eating, my knee starts bouncing nervously.

'All I have thought about in the last year is you. I have dreamed of kissing you every day since the trip and even before that if I'm being honest.' He rubs his face like he's mortified. 'I just thought...' He trails off.

'Thought what?' I hang onto his every word.

'That you weren't that interested in me.' He looks sheepish. 'You looked so uncaring when I found you at the party. Then I got a phone call from my mum. She was drunk on the phone asking me whether I knew where her car keys were, and I got worried because why would you want to hang out with somebody like me.' He pauses for a breath. I've never seen this vulnerable side of Alex, and I think I'm in love with him. He carries on, 'You haven't been very easy to read.' At that, I laugh. Hurt crosses his features.

I nudge my knee against his. 'I feel the same way about you. I can't think of anything but you. You're impossible to read. And I wasn't uncaring, I was upset. Over you.' A crease of confusion forms between his eyebrows. 'I get really nervous and tongue-tied around you and you've seemed very cold since France.'

'I was convinced you got bored of me after the trip. How should I have known you were nervous? You weren't in the coach,' he says, and I can hear the doubts in his voice.

'I took like six motion-sickness tablets on an empty stomach. I was out of it. I was surprised I strung two sentences together.'

He laughs at that.

'So, to make it clear,' he starts as he grabs my hand resting between us. I squeeze it. He tilts his head and looks at me through the strands of golden hair. 'You like me? Because I like you. Like a lot.'

'I went to a party because of you, and I hate parties. Doesn't that say it all?'

He leans forward, almost closing the distance between us. 'Say it,' he dares me.

'I like you. Like a lot.' I echo his words and warmth spreads through my belly.

*

Vicky eyes me sorrowfully. 'He has always been a dick, but you just didn't know that until the very end.' She grabs my hand resting on the bar, only releasing me when I nod. 'Don't waste your time on him. Don't talk to him. Just do your bit.'

I know she's right but for the first time in years, I feel I need closure. Whatever that means.

'Look, Holly,' she starts again, 'I know you have this guilt over what happened ten years ago, but you shouldn't. He's the one to be blamed.' She dredges up feelings that have been buried for the last ten years. I'd rather they stayed that way, but of course, they can't.

'I did some things that I'm not proud of.' I shift uncomfortably in my seat.

'Yes, but only because he made you do them,' she speaks louder this time.

I nod again because there's nothing she could say that would make me feel better about my part in what happened ten years ago. Shame is a messy and complicated thing; it doesn't take excuses or justifications. Unable to fight it, I chase it away with my drink, tipping it in like it's water.

9

The conversation with Vicky plays on my mind for the next couple of weeks. On Tuesday, I wake up on the wrong side of the bed, everything out of sync. It starts with my dreams being tormented by nightmares where a seventeen-year-old Alex hovers in the shadows like a ghost from an eighties movie and tells me in a ghoulish voice that I will forever stay alone. Halfway through the dream, he transforms into Aaron chewing on a mint leaf right in my face and laughing.

The dark thoughts continue following me around the cramped flat as I rush to get my lunch ready for school. They trail my awakened consciousness when I sluggishly dodge through the early Tuesday traffic and when I park at the empty school car park, save for one car, a fancy Mercedes.

I wonder how other teachers ever meet deadlines without putting the hours in. I always feel I'm the first one in, right after the caretaker opens the gates, and the last one out, right before the caretaker kicks me out and locks the gates. The caretaker and I are on a first-name basis by now. On a few occasions, I've tried to bribe him with a Twix so he'll close the school later, but he's a tough cookie and has so far resisted my offer.

When I lock the car, the sky is rumbling ominously above my head, making me hurry. I ignore the Mercedes parked in the corner because it's the same Mercedes I've seen almost every morning and evening. I haven't figured out whose car it is yet, but whoever is doing long shifts alongside me likes their car immaculate.

Despite the early autumnal showers, it's always spotless both on the inside and outside. It's the level of neatness that makes your hand holding the car keys itch. Not that I would ever do anything. There's only one person I've ever considered keying their car, but it's not worth the offence. Plus, scratching *dick* onto Aaron's bonnet would take too much time, and I can't think of any other words that would contain less than four letters and describe Aaron's character so succinctly.

I yawn as I put the code in. The door clicks hollowly, allowing me in without resistance. The inside of the school is cold, and I huddle in the butterscotch-yellow wrap cardigan I put on this morning. I thought it was a bold fashion choice when I bought it. I categorically disagreed with Lydia when she said I looked like a cute bumblebee in it.

I'm a circus juggler, balancing haphazardly stacked pupils' independent writing books, a lunchbox and coffee in a bamboo cup in my arms. I push through the main set of doors with my elbow, but I come into contact with something solid that makes me lose half the items I'm carrying.

My lunchbox splits open and the contents, an unappetising combination of grains and seeds with some green and red leaves, scatter across the carpeted floor. A solitary boiled potato rolls pathetically between my feet and lands next to a laptop bag that belongs to the person I so brashly ran into. Even I have to admit that my lunch, now laid out like a post-modern art installation, isn't fit for human consumption and rather looks like it was intended for rabbits.

I'm about to apologise, but a set of incredibly green eyes staring back at me stop me in my tracks.

When I unfreeze, Alex says, 'I'm sorry. I didn't see you,' as I mumble, 'Sorry. I'm never this clumsy.'

We both stop at the same time, gazes falling to his grey tie and white shirt, now decorated with Rorschach-shaped coffee stains. At first glance, it looks like somebody defecated on his shirt and the ridiculousness of the situation makes me burst out laughing before I can stop myself. This can't get any worse. I clamp a hand over my lips. I wait for him to shout at me like any reasonable adult would do in this situation, but he's only gaping at the growing stain in horror.

I remark embarrassedly, 'I've made a dog's dinner of your shirt.' To my surprise, his lips twitch before his expression reverts to the usual iciness.

I pull out a tissue from my pocket to wipe the worst of the mess off his tie, but the tissue has a pea stuck to it. I stare at it with alarm, unsure whether to cry or scream. A hoarse bark comes out of him and eradicates all my thoughts. He tries to hide it with a cough, but it's too late.

I don't know what possesses me, but I abandon all my stuff by the sign-in table and before I think it through, grab him by the tie. 'I remember reading that if you pour cold water through the back of the stain, it should remove it.'

He's so stunned that he lets himself be dragged to the disabled toilet right behind the reception.

As soon as we're inside, the automatic light floods Alex's startled face in cool white, making his freckles stand out. I forgot how small the toilet was and now standing here with somebody who looks like they hit the gym at least twice before breakfast makes the confined space crowded. We have no choice but to stand so close there's barely any space between us. The whole space smells of cheap coffee, the clean smell of laundry detergent and the now familiar woody fragrance of Alex's aftershave.

I think my mind must be working on autopilot because my hands immediately start loosening the tie around his neck and pulling it over his head. For a few painful moments, our faces are a few centimetres from each other.

'The faster we get it under running water, the more of a chance it won't stain,' I reason.

As soon as the tie is off, I abandon it in the sink under the running tap. I spin around, ready to start unbuttoning his shirt, but he pushes my hands away and shakes his head vehemently. His skin is hot to the touch and my fingertips feel singed.

'I'm capable of taking off my own shirt,' he snaps.

'I never said you weren't,' I retort before I can stop myself.

'I can't believe I've let you drag me here,' he mutters to himself, and I have to agree with him on that one.

He makes quick work of his shirt and then he's naked to the waist in a space smaller than a room in a capsule hotel in Tokyo. My tongue swells to the size of a common garden slug, and my pulse skyrockets because under the shirt Alex is solid muscle, a fascinating combination of golden freckles and pale skin. His shoulders are wide despite his slim frame. When I spot his pink nipples puckering in the cold, I can't take any more.

His eyes train on the wall. Surely, he's not embarrassed. The Alex I knew was a little on the self-aware side, but this twenty-seven-year-old man is a solid lump of muscle and an assistant head, and as such, he should strut around topless while giving people orders all the time. I shut off my distracting and unhelpful thoughts at once.

Busying myself, I run the inside-out shirt under the tap. The sleeves of my cardigan get soaked so I dispose of it on the radiator. I notice Alex eyeing my black dress, his gaze trailing down to the bow that embellishes the lower back. His nostrils flare for a moment in an emotion I can't decipher.

I redirect my attention fully to the sink. When the stain starts disappearing, I *yippee* in victory and immediately regret the sound. Momentary relief fills Alex's face before it blanches.

Bollocks, I curse inwardly. I hastily seize the tap to turn the water off, but the damage is done.

'Your shirt...' I can't find the words, but he finishes in my stead.

'...is pink. Why is my shirt pink?' His voice climbs an octave higher.

I rummage through the pockets of the garment and find the culprit. A pink mini highlighter.

'You can't say I haven't tried.' Trying not to think about how ridiculous this situation is, I force solemnity into my statement.

There's a tense moment in which neither of us speaks. Then Alex doubles over and starts laughing. His reaction sets me off and soon big tears run down my cheeks. I end up getting a stitch in my side and have to squeeze it.

'I guess I'll have to ask Jane whether we have any more PE kits in the lost and found box,' he announces in a serious tone when he manages to compose himself, but amusement lingers on his face. What an insolent bastard to be making fun of my first-day outfit.

I flush with self-consciousness but feel amused despite myself because I can't not see the humour in this. I should hate him, but my feelings are jumbled, my chest a pressure cooker full of conflicting emotions.

'If I were you, I'd ask for a Tudor House T-shirt. It would bring out the green in your eyes, and it will go really well with your tie-dye tie.' I pick up his soaking, brown-stained tie.

He's positively smirking.

He lifts his hand, but I never know what he intended to do because he halts mid-move. His voice dips. 'You've always been so clumsy. I can see that hasn't changed.'

I go still, feeling rattled by his words. The spark I felt a minute ago is gone, replaced by self-loathing and resentment that thump me right in the diaphragm, leaving me winded.

His face shuts down as soon as he realises what he's said. The atmosphere between us turns frigid. I start collecting my things, and I'm about to go when I catch voices outside the reception. Everything tenses inside me once more; this is bad.

'*Ew.* Mind the shit on the floor,' John says to somebody on the other side of the door.

Alex puts his index finger over my lips. Immediately, they start to tingle, and I swallow hard at the sudden intimacy. Seeing my reaction, he takes a hasty step back, and his gaze drops to the floor like I'm a repugnant toad and he's in need of washing the finger before it grows warts. I can't stop myself from clenching my fists in response.

Unaware of my inner monologue, he locks the door behind him with a silent click and waits. How come he's not panicking?

'There's someone's laptop here.' Danielle, the worst person possible to witness my downfall, is present and accounted for. Great. 'And somebody dropped their lunch on the carpet. Yikes.'

'I wouldn't call that a lunch,' John says with a sneer. I don't think I've ever heard him use such a condescending tone. 'It looks like regurgitated animal feed to me.'

'You're a PE teacher. Don't you mostly eat regurgitated animal feed?' she jabs and then adds maliciously, 'I bet it was that *Holly person*. She seems like the clumsy type.'

That Holly person? Did she really say that? Alex gives the door a death glare, ready to slaughter somebody.

'Don't be like that. Holly's nice.' John defends me, and warmth flickers in my chest. Alex's face darkens, if it were even possible.

Danielle snorts, and I hear her moving towards the corridor leading to the classrooms. 'You're only being nice because you want to bend her over a desk, don't you?'

I'm so shocked by her crude words that for a moment I think I must have imagined them.

Either John is not aware of what a gossip Danielle is, or he doesn't give a damn because he responds in his suave manner,

'Don't mind if I do. She's seriously hot in that quirky way. Like a kinky librarian.'

I almost choke at John's words. I don't dare to aim my gaze anywhere in Alex's vicinity because I'm mortified. But it doesn't escape me from the corner of my eye that Alex's hands tighten into fists.

'Just be careful. There's something going on between Alex and her. I don't know what yet, but I will find out. You don't want to be another person Alex gets fired.' Their voices retreat with their footsteps.

'I'm not Hayden,' John's fading voice starts saying, but the rest is too muffled for me to hear.

Did Alex have somebody fired because he was after the same job? Regardless of his arctic personality, no wonder he's so unpopular.

We wait five more minutes before the coast is clear, surreptitiously squinting in each other's direction.

Neither of us says a word until we both speak at the same time. While I say stiffly, 'I'd better go,' Alex rushes, 'About what John said…'

'It's none of my business what you do or don't do,' I say a little too harshly.

He grips the bridge of his nose and closes his eyes for a moment. When he opens them, they're cold. He pulls himself up to his full height which is only a smidge taller than me; he's back to his superior bullshit, and instantly I feel defensive.

'So, you think it's not above and beyond my practices to fire people who are my competition?' he accuses me haughtily. I refuse to rise to his words.

'Let me know how much your drycleaning is, or I'll buy you a new shirt if it's beyond cleaning,' I say with detachment, but I know my silence to his previous question is an answer in itself. I've just poured water onto hot oil.

He laughs hollowly and crosses his big arms in front of

him. My hands go automatically to my hips, ready for the fight. 'There's not a grey cloud in your world, is there? Everything can be solved with money. Start facing your problems. You better go before you cause any more damage. That's what you do, don't you?'

His words are so harsh I rear back like he slapped me. I thought offering to pay for his ruined shirt was facing my problems. Did he expect me to bow down and beg for forgiveness?

He catches my reaction and his cheeks twitch. He opens his mouth.

'Don't bother,' I snap, barely containing anger so hot it feels like it's boiling my insides. 'Whatever you were about to say, I'm sure I'll be glad to have missed it. I'll let you deal with the mess on the carpet because, as you said, I can't seem to deal with my problems.' Out of spite and unable to help myself, I add, 'At least I'm not a two-faced arsehat.'

I pick up my stuff scattered around the reception and rush to my classroom, only halfway there realising I've left my bumblebee cardigan in the toilet. It's a small price to pay for speaking my mind.

10

Half an hour later, I've gone through the lesson plan for the lower comprehension set and the higher maths set I'm teaching today. I'm setting out the starter tasks ready for the kids as soon as they come in when my phone buzzes. It's Catherine.

'Hey,' she says sweetly, but there's a definite strain in her voice. We've always been close and even though we often went without seeing each other for weeks during uni and our life paths couldn't have been any more different, we've stayed best friends. So it's no wonder we work on an almost telepathic level. Cheryl and Jason Blossom from *Riverdale* have nothing on us.

'Is everything OK?' I start gently, happy to be dealing with somebody else's problems for once.

'Of course.' Her voice wobbles a little.

'If you're keeping it in out of any sense of misplaced solidarity to my current pathetic existence, I can assure you I'm all ears. I welcome any interruptions to my drama. I'm here for you. Always.' I try to sound as supportive as possible even though less than half an hour ago, I was mere minutes away from an emotional breakdown or walking out of this school forever.

There's silence on the other end, and so I wait. When she doesn't say anything, I try a different strategy. Cheering up Lydia-style it is.

'Let me prove to you that I can take on whatever's worrying you. Let's start. My mother is the living embodiment of Pamela

Jones and can't seem to understand that a woman can be happy without a man. A few weeks back, she tried to match me with a guy who turned out to be so nice, he invited me for lunch with him and his boyfriend. The only reason I didn't tell you and Lydia was because I didn't think I'd ever live it down.'

The line is dead.

I plough on. 'I was cheated on by a boyfriend who liked to have needles stuck into his buttocks. He liked to polish his very small and disgustingly greasy…' I pause there for effect before I continue. '…car every Saturday so that all the neighbours noticed it. He would sit in it for hours because he couldn't afford to fuel it.'

Still nothing.

'He made me move out into a tiny studio where I suspect at some point somebody tried to hide a cadaver under the bathroom floor.' I hear a small giggle.

'And my neighbours like to do it at two o'clock in the morning while one of them is neighing like a horse.' She chuckles. It's almost like a sigh of relief.

I top it up. 'I'm so poor that I have less than ten quid in my bank account and have no food in my fridge. My ECT mentor, who is also my first-ever boyfriend, just tipped the only food I had onto the floor, his tie and his shirt. I, being the nice person here, tried to wash it for him. I made him strip to the waist and actually managed to ruin his shirt forever. Who knows, he might still be stuck there. Crying and topless.' She's fully laughing now. 'Better?'

'You did not?' she questions with disbelief. I have to admit it does sound far-fetched.

I look up at a sliding sound and just see the door to my class closing like somebody was about to enter but changed their mind. I hope that whoever it was didn't hear me.

'You're stronger than I think you are sometimes. I just hate adding extra stress to your shoulders, Holly. You've had so much going on recently and my problems seem so petty next to yours.'

I swat my hand before I'm reminded she can't see me. 'Don't be silly. What do you need? I'm here for you.'

'I'm feeling a bit swamped lately. Gabby hasn't been sleeping, and Richard has been working late. When he comes home, he's tired, we both are, but sometimes I just feel alone in this parenthood thing. You know me. I'm logical and analytical, I don't get overwhelmed that easily, but I have a conference today. I've slept three hours, and our babysitter pulled out last minute because she's got the flu. And Lydia has a date.'

There are unshed tears in her voice. She's so strong, but parenting is hard, and whoever says it's not is an idiot.

'I'm free. Besides, I have so much marking to do, I'd rather do it at your house where it's warmer and doesn't smell of mould.'

'I've got a fridge full of food and you're welcome to anything in it. Even the Strings & Things Yollies and you know how obsessed Gabby is with them,' she offers happily. 'You are the best, and if any idiot tells you otherwise, you send them to hell, or better, to Lydia.'

My brain rewinds to what she said about Lydia.

'Lydia's got a date?'

'Some guy from work. Ted, I think.'

'Not *Ted Talk* Ted?' I ask incredulously. That guy cannot stop engaging people in intellectual one-sided conversations. Lydia called it a disease. She must know what she's doing. 'Anyway. What time do you want me at your place? I can swing by straight after I have a shower and get changed.'

After the call, the morning proceeds without any hiccups. Apart from my terrible lower comprehension set that I dread every week. They're just a bit too rambunctious and unfocused. Despite all the positive reinforcement I've been putting into building a relationship with them, I can't get through to them.

I expressed this to Alex at the last meeting, but I still almost choke when I catch him quietly slipping to the back of the classroom when the kids start streaming through.

Out of all the days, he had to choose today to observe me. I can't stop myself from feeling satisfaction when I notice he's wearing what looks like a borrowed blue polo shirt. It's a bit tight on him, and I can tell from here it must be itchy as hell.

He doesn't acknowledge me, his expression indecipherable and unapproachable as always. However, when a few pupils wave at him, his demeanour changes completely. He's obviously popular with the children. He even asks Kyle about his hamster called Kevin. Why didn't I know that Kyle had a hamster called Kevin?

'OK, settle down, class,' I call out in what I hope is my best authoritative voice. I reward a few pupils for being ready and ask everyone to put their names and dates down on the recap sheets in front of them. Alex scribbles something down. There hasn't been any time to get anything wrong, or has there? My stomach feels scraped out like a hollow tree trunk, but I'm not sure whether this feeling is connected to the lack of food in it or the dread caused by Alex's presence.

'Before you start with the recap, can anybody tell me what literary genres we learnt last week?' There's a moment of silence when not a single person raises their hand, the fear of all teachers during an observation.

Alex is about to speak, probably to jump in with something spiteful, when I start re-enacting Harry Potter brandishing a wand with dramatic swings. When there's only confusion in my pupils' eyes, I channel my inner Hagrid, and in a very bad West Country accent, I holler, 'Yer a wizard, Harry.'

The class erupts into laughter, and a good half of the class start shouting out *fantasy*. For somebody so sombre and serious, I've always been a comedian in the classroom.

I motion with my hand for everyone to settle down and

mimic putting my hand up. Most of the hands shoot up, ready to answer. I do a little victory dance at my success which makes everyone giggle.

'Evie.' I point at a girl with black pigtails and dark grey eyes. She's always very quiet, and I have the feeling she needs a bit of confidence-boosting.

'Fantasy,' she mumbles, and I immediately peel a star from my reward sticker chart and stick it onto her hand.

'Ten points to Gryffindor.'

I continue, re-enacting *Diary of a Wimpy Kid*, *Frankenweenie* and *Gnomeo and Juliet*. I try to avoid any human contact with Alex, and for a moment, I almost forget he's there. I think I'm a good teacher, and one pompous idiot at the back of my classroom isn't going to make me forget that. I carry on proudly with my newly found confidence until I start re-enacting *Star Wars*.

'*Star Wars* is a space opera,' Alex mutters almost to himself. He blinks rapidly when all the heads turn his way. He couldn't stop himself from having a dig.

'Thank you, Mr Bennet. You're right, sometimes genres are not so clear-cut and can blur into each other.'

I take his remark in my stride, and he dips his head to the sheet of paper in his hands in what almost looks like embarrassment. I feel almost giddy. I can't leave it there, 'Take *Star Wars* for example.' He tips his head up, his eyes boring into mine, but I don't break the contact when I speak. 'We don't know where the force comes from, and in a way, it acts like magic by following no logical or scientific boundaries or abiding by physical laws. So, we could call the Jedi space wizards if we wanted to be accurate. However, we could also consider all the technology that isn't powered by the force and say that the technology is very advanced which would almost make us think of the sci-fi genre.'

Our gazes lock, daring each other to take the next step that might tip the balance. The air sizzles and sparks with frantic energy similar to seconds before dancers' bodies slam against each other in a mosh pit. I feel there are only two possible outcomes – a profanities-ridden argument or a fight. But at the last moment, Alex clears his throat, and the tension shatters like a sheet of glass struck by a sledgehammer. I'm reminded I'm in a class full of children who are staring at me like I'm having apoplexy and that having a wrestling match with their assistant head in front of their eyes is career suicide.

'OK, time for a recap. You have five minutes. Off you go,' I say hastily and pretend to tidy my desk. I can hear the door close shut behind Alex, but I'm not composed enough to check whether he's really gone.

The rest of the lesson goes swimmingly, mainly because of Alex's absence.

Once I take my class to the hall for their lunch, I come back to my classroom, my empty belly rumbling pitifully. When I reach the desk, I stop in my tracks at the sight of a brown paper bag full of food with a familiar yellow cardigan lying neatly folded next to it. When I bring the fabric to my nose, it's not only soft but also smells heavenly like it's been laundered.

Attached to the paper bag, a curt note says, *I am sorry. I had no right to judge you. A–*.

I open the bag unsteadily, flabbergasted by the sheer quantity of food. There are two sandwiches, my all-time favourite BLT and Ploughman's, two flapjacks, a muffin and two pieces of fruit – an apple and a banana. My cheeks heat because he must have heard me speaking to Catherine on the phone. I quickly snap a picture of my lunch with the note attached to it and send it to our group chat.

I think I need some context, unless our friendship has grown so comfortable and our lives so boring we now share photos of our lunches, Lydia immediately messages.

That's unexpected, Catherine types.

I pop to the loo and when I return, a missed call from Lydia embellishes my screen. I judge by Lydia's next message that contains a long string of emojis, a bucket of water, a shirt, a flame and for some reason a large aubergine Catherine must have updated her on the phone while I was away.

I message back, *To top it off, I basically accused him of having a teacher fired because they were after the same job.*

The question is why did he buy you lunch? Men don't do shit like that for no reason. Call me a sceptic. Lydia ponders.

He said some awful things. I think he might have bought me lunch to genuinely apologise, I admit with confusion because the Alex I've worked with for the last few weeks has been nothing but emotionally unavailable and hostile.

I don't know what to think of him. Before he got me lunch, he made me look like an idiot in front of my class. Not to mention all the stuff from the past.

People change, Catherine responds. She always wants to see the best in people, but this time her comment hurts a little because I don't want to see anything good in Alex.

He was a dickwad to her ten years ago, Cat. People don't change that much. Some things can't be forgiven, Lydia messages resolutely.

I'm not forgiving what he's done to Holly. I hope you know that, Holly.

A weird knot tightens in my chest that won't go away. I take a swig of a bottle of juice that was at the bottom of the bag to loosen it.

I'm sorry. I've upset you now, Catherine types.

I know she overthinks things and will worry if I don't put her at ease.

I'm fine. Really. I just don't want to feel any particular way about Alex or have anything to do with him. But for the first time, I doubt my own words.

I'm halfway through my lunch-for-two when John barges

into the classroom without a knock. I've learnt that's his customary way of entering any school spaces, so I simply wait until he reveals the purpose of his visit.

In his hand, he's holding a bag of triple chocolate chip cookies, and I'm reminded of the comment he made about me to Danielle and scowl.

'Hey, Holly,' he greets me with obnoxious over-familiarity and struts towards my desk. I can't deny the animal magnetism he spreads around the room. It's like every piece of furniture is covered in a thin layer of musk as soon as he enters. I don't think that's necessarily a bad thing for some, but I feel choked by it.

He leaves the cookies on my desk, and I arrange my face into some semblance of a smile. He brought me something sweet almost every day last week. I don't wonder about his intentions any more, but his sugary gestures have turned into bitter blackstrap molasses on my tongue after overhearing his conversation with Danielle.

'A few people are going for a few drinks tonight after work. Did you want to join us?'

I pretend to be gutted. 'I'm babysitting my friend's daughter tonight. But maybe next time?'

He nods, but I read his disappointment. That is until his attention lands on the incriminating note that I stupidly left on the desk in plain sight.

His eyes widen a fraction before he nods. I don't like the look he gives me before he leaves. It's not unkind per se, but there's a definite edge to it that makes me nervous.

I have no doubt this will spread around the school like wildfire. There's no limiting damage. I've learnt over the last five years in education the best way forward is pretending ignorance. As Queen Elizabeth I would say, 'I observe and remain silent.'

11

All the way to Catherine's house, I think of Alex. It was much safer when he was a hostile and inconsiderate arsehat, but discovering that under the veneer of a robot is a human being after all, is unnerving. The possibility of Alex being capable of feeling pity and shame raises my own shame and guilt. It makes me hate him even more.

I arrive at Catherine and Richard's house at ten past six. Their house is a 1960s red-brick semi with two tight parking spaces, one of which is currently empty for me to tuck into. All the lights are on, and heavy curtains are drawn over upstairs windows to block the bedrooms' view onto the residential road crammed with identical houses.

A part of me wonders whether I should feel discontented with life because I don't have any of this. A house, a husband and a kid, but when I visualise myself in that alternative reality, I can't quite see myself there or the man next to me. Even when I was with Aaron and things were good, I didn't really see us in that future. As much as I'm reluctant to admit it, maybe Aaron was right, and I never gave it my all.

Now, his future is going to look a lot like this, but I won't be in it. With surprise, I realise that for the first time, it doesn't hurt. There's no feeling of betrayal or anger – only relief.

I ring the bell, but instead of Catherine, little Gabby opens the door and immediately jumps into my embrace; I'm the mangrove to her spider monkey. She mumbles *Auntie* as she detaches herself from me, leaving red-berry stains in the shape of her tiny fingers all over my top. But I'm prepared, and everything I'm wearing is shabby and threadbare, including me.

'Where's your mummy?' I follow her in, hand in hand. Her skin feels warm and sticky as she pulls me in after her.

I abandon all my bags on the floor with a thud and breathe a sigh of relief. I've brought some games and sleepover stuff. Because it would be too late to travel home after, we agreed I'd go to work straight from here.

I can't count how many times I've stayed in the tiny spare room overnight. If there's anything like a home away from home, for the last five years it's been this house. It's the place where the three of us, Catherine, Lydia and I, put the world to rights when it seems like it's falling apart around us. It's the place I stayed when I found Aaron cheating on me and where Lydia spent a week drinking schnapps and eating Cadbury's Creme Eggs after her mum died. It feels grounding and uncomplicated compared to my childhood home.

Catherine, rushing from the master bedroom and buttoning her white shirt while closely avoiding Gabby with the ease of an inflatable stick figure, breaks my train of thought. I laugh, and she rolls her eyes, but there's a serious glint in her look that worries me. I watch as she pecks her daughter on the forehead.

'Can I show Auntie Bing?' Gabby asks with poorly disguised hope on her face, and it gets me all over again how much it was great being a kid. All the decisions were made for you, and all you cared about was showing off your favourite toys.

'Only after you wash your jammy fingers, munchkin,' I say and pinch her cheek. She rushes off to the kitchen after Catherine nods.

'You're a lifesaver.' Catherine's dark eyes are too big in her face, like she's been close to tears this entire time.

'Hey, what are childless friends for,' I joke.

'Holly, I'm so sorry if I upset you earlier.' She breaks the playful atmosphere.

I interrupt her before she gets into it. I've been rehearsing this all the way to her house to make it sound at least semi-convincing. 'You were right. I don't know the person Alex has become, and people do change. I've certainly changed since I was seventeen. It's alright.'

She squeezes my hand gently. Sometimes, she's so sensitive, and I love her even more in that moment.

'I hope I haven't spoilt your plans for tonight.' She bites her lip as she rummages through her bag abandoned on the closest sofa. She takes her purse and a lip balm out of it before she carries on rifling through it.

'Actually, you were a great excuse to say no to drinks with John and some of the other teachers.' I admit. 'I needed to clear my mind anyway.'

She stops going through her belongings for a second and gives me a knowing smile. 'How was your lunch?' The grin her face spreads into looks lighter.

She swipes all the stuff on the armrest of the sofa into another bag before resolutely zipping it close. My lips twitch, she's never been a particularly organised or tidy person.

Shrugging, I park myself on one of the comfy armchairs. 'Predictable. The sandwich tasted of lies and deceit, the muffin had a hint of self-importance, and the juice was spiked with ill manners. You are what you eat, after all. Or buy what you are in this case.'

Now she has nothing to do, her eyes bore into me with an unblinking directness that forces me to add reluctantly, 'I must admit it tasted OK. He even got me my favourite sandwich which even my mother gets wrong most of the time. I find it extremely frustrating.' I sound like a petulant child, but I can't help it.

'BLT on seeded bread, no mayo?' She pauses before she

angles her head towards the small footsteps thudding upstairs. Then, her attention falls back on me.

'That's...' she starts, but she must spot the red flags manically waving in my eyes because she restrains herself.

I draw my knees up, wrapping my arms around them in a protective cage. 'Don't say that's nice. I know your default is to always be kind to people and see the best in them. Don't get me wrong, I love that about you, but I don't think I can cope with *Alex* and *nice* in the same sentence yet. Or ever. He was really awful to me in the toilet, so he bought me lunch to redeem himself, or maybe he just didn't want me going snitching to Jane that he was unprofessional. Who knows. So now, we're even-steven. What happened in the past stays in the past. There'll be no more drama between us. No more *Waterloo Road*.'

She nods knowingly but can't help herself and adds, 'Somehow, I get the feeling Alex and you aren't finished yet. The past sometimes has a way of leaking into the present.'

'We both did some awful things ten years ago, and I'm not proud of myself and my actions back then. It's better if we keep it untouched. We're not teenagers any more.'

'It's not all your fault what happened back then.' She tries to make me feel better.

'I know that.'

'It's never too late to clear the air. You can't carry on like this, being at each other's throats – this is an important year in your career.'

I suppress an unhappy snort. 'At this point we'd need a catalytic oxidizer to clear the air between us. You forget that to have a reasonable conversation you need two reasonable people who have a common desire to resolve their messy history. We're beyond explanations; Alex doesn't care about the past or me so there's nothing to discuss. We're just two strangers who happen to share an uncomfortable past and have to learn to navigate the present, that's it.'

She reads my hurt expression but ploughs through, nevertheless. She must find it important to say the next words because she's never been the insistent type.

'I've never said this so please let me say it once, and then I won't speak about it again.' She tugs at her shirt, belying her confident words. 'Someone who looked at you the way he did ten years ago doesn't just forget and move on. He was smitten with you long before he wrote you that first message. He couldn't keep his eyes off you whenever you were around. I noticed. Vicky did too. That kind of attachment can't just vanish into thin air. I think he's only pretending to be indifferent because nobody is completely immune to their first love. The sooner you two get past that, the sooner you can really move on.'

At the mention of Vicky, I can't help but grimace. After what happened between me and Alex, I always assumed I was a passing fancy to him. The fact that Vicky knew he liked me long before I did is an unwelcome revelation, and I can't quite fathom why it bothers me so much. It didn't stop him liking other people at the same time though, I think bitterly.

I know she's making a valid point, but because I want to make Alex the villain of my story after being decimated by his words in the toilet, I declare defensively, 'I doubt he's changed that much. Everyone's saying that he's sleeping with the principal and that's how he got his job.' I feel a little ashamed of myself for turning into one of the gossipmongers at my school, but I can't help it.

'Who's everyone? John the guy who thinks you're hot in a quirky way, like a kinky librarian?' Her comment is infused with amusement.

I slide my hand off my knee and lift it in defeat. 'OK. I must admit John is not the most reliable person. Last week, I caught him sticking used chewing gum under one of the tables in the staffroom.'

Little feet scatter down the stairs and effectively conclude our conversation. I feel almost relieved.

I laugh hollowly. 'How have we ended up talking about me again? Aren't you the one upset?' We both laugh for real this time.

She stands and picks up her bag. 'Well, talking about other people's problems always makes me more objective of mine.'

Gabby bounces into the room with a strange-looking rabbit with a slightly overlarge head and jumps straight into my lap.

After that, Catherine rushes to the conference, leaving me and Gabby to our evening. But before she goes, we hug tightly and don't let go for a long time. I've never been much of a hugger, my family not being a touchy-feely kind, but Catherine is the best hugger there is.

Later, I prepare milk and biscuits for Gabby, and together, we watch an episode of *Paw Patrol*. I tuck Gabby into bed not long after and mark books until ten thirty. When I get into my pyjamas, I mindlessly switch through programmes until I finally end up playing *Return of The Jedi* on the Disney Channel.

I get a link for a dating website from my mother that I ignore and a few messages from Vicky that I don't. She asks me how I am, and for a few minutes, we chat on the phone about nothing. It's always been so easy with Vicky because she makes me forget about things going on in my life. That is until she asks about Alex and whether there have been any new developments. For the first time, I decide to lie and text, *No, we rarely see each other. It's a big school.*

My cheeks heating at my untruth, I realise that I want to keep what happened between me and Alex to myself for a little longer, even though I'm not sure why. The thought scares me because even though I was the one who broke up with Alex via text message without any real explanation and then ignored his pleas to tell him why ten years ago, he was the one who moved on a day later and found the first available female to make up with, effectively breaking my heart. By the time I found out I wasn't even the only one who he tried it on with, the blood-pumping organ was ground to a pile of ash. Because the truth is I never mattered to him.

Despite all my earlier bravado in front of Catherine and dismissing words, I have not forgotten, nor have I let go of the past.

12

The following week I have my first formal observation with Alex followed by a customary weekly meeting. As usual, he highlights all the areas I need to work on and then smoothly moves on to praise my behaviour management and curriculum knowledge. He says all this in such a monotone I miss the fact he's giving me a compliment until it's well and truly over.

Then, he coolly informs me that I'll be planning a school trip. He gives me a sheet with details of potential places and a stack of forms to fill. A trip proposition with a budgeting section, a draft letter to parents and carers and a permission slip. It's all Greek to me, and I'm frazzled by the foreign paperwork and the weight of responsibility that settles on my shoulders straight away. He finishes by saying the trip needs to take place at the end of October, which is over a month away. When he leaves, my mind is playing a game of Tetris, attempting to slot all the new pieces of information into an orderly pile but failing. Thanks for the heads-up.

Over the next few weeks, I get to the manic state of working before work, working through my lunches and working past sundown. Not only am I planning and marking books well into late evenings, but at the weekends, I also do my ECT coursework while trying to organise this blasted trip.

As the autumnal chill starts creeping into the classrooms, a few changes happen around the school. A week after my altercation with Alex in the toilet, school lunch leftovers began appearing in the staffroom. The selection usually includes a tray of stale flapjacks, a bowl of dried chips or rubbery macaroni cheese, but I always happily tuck in. When I question the sudden influx of canteen food in the staffroom, Becky informs me that Jane said it was a waste to be chucking leftovers away. I can't complain about this, but not all changes are for the better.

Noticeably, a few members of staff start avoiding my eyes, and a few even give me a direct cut. For a few days, I puzzle over this occurrence until I walk past Dan and Samantha, key stage one teaching assistants, chatting by the staff toilets and overhear Samantha telling Dan how Danielle told her that I got my job because I was sleeping with Alex at the time. The speculations evolve further over the next day, and it reaches my ears that apparently after I got my job, I refused to continue sleeping with Alex and that's why he's been so hostile to me.

The gossip makes me so livid I spend my lunch in the disabled toilet on the phone with Lydia who is ready to gut them all with the teaspoon she's currently scooping out her low-fat yogurt with. I prevent her from storming into our school and committing multiple homicides. We dissect the topic thoroughly over Indian-Nepalese food at Lydia's the next day. Catherine, always the voice of reason, eventually manages to dissuade Lydia from pursuing her violent urges.

On the other hand, Becky and I have become friends of sorts. She's still on the shy side and can be very quiet at times, but she's always nice and never imposes on me. She checks on me during some lunches, and I sometimes buy her coffee from the local Costa in exchange. We often get into small talk about cats, food or The 1975, a band we both like. Everything about our camaraderie is uncomplicated and comforting.

Despite all the gossip harrying my person, Becky openly condemns it, which is a fresh breath of air compared to the covert Cruella de Ville vibes from Danielle who always beams my way whenever we're in the same room. John doesn't help the situation by openly flirting with me whenever Alex is around. I've long had the feeling he's got a hidden agenda of pissing Alex off.

My bank account balance dips dangerously to two-digit numbers mid-month thanks to too many friendship-building coffees, so I once again text Aaron about not receiving his repayment plan, but infuriatingly he stays AWOL.

A few weeks later, the trip day arrives, and I find myself trapped in an odd feeling of déjà vu. The coach is cramped with twenty-eight ten and eleven-year-olds and six members of staff plus the coach driver. I'm sitting in the front because I still haven't gotten over my travel sickness. The subtle smell of budding teenagerhood, salt and vinegar Pringles and Danielle's Carolina Herrera perfume is not helping with the queasiness.

The tension in the coach is denser than wading through Oobleck. There seems to be a below-average amount of blinking, and everybody is watching everybody like we're playing Wink Murder and I didn't get the memo. Becky's attention keeps steering towards Alex who's sitting in the middle of the coach next to John, and the two males keep throwing daggers at each other.

At the back of the coach, Danielle is seated next to Rob, the year three teacher roped into the trip despite his best efforts. When spying on Alex, she keeps yawning into her hand while Rob is talking one hundred miles per hour and scrolling down his phone. I bet he's talking about his copywriter girlfriend. He'll talk to anyone about her, whether they're willing to listen or not. A vindictive part of me feels like gloating, but I'm a fully grown adult so I only gloat on the inside. Maybe the corner of my lip lifts a notch, but who cares?

A commotion in the middle of the coach makes my gaze fix on John who is manspreading and encroaching on Alex's personal space. Alex looks like he's ready to gut him. He tells

John to move, but John frowns and says something that makes Alex's eyebrows rise in a challenge. A moment later, John shifts his invading knee, and Alex goes back to gazing out of the window. When Becky catches me watching, she leans in.

'Apparently, Alex had a stern conversation with John last week, and since then, they've been ready to challenge each other to a duel.' Despite Becky's over-dramatic words, I appreciate her forthcomingness.

'What was it about?' I lean closer. The school's ways must have rubbed off on me because I can't seem to stay away from any gossip that involves Alex. I feel deeply ashamed but not ashamed enough to stay silent.

'Unprofessional behaviour on school premises and spreading slanders.' She pushes her chestnut hair behind her ears with jittery hands. 'I know John can sometimes be a bit *cheeky*.' She pauses before she adds, 'But I feel this is only going to fuel John and Danielle further.'

She gives me a meaningful look, not wanting to directly say that the gossip was about me, but I catch her drift. I can't stop the sigh that escapes my lips. I feel so enraged at the unfairness of the whole situation. I've landed in the middle of something that has nothing to do with me.

As soon as my insides start gurgling halfway through the journey, I pop a mint leaf in my mouth and chew. Someone coughs somewhere behind me, and when I turn my head, I catch Alex looking at me strangely. I force myself to face the front again, but my cheeks are heating, a well of memories flooding my mind.

John and Rob swap seats, Rob ending up sitting next to Alex who is as antisocial as they come. When Rob tries to initiate a conversation, Alex freezes him mid-sentence. Rob hurriedly plucks out his phone and carries on scrolling. Lydia would have had a whale of a time on this coach. She'd probably ask for a bag of popcorn.

Finally, after an excruciating hour, we arrive at Newley Farm. All the children line up, eager to embark on their adventure, while I fight hard not to puke in the nearby bramble bushes, visualising taking in the fresh air, a wildflower meadow and butterflies, my pretend happy place.

After all the kids are counted, they're led by Alex and Danielle, closely trailed by John, Rob and Becky towards a red-brick farmhouse surrounded by kitchen gardens on one side and a paddock and vast fields on the other. I hang back, pretending to be busy looking at an oak tree with a rope swing dangling lopsidedly in the chilly wind to my right while I'm trying to persuade my body not to vomit out my breakfast.

Life is good. The sun is shining, and I haven't embarrassed myself and gotten the nickname Miss Pukey. That is until I realise they'd abandoned me with all the lunches and equipment. The coach driver gives me an impatient look, informing me while loudly chewing spearmint gum that he needed to be on his way about five minutes ago.

Dressed in my favourite '90s green-and-grey lumberjack shirt tucked into high-waisted flared jeans decorated with embroidered flowers, I fear I'm overdressed for the task. I scan the muddy path decorated with four-by-four tread marks leading towards the house, trying to find an easy route that doesn't exist. The brown cowboy boots that I bought on Vinted for twenty quid are already caked in the slimy greyish mud that surrounds the farmhouse. It can only get worse from this point. I sigh but heft the heavy bags, nevertheless. I can show Alex I can fix my problems and that I'm not a quitter. Also, I know that nobody will need the equipment until after lunch so nobody should notice me gone or witness my embarrassment.

Five minutes later, I'm lugging three massive bags filled with lunches, water and equipment towards the house. I've only made it halfway when my left arm starts going dead. There's a fifty-fifty chance they'll have to amputate it if I don't do something about it right now, but I know that if I put the bags down, I won't be able to pick them up again.

The nape of my neck starts sweating, and I make an exaggerated huff slash growl to defuse the tension in my body that I hope nobody will ever hear.

Just as I'm thinking I might have avoided anybody witnessing the lowest point of my career so far, a familiar person strides purposefully towards me with a frown. When he realises what I'm doing, he sort of freezes mid-step. It would have been almost comical if the person didn't have a mop of ginger hair and the coldest green serial-killer eyes. Once Alex is back in motion, like Frankenstein's monster reanimated, his frown deepens and the corners of his lips shape into an unpleasant upside-down 'u'.

My body simply stops collaborating. My gaze snags on the shape of him and refuses to move away from his form. It's the way he moves that sends my pulse off the charts and into outer space. His walk has always been predatory, like a panther. Both the forest green jumper and dark blue jeans he's wearing mould around his athletic body perfectly, making my breath uneven. Despite his off-putting scowl, my heartbeat speeds up and it angers me to no end that my body still reacts this way to him. I'm sure that if I were a guy, I would have a massive boner right now.

'Why are you carrying the bags on your own? Everyone's waiting inside,' Alex grumbles. My proverbial boner is gone. He huffs something under his breath that sounds a lot like *John* and *arsehole*, but I would not imagine in my wildest dreams this version of Alex would ever say anything this unprofessional.

I get all defensive, and the bags drop to the mud with a splat. A fine spray of mud covers his jeans from boot to knee. I don't feel regret at the sight of what I've done. Instead, my achy arms cross and my chest puffs up like an over-inflated balloon ready to pop with the lightest of touches. I've had enough of being people's pincushion. Just because I like to keep to myself doesn't mean I will let people walk over me.

'You can't seriously be angry at me. I'm trying my best here, but it's only me and a lot of bags that seem to be packed with sand and bricks just to spite me. Nobody prepared me or informed me I'd be a porter or that I would get involved in heavy labour because I would have worn my combat boots.' I point to my ruined mud-dip-dyed jeans and add, 'And overalls.'

I huff hair out of my face with irritation and push it back, hoping it stays there forever. When I push it back for the third time and it falls back, I'm ready to explode. What happens next makes me utterly still. Alex invades my space and pushes the stray hair behind my ear, skimming the shell of my ear with his fingertip for a moment. I'm so shocked I run out of steam, and words. Officially, my rant is over.

'I'm not angry,' he starts. My eyes narrow in disagreement. At seeing my reaction, he presses his lips together, making the rosy colour go deep pink. '…with you,' he finishes. Suddenly, he seems oddly out of breath. Startled, I realise that he's holding in his temper, and what shocks me more, I believe him.

I shift my weight from left to right because I didn't expect him to say that. I'm suddenly reminded of his impatient flare-ups aimed at his mother, the world and general human stupidity. I'm starting to gather that maybe his detached air has been a mask all along because one moment he looks utterly beyond himself but the next, he seems composed. I guess he hasn't changed that much after all.

He picks up all three bags off the ground, hefting two of them over his shoulder with ease, not caring that he's smearing mud all over his jumper. We carry on walking towards the farmhouse in tense silence.

With a quick glance over his shoulder, he informs me, 'John and Rob were supposed to help you with those. I specifically asked them to carry those bags so you could lead the trip. You deserve to reap the benefits after planning all of this.'

A surprised *oh* escapes my lips. I think that it's sort of nice that somebody is vexed on my behalf, that is until he spoils it with, 'You should have asked somebody to help when you realised you weren't getting any.' Either he's really bad at this social communication thing called polite conversation or he's trying really hard to piss me off again. I can't quite decide. Either way, I've reverted to *grrr* mode.

'I can fix my own problems. Thank you very much.' I throw his previous words back at him. At my comment, his shoulders stiffen, his cheeks turning radioactive hot. I think he's feeling embarrassed.

We've reached the door of the farmhouse when John's cheerful voice announces from behind us, 'I've got this.' I grimace at his unhurried approach. He offers me a quick grin, not reading my rigidness. 'Sorry, Holly. I promised to help and then I got stuck.' His unhurried attempts to take the bags from Alex's hands don't give me apologetic vibes.

Alex's frown becomes glacial as he moves out of John's reach. I wouldn't want to be on the receiving end of that look. 'Is that why Holly was hefting all this baggage on her own?' He speaks to John in deadly slow words. 'Because you got stuck?' He says *stuck* like it's a foul word. 'Stuck doing what precisely?'

'I told you I was fine,' I say to Alex, not wanting to make a big deal of this, but he's not listening. I can tell John is enjoying this a little too much.

'What if she'd had an injury? The school would have been liable.'

My breath lodges in my lungs like a ball stuck in a blind turn in a ball-in-a-maze puzzle. Is that why he's so angry?

At first, John only puts his hands up in defence. Then he does something that puts me positively in a fouler mood, if that's even possible. He places both his palms on my shoulders.

Alex looks like he's going to breathe fire and incinerate him on the spot.

'Holly, all good?' John mumbles into my ear, digging his cold hands into my shoulders.

I shake him off, step out of both of their reaches and nod stiffly, wanting to be anywhere but here. From now on, I'm Switzerland.

'See, Alex? No harm done. You need to loosen up a bit. Come on, Hols,' John says jovially and takes my arm like I'm a Victorian lady in need of a chaperone. I only follow out of shock.

Once safely inside the house, I step out of his reach once more. I barely notice my boots leaving a muddy trail on the white tiles as I try to lose John, but he's hard to get rid of, like a tick. He's happily chatting about something like nothing has happened, but his words are going straight through me.

'Stop this,' I grind out and turn around, coming face to face with him.

In an instant, his easy demeanour vanishes, and his eyebrows rise in question.

I elaborate, 'Stop using me to get a reaction out of Alex. Is this some sort of a twisted game of yours?'

'That's not…' he starts but trails off as soon as he catches my expression. 'OK. I'm sorry.' His eyes lower in what looks like shame, or a very good attempt at appeasing me. 'It's not a game. I won't lie, I get a kick out of needling him. For some reason, whenever you're near, he's easy to rile, but I really like you.'

I huff in disbelief.

'Really.' He moves closer to me, but I step back. He pauses, uncertain. 'I just don't like the way he talks to you, and I feel a bit protective of you. That's why I keep winding him up. I know you don't see me like that, but if you ever wanted to go out or something, let me know.' He scratches his ear like he's nervous. Before I have a chance to say anything, he leaves me behind, gawking in puzzlement.

When I finally join the rest of the adults, Alex has split people into two groups for the first two activities. I end up with Danielle while John ends up with Rob and Becky. Go figure.

The paddock smells distinctly of rotten chestnuts and pigs. The bucket in my hand is heavy, and whenever my arm wobbles, the apples bob from side to side. The strong smell of too-sweet apples reminds me of the homemade cider my nan used to make.

A hairy brown pig with a button-like nose approaches two girls from my group. Evie, the quiet girl from my class, and Amira, a much chattier girl with curly hair, snort with laughter as Rupert the pig makes some truly disturbing oinking noises after they shake their bucket and a few loose apples escape over the edge. I watch with amusement as another pig joins the feast, a truly feisty sow called Molly, who quickly polishes off all the leftover apples Rupert hasn't had a chance to scoff. At finding out that Molly has eaten his breakfast, Rupert makes an angry burp-like sound that sends the girls into another fit of laughter. I can't stop the grin spreading over my features because I'm happy for someone to finally draw a laugh out of Evie. I wonder whether Alex paired them together knowing they would hit it off.

Absentmindedly, I gaze at the adjacent paddock that houses guinea pigs and rabbits in wooden hutches. Not for the first time, I focus on a ginger head that's shining in the sun as bright as a new copper coin. From this distance, I can see his hands are full of fluffy white bunnies. I start walking towards the fence to get a closer look, persuading myself that I need to check on Evie and Amira who have wandered off.

When I get close enough to distinguish the words between Alex and a blond-haired boy I have in my lower maths set, I hide from their sight behind an oak tree while pretending I'm collecting acorns for the pigs.

'If you don't want to hold the rabbit, that's OK. I used to be scared of rabbits when I was your age. It was the big front teeth.' Alex pushes his front teeth over his bottom lip, and the boy laughs. Alex's voice is so soft my knees feel unsteady. I don't think I've ever heard him speak like this before.

He carries on, 'If you want, I'll hold Eddie for you, and you can stroke him or just feed him. I'm told Eddie really likes dandelion leaves.' The boy nods eagerly, and Alex smiles in encouragement. My insides semi-melt until I'm reminded that he was a right pain in the arse to me a mere hour ago.

Alex lifts his eyes as if he can read my thoughts, and his lips open slightly. At the fear of being discovered eavesdropping, I stumble back, but my arm snags on a low-hanging branch, and I lose my footing. The bucket in my hand topples and half of the apples spill to the ground with multiple thuds.

I refuse to see whether Alex has spotted me and start picking up the apples without delay, my cheeks reddening.

After picking up most of them, I straighten, but something nudges against my calf with such force I have to hold on to the fence to not topple over. Something wet and rough scrapes the leg of my jeans. In a panic, I spin to be confronted by Molly's hairy, and a bit too eager for my taste, countenance. I peek down my leg and sigh. A long trail of drool decorates my ruined jeans. I put two and two together and just about push down the bile rising in my throat. Thankfully, I can't spot Alex anywhere.

'Oh my god, Holly, are you OK?' Danielle's affected voice comes from my right. I throw a few apples to my left just to divert Molly's attention elsewhere, and she happily trots in the direction of the tossed crunchy treats. If only Danielle could be distracted that easily.

When I spin on my muddy heel, Danielle is hovering by the oak tree, judging my slimy, muddy jeans while pretending to be concerned. To my annoyance, her black hair is gleaming immaculately in the autumnal sun, and her cream mohair jumper and Hunter wellies only add to her posh country airs.

Next to her, I look like I've waded through various bodily fluids. I get so angry at her pretending to be nice and at having the worst day ever while everyone is seemingly having a blast, I'm close to letting loose. If Danielle knew what was best for her, she would have left it there.

'That was so awful,' she coos, like I'm a baby that needs to be pacified, and her long gel nails clutch my shoulder. I try to wriggle out of her grip, but she's a vulture gripping a carcass.

What is it with people and pigs today? Everyone seems to want to touch me or invade my personal space.

'You were so distracted there. I thought the pig was going to pull you over.' When she says the word *distracted*, her eyes land somewhere over my shoulder. Unable to stop myself, I follow their direction, searching for Alex who's no longer there. It's an automatic reaction, but I pay for it dearly when I turn back. Danielle looks victorious, her pouty pink lips split into a ghost of a grin.

Fake concern scrunches up the sides of her nose. 'Do you need to sit down for a minute?'

What a two-faced bitch. I bet there's a story brewing in her head already. She's probably wondering how she can spin it to get the most reaction. *Attacked by a semi-wild pig while staring longingly at her ex-lover.*

'Cut the crap, will you?' I say without preamble, surprising even myself. Between her and John, I've had my fill of people trying to manipulate me. Everything in her expression changes with my words. At first, she looks shocked, her painted eyebrows almost disappearing in her black fringe, but when I don't back down, her expression turns nasty.

'You should be careful what you're saying around the children, Holly.' She scolds me like I'm one of her pupils. It vexes me to no end.

I instil zen into my voice. 'And you should be careful what you spread around the school about me. I've had enough of your toxic gossip. If you have anything to say about me, you can say it to my face.' Judging by her stunned expression, she didn't expect me to be so direct, but I haven't finished. 'I don't appreciate you talking about me behind my back, and I can't imagine Alex does either. We're both human beings and deserve more respect than that. Just because you work in a primary school doesn't mean you should behave like a ten-year-old.'

At the mention of Alex, she perks up. I stop her there.

'If I hear you spreading any more gossip, I will go directly to Jane and accuse you of defamation. I don't think you would appreciate a warning on your record. Also, I wouldn't be able to stop myself from telling her how you fiddled with the maths mid-term test results spreadsheet so it looked like you got better data than you actually did.' She blanches. She didn't expect me to know, but I'm not stupid. Plus, I regularly rummage through her folders.

I put my hand up before she spouts any more venom.

'Enough gossip about Alex. If you have any issues with him as your manager, fair enough. Go and speak to Jane or Alex himself. Those are the appropriate channels. If you have a problem with him on a personal level, I guess that's your own issue, and as such, should stay where it belongs. One would think you're obsessed with him.'

'Don't stick your big nose into other people's business,' she lashes out. I suppress an urge to touch my nose and check its size. Her voice dips low like my words have hurt her, and I see it then and there. I just about stop myself from flinching at the realisation. Something has happened between her and Alex and for a short moment, I squirm uneasily. Did they date? Or worse, did they have a fling? Various scenarios flash through my head until it starts spinning. I shake to clear it.

I feel like screaming, like I need to be anywhere but here, so I thrust my bucket forcefully into her hand. 'I've had enough of swine for today. You can take over.'

When I spin on my heel, my eyes catch something coppery through the trees on the other side of the fence, but I walk away too fast to really focus on it.

13

I end up feeding goats with four year-three boys and one year-four girl. Compared to the stressful start of the trip, I spend a peaceful hour just watching children having fun. Maybe it has something to do with the fact that I haven't encountered any adults since the incident with Danielle. I wouldn't be surprised if she's already spoken to John about my mad ways.

'Who knew that goats pooed so much,' I mumble to myself, distracted.

Being a city girl, I somehow had completely unrealistic expectations of farm life. I visualised rolling hills, long grasses gently swaying in the wind and sheep and goats bleating in the distance. Instead, everything smells of faeces, and both the sheep and goats are so loud it hurts my ears. Also, the goats are sort of cross-eyed which unnerves me.

'Yes. They do,' someone agrees to my right.

I steel myself; there goes my peace. Where's the chain mail and armet helmet when one needs it? But instead of emanating annoyance per usual, Alex pulls his lips into a rare smile as he passes me a bucket full of dry food.

I shake my head vigorously. 'Over my dead body.' When his outstretched arm doesn't move, I elaborate, 'They're prone to attack when food is involved.'

I speak from experience here because earlier when the animals were herded for feeding, they went into a mad rush to get to the bucket first, ramming each other out of the way like it was a rugby game. I was surprised red steam didn't escape their furry nostrils, their eyes didn't turn red, or their horns didn't grow and curve like the Lord of Darkness in *Legend*. I really admire the kids feeding the beasts, but I wouldn't touch them with a stick.

I must say some of this out loud if not all because Alex snorts. I frown, dismayed. 'My distress is hilarious to you, is it?' Why he's suddenly in such a good mood is beyond me.

'Well, I must admit that your sense for drama has not abandoned you. Duty calls.'

'What if they charge?' I'm so nervous I've lost my ability to filter my words.

'Then I'll jump in your way and be trampled by goats. I'll be labelled a hero.' He grins, and I keep wondering at his sudden change of tune.

'A vice principal in a local primary school gets smothered by goat poo in a heroic attempt to save one of his teachers. The article is writing itself in front of my eyes as we speak,' I announce with the gravitas the statement warrants.

'Are you stalling for time?' He's not impressed by my journalistic skills.

I mentally brace myself when I climb over the fence, but because I'm holding the bucket while scaling a metre-high fence, it's a too challenging task for my mediocre coordination skills. Alex ends up steadying me by holding my arm. His hand feels warm and firm on mine, and the contact sends a tingling sensation across my body. I can't pull my arm out of his without diving headfirst, but as soon as I'm steady, I take a step back to regain my equilibrium because my internal organs have turned into jelly cubes. I'm not sure whether it's the prospect of being trampled by ravenous goats or Alex's hand on me that makes me lose my composure.

I check the watch on my free wrist and then tug at my shirt. I'm about to retie my hair, but a clearing of a throat stops me in my tracks. When I can't use any more delay tactics because I've been caught red-handed, I steady myself and shake the bucket, the contents rattling ominously. I embrace the incoming death.

A few goats lift their heads, their bulgy eyes growing big with frenzy as they register the bucket full of goodies. Excitement is palpable in the air, my knuckles stiff around the handle.

'This is like a start to most horror movies,' I mumble, and somebody barks behind me, snapping the tension in half.

'How many horrors with goats as the main villain have you seen?' Alex is sceptical.

I throw him an unamused side glance because I refuse to look away from the gathering flock of animals.

A few goats start marching stiffly towards me, unable to decide whether I'm a friend or foe. The hunger must win because, within a few seconds, those few brave goats venture all the way to me and start munching on the hay pellets.

Tentatively, I stroke the closest black-and-white goat. Its head feels bony to touch, and its fur coarse against my palm, like an old rug. But it's strangely comforting. From my peripheral vision, I can see Alex is grinning. It completely transforms his face.

'Not a word,' I grind out.

This isn't too bad. For a few moments, it's sort of nice, and I understand why the children are enjoying this so much. That is until the rest of the herd and the few goats being fed by the children decide they want the contents of my bucket too. As one, they set into motion with the sole purpose of reaching the source of food, determination glazing their eyes and speeding their hoofed legs. In my panicked mind, Kelis' *Milkshake* starts playing on a loop.

I shrink back, the bucket rattling loudly. I take another step back, but the heel of my boot catches on a tree stump. Pellets fly in all directions, hitting me and Alex like an apocalyptic meteor shower. Everything slows down. I start toppling backwards, but

Alex's hand snatches my elbow just before I connect with the ground. The movement propels me sideways. I ram my knee into the stump, and I slam into the dirt, taking Alex with me. All I feel is a sharp sting of pain across my shin and the heavy weight of Alex's body crushing me whilst his arms shield me from the goats that descend on us like vultures and pick at the pellets between our tangled bodies. It's like Hitchcock's *The Birds* but instead of birds, we're pecked to death by domesticated ruminant mammals with backwards-curving horns and crossed eyes.

Ten minutes later, I'm sitting in a dingy utility room being nursed by Alex who is also, to my luck, the designated first aider for the trip. Straight after we picked ourselves up, I realised that not only did I cut my shin open, but I also managed to twist my ankle. All the adults gathered around me like I was an invalid. I flatly refused Alex carrying me into the house, so I had to hobble with Alex and John on either side, scooping me up like I was a bunch of bananas. Danielle didn't look very pleased about the fact that both of their attentions were on me and not her. I wasn't particularly pleased that the attention was on me full stop.

Now, the silence of the utility room is pressing against my ears. Everything here smells of mud and bleach. One of the only two plastic chairs in the room is propping my leg that is currently strapped up tight and iced. The other chair is digging painfully into my bottom. I try not to fidget but being thrust into a small space with Alex again makes me fidgety because I just don't know how it's going to go. Are we going to shout at each other, share jokes from the past, be coolly hostile to each other or pretend that the other doesn't exist? Just thinking about the multiple possibilities is giving me whiplash.

My gaze keeps getting dragged to his previously immaculate jumper that, even now splattered with mud and grime, fits his solid torso too well for my comfort. His jumper must have gotten soiled when I took him down with me. He should be angry with me, but instead, he's collected. Alex in crisis has always been solution-focused and level-headed. That was one thing I loved about him. I flinch at my internal monologue.

I watch as he takes the slightly beaten first-aid kit out from a wooden cabinet attached to the wall and starts rifling through it. I shamelessly study his profile because I haven't had a chance to watch him unobserved since our reunion. I've always thought his profile was full of contrasts, a sharp nose and cheeks sloping down to the softest, pinkest mouth, together creating delicate features offset by a freckled complexion. I used to dream of those freckles.

He must find what he's been searching for because his expression turns victorious like he's hit the jackpot on a fruit machine.

To my dismay, he kneels in front of me. I blink in confusion until it dawns on me he intends to nurse me himself. It was enough I had to let him strap my ankle, but because there was no contact of skin as I kept my sock on, I just about managed it. But I draw a line right here and shake my head vigorously, my short hair sending additional mud flying around the room and onto him.

'I categorically refuse.' I snatch the non-alcoholic wipe from his waiting hand and try to shift sideways which is a feat of its own with one leg propped up. Even though the contact didn't last more than a second, I registered the heat pouring from his hand to mine; Alex has always run a few degrees higher. Where my hands are ice blocks, his body is a self-sustaining kiln. He doesn't budge, and his knee blocks my side so unless I want my thigh to touch his leg, I have no choice but to surrender.

'I'm capable of doing it myself. Thank you very much,' I snap.

His expression turns unreadable for a moment until something that resembles amusement flickers across his features. 'OK,' he announces calmly, staying put. There's a challenge at the curve of his lips. 'I'll wait.'

'I will manage, but I require some privacy. This isn't First Aid Challenge on *Blue Peter* – I don't need an audience.' I sound petulant, but it rubs me the wrong way when he's being smug.

He shifts in his position but doesn't get up. His legs must be getting stiff, but he's stubborn. 'The fact that you haven't so far managed to roll up your trouser leg and look at the cut tells me a lot about how you're planning on *managing* it.'

I won't admit out loud I was planning on ignoring it and pocketing the cute red and blue plaster for tougher times or for a tougher Holly who would be OK with looking at blood without fainting.

He smells my bullshit straight away, like a truffle hog finding a particularly large growth of the expensive tubers. 'Admit it. You weren't going to put a plaster on the cut, were you? Or even look at it.'

'Maybe I was.' I lean against the back of the chair, trying to gain some distance. I don't like being cornered. 'Maybe I wasn't. None of your business either way.' I go in with a directly offensive tone because one never plays darts without intending to hit a bullseye.

'It's my business. Because if you get an infection because of an untreated scratch and they have to amputate your leg because you were *too chicken* to check it, I might be liable for not giving you first aid.' Did he really call me chicken or am I delirious because of potential infection coursing through my body? I'll never know because I'm not going to look at the cut.

'I'm not *chicken*,' I spit out, but there's no real spite in it because I think he's having fun at my expense. 'It's called hemophobia, and it's a real thing.' It occurs to me he's being almost human here and wonder at the change from the cold, hostile Alex I have encountered for the last few weeks. What has gotten into him?

'Fair point,' he acknowledges and snatches the wipe from me again while I'm preoccupied. 'Ready?'

Before I have a chance to react, he grabs the jean leg, tugs at the end so my foot slips between his and starts rolling up the trousers. 'Look away if you must,' he orders, but I'm so fascinated by his hands that I'm deathly still.

A thought occurs to me. Have I shaved my legs? A part of me hopes that I haven't shaved them for at least a year so as soon as he sees the growth, he lets go and leaves me in peace, but no luck. My calf is as smooth as a baby's bottom and there's blood trickling from a long cut located under my knee. I gulp heavily, my sight spinning. Then my eyes shift to his freckled hands, and I wonder at how gently they're holding my leg in place, and that's all it takes to redirect me; I'm like a baby being presented with a brightly coloured rattle. His hands have always been my fetish. And he knows that. We both stare at where we are touching, white against slightly tanned skin. Multiple entities like butterflies flutter in my heart cavities, making them convulse. I get light-headed, but this time, I have a feeling it has nothing to do with the blood.

Alex coughs awkwardly, stopping my dangerous thoughts. 'What is it about the goats? I have never seen anyone this panicked about goats.'

I think he's trying to distract me, and it's working because I can't stop myself and spill the truth.

'I guess I've developed a lifelong distrust of galloping goats after Auntie Eugenie's pet goat Mabel rammed me into a freshly painted picket fence. I only had one pair of jeans and ended up walking with the print of the fence on my bottom for four days. All the neighbouring children started calling me the Zebra Girl. I was twelve, the tender age when nobody wants to be called the Zebra Girl. Plus, their eyes unnerve me.' I shudder.

He shakes his head in disbelief. He disposes of the used wipe in the sanitary bin and inspects the cut to see whether there's anything wedged in it.

'I don't think goats are capable of galloping. That's more of a horse thing.' Is he mocking me? Once again, I wonder why he's being almost nice. Maybe he has a split personality disorder I never knew about. It would explain a lot.

'Well, running didn't sound dramatic enough. They sort of hobble like pirates but saying a hobbling herd of goats attacked me sounds pathetic.'

'I agree,' he offers in a deadpan fashion so characteristic of Alex.

He gently applies a plaster to the cut, smoothing both ends down. Fingers swiping side to side, he keeps rubbing the plaster, like he's got stuck in the motion. There's no blood in sight so I let myself fully focus on the sensation. At the sight of goosebumps spreading up my calf, he realises what he's doing and stops with a self-conscious cough.

'Why are you being so nice to me?' The words spring out of me without volition. I roll down my jean leg to give myself something to do.

He lowers himself in resignation until his bottom is parked on the cold tiles. 'Because I've been unfair to you.' I quirk an eyebrow. 'I heard what you said to Danielle.' He looks momentarily embarrassed.

I bite my lip. 'I don't like gossipmongers.'

'I don't either. I got you all wrong. We're adults, and I know I haven't been fair or particularly welcoming.'

'You've been an arsehat,' I interject. To my surprise, he chuckles at that. Maybe Catherine is right, and he has changed.

'I have, haven't I? As your mentor, I'm supposed to support you. We're colleagues. I want to lay our weapons down and let go of the past.' He echoes Catherine's words.

'A truce?' he offers, and his voice is laced with urgency. I think about it for a moment, but the alternative of continuously arguing is exhausting just to consider. I can't forget the past, but I can ignore it for the time we have to work together.

Eventually, I nod and test the word on my tongue. Then, I proceed to unbuckle my invisible gun holster, gingerly placing it down on the floor next to him, followed by an invisible dagger plucked from my boot and lay it by his feet as a peace offering.

Shaking his head in amusement, Alex releases a breath I didn't know he was holding. He utters, 'I've had enough of swine for today. I can't believe you said that.'

I can't help but grin.

A strange warm sensation bubbles in my stomach. I try to shut it down, but it lingers. Who knew that Alex and I could share a joke?

14

I don't participate in the rest of the activities on the farm and only watch from afar. During lunch, we all sit at the back of the house on makeshift benches, eating our various sandwiches. John sits next to me for a while, sharing his Coronation chicken sandwich with me, and this time, he doesn't attempt to flirt. He's extremely polite which is very unlike him.

I try to filter out Alex's presence two benches away, but his eyes bore into the nape of my neck with unnerving intensity. Since our truce, he hasn't stopped peering in my direction when he thinks I'm not looking.

To avoid kids overhearing him, John leans closer, and his head ends up in my personal space. As soon as he realises what he's doing, he respectfully pulls back.

'Are you going to Becky's birthday party next Friday?'

Despite not being much of a party girl, I said yes to Becky because she's been nothing but nice. 'Yeah. Are you going?' I enquire politely.

'Hell, yeah.' He raises his hand to high-five me. I end up high-fiving him back like a ten-year-old because I don't want to create any more tension today. He must misread my assuaging gesture because a brilliant smile spreads across his face. I thank whoever above for the fact it's half term next week and I won't have to see anyone for a week.

He leaves to sit next to Danielle after that, but to my surprise,

I'm joined by Becky, and then Alex, himself, who says he just wants to check on me but stays with us until the end of lunch. Immediately, Danielle's expression turns distinctly sour like an unripe lemon. I can smell her *eau de disapproval* all the way from the back bench she's sitting on with John.

Alex ends up sharing a cinnamon madeleine with me, professing he's too full, but I know that Alex has always been obsessed with madeleines. I guess he's really trying this truce thing.

That night, I fall asleep as soon as my head hits the pillow despite my leg being uncomfortably propped up on two pillows. But I'm not given any respite as one vivid dream chases another.

In one of them, I'm swarmed by an angry herd of guinea pigs, ill intent glowing in their rat-like eyes as they're swiftly closing the distance. When I look about for a weapon to fight against the deadly rodents, I notice I'm wearing denim head to toe. It's the most ridiculous thing I've ever seen, and now that I think about it, it reminds me of the infamous double-denim outfits worn by Britney Spears and Justin Timberlake in 2001. I'm also shrieking like I'm in one of those B-movies while my fake cowboy hat attached to my head with a red plastic string keeps falling into my eyes.

A thunderous galloping of a horse and the heavy breaths of an animal pushed to their limit are sounding in the air. Blocking the flaming sunset, a lonely rider rushes to my rescue. His heavy hat hides his face, but I catch glimpses of brown hair that resembles John's. The urgency of the situation is forgotten for a moment as I take in the powerful thighs dressed in heavy cowboy leathers. The rider's long limbs dig into the beast's sides when he speeds up. But then the thighs morph under the leathers into slimmer, more athletic legs and when they press against the horse's body, something clenches inside me almost painfully. The rider's shoulders broaden, and his waist, strapped with a heavy belt, tapers. My pulse picks up at the familiar shape of the man's body.

The cowboy's pale throat, not obscured by the hat's brim, is glistening with sweat. When he closes the distance, his hat slides to the side and reveals Alex. My body clenches deliciously. His hair is longer, like it used to be at school, and his mouth piercing is back in place, gleaming on his bottom lip. It makes me think of what it would feel like between my thighs.

During my torrid thoughts, all the guinea pigs have progressed close enough to nip my feet, which are suddenly bare. Just as the closest guinea pig opens its maw to bite down on my left toe with its overlarge front incisors, Alex's long arm releases the reins and grabs me by the waist. He heaves me in front of him with an easy swoop. His warmth surrounds my body, and the solidness of his chest presses against my back, his upper body muscles shifting as the horse spins. Alex's powerful thighs squeeze my legs as he urges the horse to move faster and away from the danger.

The feel of his physique raises all the hairs on my body, the anticipation of what might happen next unbearable. The front of the saddle digs into my intimate parts in an almost painful way, and the motion of the rocking horse and Alex's body pressing against me is making my core melt.

My body starts moving. Up and down. Up and down. Until I fall apart so hard I wake up. I curse and wipe the sweat from my forehead. I feel ashamed and angry at Alex for being the main protagonist of my dream. Now I definitely won't be able to look him in the eye. Truce or no truce.

So, I just had a sex dream about ALEX, I message Lydia and Catherine.

Within thirty seconds, three dots appear next to Lydia's name as she's typing furiously despite the clock's hands pointing towards four in the morning. When I got home after the trip, I updated them on everything, including the fact that Alex and I buried the hatchet.

What the fuck? How hot on a scale from one to five?

I miss sex dreams, Catherine types wistfully and then adds, *Gabby has been on one tonight. I've slept less than two hours.* She must be eager to know too because another message pings straight after. *How was it?*

I would need to go into two-digit numbers, I message as my cheeks burn in the dark. My body shifts against the bed covers, but my skin feels too sensitive and hot, so I push them off with my legs.

Lydia's next message includes some very descriptive images of emojis with flushed cheeks and a plethora of vegetables. Cucumbers, courgettes, aubergines and such. She must have raided all the phallic-shaped emojis available on WhatsApp. She adds enthusiastically, *Tell me more. How did you do it? I've just returned from the most boring work do, and I need cheering up.*

Why would you stay at a party that was boring until four? I question.

Free booze. A few hot individuals. Now, tell me.

I retell the dream as succinctly as I can, but Lydia keeps asking probing questions.

I was with Aaron for years and had precisely zero sex dreams about him. Our sexual experiences were OK, sometimes even good, but he always cared more about his needs than mine. He rarely touched me the way I needed him to, and I was too shy to tell him what I wanted. I didn't feel exactly unsatisfied, but it always felt a little one-sided, a glass half empty. Maybe that's why he strayed and looked elsewhere.

Even though Alex and I never did it, the things we did never felt unfulfilled. However, I know that time tends to wash away the finer details and maybe I've just put my physical experiences with Alex, despite his betrayal, on a pedestal over the years because he was the first one to touch me like that.

Lydia pulls me out of the dark, spiralling pit that my mind has turned into. *Dinner tomorrow night? To celebrate the start of the half term?* Her message, as per custom, is trailed by a line of emojis of all the alcoholic beverages available on the chat. One must love her enthusiasm.

I message a thumbs up. Immediately my response is liked by Catherine.

I wish I could join you. My mother is staying over, but I want all the details. Especially what Alex looked like in a cowboy outfit.

I snort despite my misery. Catherine is never dirty, so her message amuses me greatly.

Around seven o'clock, I give up trying to fall asleep. Still dressed in my silk pyjamas and with a bad case of bedhead that would totally secure me an audition for an *Edward Scissorhands* remake if there was one, I log into one of my favourite auction sites that sells vintage shoes and start bidding on a few items. This is my happy place. That is until the internet connection goes. I *grrr* and pad barefoot to the router to see what the issue is. Unfortunately, never having been tech-savvy, I can't fathom a reason why it's not working even after I reset it. I check my phone, but my data plan is shocking. I *grrr* some more, hoping that my discordant interjection will work magic in the ether, but no luck.

I pull on my baggy jeans and threadbare grey sweatshirt that always makes me feel I'm ready to weather a storm and pack my laptop. There's an independent café nearby that sells OK croissants and offers its customers decent-speed Wi-Fi.

As soon as I walk into the café, the smell of roasting coffee beans envelops me like a fluffy blanket. I breathe it in, finding my inner zen. Even the loud noise of a coffee grinder, a milk frother and various whirring machines create a cacophony of sounds that's music to my ears. I've always loved coffee shops. And because I got paid last week and it has filled my bank account with hope and a few zeros preceded by an actual positive number, I don't regret spending a few pounds in the establishment.

With my still tender ankle, I hobble towards a tucked-away corner of the café and focus on the auction unravelling in front of me. A few minutes later, I'm glad I made the choice of coming here because one item in particular, a pair of 1940s blood-red ballroom shoes, is causing all bidders to go full loco mode like it's Bonhams Auction House and not a small niche online auction site.

I've always loved the auction environment, both online and offline. Knowing when to start and stop bidding and how high to go is an art. I love the way my bid can spur others into action or freeze them. It's all about timing, and I've always been good at it. I get hot from too much thrill and take my hoodie off, realising belatedly that underneath I'm wearing a vintage Spice Girls top that, despite being able to fit at least two of me, barely reaches my belly button. I think during my crop-top phase in my early teens and my obsession with '90s bands, I just decided to cut off the bottoms of all my band tops with scissors and never bothered to do anything else with them due to my inferior dressmaking skills. Only Spice Girls and Aqua crop tops have survived, but I'd guard them with my life.

The image of the girl band in their prime with Ginger Spice in the iconic Union Jack dress posing in the middle is so bleached out it would be nearly impossible to see which Spice is which if it wasn't for their distinct outfits, a combo of latex skirts, strappy shoes and brightly coloured tracksuit bottoms. Because I don't ever see anybody familiar in the café, I don't mind too much that I look like I've just stepped out of the '90s.

After obtaining the said 1940s shoes for peanuts, to celebrate, I head to the counter where a small queue of five people has gathered in my absence. I consider what to order when I notice a familiar ginger-haired man dressed in a blue zip-up jacket and grey joggers with one earbud of his earphones still plugged in while the other is hanging over his shoulder is standing in the queue two people ahead of me. My insides turn into a can of wiggly worms. Next, the bell over the front door rings and Aaron and Eva walk through. My already-queasy stomach flips upside down, threatening to send all the food I've eaten today back up. I consider my options and come up blank. I try to find a safe route that would lead me back to my table without being discovered, but the café has transformed into the Ninja Warrior obstacle course in front of my eyes, and I cannot see a way through.

As if reading my thoughts, Alex turns his head, and when he spots me, he smiles before his forehead puckers up as he registers my panicked state. I can hear the couple talking, coming closer to the counter with every step. The end is nigh.

All the blood drains from my face. I must look dreadful because when the barista asks Alex what he wants, he steps out of the queue and heads towards me.

'Holly?' Concern lends his voice a soft undertone. I almost don't notice his hand on my elbow because all I'm trying to do is stop myself from looking behind me. But I must not succeed because Alex glances over my shoulder. I could still run, but vexation makes my shoulders stiffen. Why should I cower? They're the ones that should be ashamed. This is my territory. I know I sound ridiculous, but Aaron has taken too much away from me already.

Trying to suppress the image of Alex in riding leathers, I say the most insane thing I possibly could. 'I'll buy your coffee and whatever you're having if you pretend you're here with me.'

Alex is the last person I want to witness my despair, but beggars can't be choosers. I'd choose beggars over losers right now. Despite my urgency, his musky smell combined with Lynx, my favourite deodorant, takes my nose by surprise. I can't not notice the sweat on his brow and how it adds to his masculinity. I shake my head, trying to empty it of unhelpful invasions while I'm in the middle of a crisis.

His eyes fill with confusion for a moment until they widen at reaching a realisation about who the person approaching from behind might be. I shove my embarrassment into the most remote compartment of my brain and throw away the key;

there's no room for it now. I've made a choice and there's no going back. I remember he heard me speaking to Catherine all those weeks ago and that he potentially knows everything.

'OK,' he says breezily, like I've just asked him about the weather rather than pretending to be my something in front of my ex and his very pregnant girlfriend. Alex's expression doesn't betray any emotions, and I can't fathom what he's thinking.

Before I have a chance to ponder further on this, he spins around because it's our turn to order. Because I'm still having a mild panic attack, I can't focus on what he's saying to the barista, but I watch her fill a tray with two hot drinks and two plates of pastries. Before I can stop him, Alex pays.

When we're about to move, a familiar hit of too-strong cologne accompanied by a sickly floral scent fills my nostrils. Aaron and his mistress-turned-mother-of-his-child have joined the queue. I remember smelling the exact fragrance in the bungalow months before I discovered he was cheating on me. I kept complaining to Aaron, the gaslighting bastard, about it, but he pretended he couldn't smell anything. My shoulders shudder at the memory, but Alex wraps his arm around my waist as he leads me away, slowing down to match my hobbling pace.

He leans into me. 'Where are you sitting?' His breath is hot against the shell of my ear.

I nod towards the table in the corner, and he seats himself in my chair, forcing me to turn my back on Aaron and the rest of the café. I shut my laptop, but before the screen turns black, Alex catches a glimpse of my online activities. His lip twitches for a moment before his features become unreadable again. Right now, I envy his ability to look casual.

My name is spoken somewhere behind me, but I don't react. Let Aaron come to me if he really desires to see me that much.

Instead of having a sip from his own coffee cup, Alex moves my drink in front of him and starts gathering all the sugar sachets on the tray into a small pile. Then, he opens them carefully one by one and empties the contents into my Americano. He's remembered not only my favourite hot drink but also how I drink it. For a few moments, I watch him as he empties sachet after sachet, my mind wandering to another morning in a different café ten years ago. Again, I wonder how somebody can change so much, and yet, stay the same. Suddenly, I'm transported back ten years.

15

It's six o'clock in the evening and the window of the dingy café is steamed up. Water droplets slide down the outside surface of the window in rivulets, creating small waterfalls. The inside of the café is cosy despite the smell of fried food, unyielding plastic furniture and Formica tops. But maybe I'm feeling cosy because Alex is opposite me.

He pours the fourth sachet of sugar into my black coffee, his long fingers ripping each packet as he goes, meticulously emptying every last grain of sugar. His pink lips are pursed, lip piercing shining almost golden in the artificial light. I can feel he's itching to say something.

'Spill it,' I challenge him.

He pauses, his green eyes gleaming with mirth.

'I will sound awfully pedantic, but I can't help it so don't judge me.' I can't stop the grin. It's so like Alex, acknowledging his mistakes before he's even made them, yet unable to stop himself. 'You know that that amount of sugar will only turn into glucose, give you a short energy boost and then once it's metabolised, your energy level will drop rapidly and make you feel even worse?'

He cares so much about so many things, including me. I love that about him. At the word love, my brain goes into total override, buffering and buffering until it halts, flashing a message in CG Times Roman Bold font stating *401 – Unauthorized. Your request could not be processed*. The word has been sneaking up on me for the last few weeks, and I can't quite figure out what to do with it.

'You're right – it does make you sound pedantic.' He pushes against my shoulder playfully, making me laugh. 'You're such a smarty-pants.' I lean over and muss his hair to dispel the thickness in my throat. The amber strands run silkily between my fingers.

When I'm ready to pull away, he quickly catches my hand and kisses my palm. Heat crackles in the pit of my stomach like fresh firewood chucked onto a well-established fire. That's what it's like being with Alex. Over the weeks I've been going out with him, I've been unable to suppress the growing reaction. My body is ablaze whenever he's near me, every touch kindling this feeling further. If we carry on in this vein, one day I'll just spontaneously combust. My face must show my not-so-subtle, and frankly crude, desires because he leans closer, and his lips caress mine in an unspoken promise of more.

'When you look at me like that, you drive me insane.' His breathing picks up. We're a complete electrical circuit whenever we touch. The source, conductors, load and all. Whenever our skins connect, we create a fixed path for electricity to flow through.

'Like what?' I ask, suddenly as breathless as he is. I've never been bold, but my shyness is defeated by curiosity.

'Like I'm everything.' His words make my chest explode into a million pieces, sparks of heat flying into the crevasses created by the rupture.

I'm ready to share feelings with him that I haven't dared to say even in my own mind when the door to the café opens, followed by a loud bell chime.

A couple seat themselves in the faraway corner. I barely look at them, but something about the man snags in my brain, and I have to check what it is. My mouth dries up when I recognise him.

My dad's shaggy brown hair and old-fashioned glasses stand out in the rundown café. I watch him as he helps a woman in her late twenties out of a fluffy pink coat. Everything about them, their age, their outfits and even their body postures, makes them look jarring next to each other. I don't realise I've flinched until my chair scrapes loudly against the lino floor and Alex asks whether I'm OK. I nod, unsure whether I mean it.

I wonder why my dad's here. He's supposed to be at a conference, something to do with his post-doctorate project.

My dad stands up when he catches sight of me. He winces at first but then his whole posture changes as his eyeline snaps sideways to Alex. With a deep scowl, he walks towards us. My dad has never been angry or aggravated with me because he's a placid man, but this man is nothing like the dad I know.

'Holly? What are you doing here?' When he asks the question, all he does is stare at Alex. I'd never thought my dad could be condescending, and immediately, embarrassment colours my cheeks.

'Dad, this is Alex. My friend from school.' Even despite my dad's even-tempered nature, I'm not stupid enough to call Alex my boyfriend in front of him.

Alex is about to introduce himself when my dad stops him with a hand up like he's teaching a kid a lesson. Frowning, I sit up.

'Aren't you supposed to be at Victoria's studying for tomorrow's maths test?' He doesn't acknowledge Alex again; it's like he's turned invisible.

To my dismay, apart from an almost imperceptible twitch at the mention of Vicky's name, Alex looks impassive. I've seen him amused, content, cross and even grumpy before, but I've never seen him this expressionless. It's like he's erected the Great Wall of China in his mind in the last two seconds and nothing will penetrate through it.

'Vicky had to go to her nan's. What are you doing here?' I lean to the side to check out the blonde who's staring at me with curiosity. When she catches my stare, she busies herself with the menu.

'Watch your tone, young lady,' my dad warns, and it's so out of character, I cringe. 'The conference was cancelled so instead I've had consultations with my undergrads the whole afternoon. It seems we're both in different places we said we would be, but only one of us has a good reason for it.'

'Consultations in a café?' I can't let it go. Even the idea of what I'm thinking makes me feel sick.

'Not that I approve of your interrogation methods, but my office got flooded this morning, and this was the closest place to hold the consults,' he says sternly, and I realise he's right. His office is just across the road.

Relief hits me like a stray missile. It was stupid of me to suggest he was lying. Now that I look back towards the table, I can see my dad's laptop bag resting against one of the bent metal legs, and the blonde has fired up her own laptop and is now typing furiously away. It still doesn't give him the right to be rude to Alex.

'Go home,' my dad orders me, like I'm a little kid. He's never been this high-handed or direct with me. From the corner of my eye, I watch Alex passively observing the scene, seemingly bored. My chest squeezes so hard that I think I'm experiencing a cardiac event.

'No,' I say defiantly, not recognising the voice that leaves my mouth. I've never talked back to my parents before despite the fact I rarely agree with my mother on anything.

Alex grabs my wrist under the table and squeezes gently, stopping me in my tracks.

'I've got somewhere to be anyway,' Alex says dismissively, carrying a strong Yorkshire accent. I know his mum is from Yorkshire, but he's never sounded like it; his words are usually enunciated to the point of perfection. 'I'll walk you home.'

Alex gathers his things. He walks past me, giving himself so much space as though I've developed some viral infection in the last two minutes.

'I'll wait for you outside,' Alex mutters without looking at my dad who is just standing there and silently fuming like he's a little boy rather than a grown adult.

I have no words left in my brain because the space is filled with white noise. When I train my eyes on my hands, they're shaking with frustration.

'How old is that boy?' My dad interrogates me as soon as Alex is gone.

'He's in my A Levels year group.'

'I'm surprised he's gotten that far,' he mumbles.

'Are you for real?' My voice rises a few octaves, and the blonde coughs loudly. Despite her best efforts at pretending to type, it's clear she's eavesdropping.

'I don't like the look of that boy; he seems like trouble. I don't want to see you with him ever again. I'll call your mother to check you've arrived at home.' He checks his watch which is his default sign he's finished with this conversation. Without another word, he returns to his table.

I feel so disappointed my vision blurs for a moment. My benevolent father, my hero, has turned into a petty, prejudiced man. It's always been my dad and me against the world.

When I exit the café, Alex is toeing a piece of rock.

Still stunned, I start apologising, but he interrupts before I get a chance to finish, like he's not interested in anything I have to say. 'Let's get you home.'

I'm ready to ask whether he's being serious, but his expression is completely shut down. I have the feeling if I said anything, he wouldn't be able to hear me anyway.

The rain has settled into a steady drizzle, and I'm almost glad for it because it fills the space and silence that the scene with my dad has created between us. Over my sodden hood, I can't see where we're walking until we stop in front of a block of flats on a small council estate. The front of the building is littered with cigarette butts and a few broken bottles whose shards reflect the light from the nearest streetlamp.

I don't ask which one of the dark windows staring blankly down at us is Alex's bedroom. He's never invited me to his place, and I've never asked, never feeling like I could. My house has been out of bounds because my mother is always there, pottering about and prying into other people's business.

'If you wait here, I'll lend you an umbrella.' His words are almost harsh, his green eyes gazing at me without any expression. A sound akin to a whimper escapes my mouth, but I can't stop it. Why is he being like that? Have I done something wrong? At hearing it, Alex squeezes my upper arm through the soaked layers of my shirt and hoodie and says almost softly, 'I don't want you to catch your death.'

'Can I use the loo please?' I shift my weight from left to right. I didn't want to ask, but my bladder is bursting. I can feel his reluctance, but it's either that or I'll have to pee in the bushes, and he knows it. Eventually, he nods.

Inside the building, the corridor is lined with old-fashioned red carpet. It's threadbare and dirty in some places and smells faintly of dog. We walk up the stairs to the second floor.

When Alex unlocks a white door with a scratched seven on it, he beckons to indicate I can come in. I scan the small space nervously. It's a studio flat, and the room is divided into a tiny kitchenette in the corner, a green sofa and a coffee table opposite. To my left, a corner of a double bed peeks from behind a wooden screen.

Despite all the furniture being old-fashioned and slightly weathered with age, everything is immaculately clean and tidy except for the bed behind the wall that is covered in female clothing and the contents of a make-up bag scattered around as if someone was in a rush. Alex's lips press into a thin line at the sight of the mess.

My eyes drift to the coffee table that has a neat pile of books, some on classical guitars and others by Orwell and Hardy. On top of the pile, a pair of familiar headphones rest; I realise with overwhelming tenderness that this is where Alex sleeps. When I inhale, I recognise the familiar smell of cleaning products and cigarettes because that's the smell I associate with Alex.

A handwritten note on the fridge that lists a few shopping items and bills that need to be paid, including the council tax and water bill, confirms my uncomfortable feeling. The handwriting is familiar, the ticks next to some of the items on the list have an extra flick at the start. Alex is a young carer. All those phone calls with his mum make sense now.

Turning to face Alex, my mouth opens, but when I catch his look, tense and vulnerable, my words die on my lips.

He doesn't look me in the eye when he points directly to my right. 'Toilet's that way.' I nod even though he can't see it.

The small toilet is crammed with hair and body products that I rummage through after I've peed. I find a can of Lynx in the only wall cabinet and when I pop the lid open, Alex's smell envelops me. Unable to stop myself, I spray it in the air and walk through the mist, inhaling deeply.

At some point, my hands start shaking, because in my naïve mind, I've always thought when Alex said he lived in a flat, I imagined one of those punky urban loft conversions with skylights and brick walls. I can't fathom how both his mum and he can coexist in such a small space. When I picture our house, the thought makes me feel itchy, like there are ants under my skin.

I stare at myself for a long moment in the cracked mirror. I'm too neat and preppy-ish in my blue shirt and yellow-and-red zip-up hoodie. How can he stand me being here? I would hate it if I were him. I think back to my dad and the way he behaved towards Alex. A strange pang of rage at my dad and this whole situation colours my vision red; I want to smash things, but that would be highly counter-productive right now.

I tug at my shirt nervously before I walk back to the main room, my heart in my throat. Straight away, I notice that the heap of clothes on the bed is neatly piled in a column and the make-up bag has disappeared. His back towards me, Alex is standing in the compact kitchenette, making tea judging by the sounds and smells.

He confirms my guess. 'Sorry, we ran out of coffee, and I haven't had a chance to do a shop this week. I know you don't drink tea, but it's all we have.' He seems so coolly polite and distant, and I can't bear it anymore.

I want the opposite of distance. Until now, I've not realised how much I need him. It's developed into this physical ache, and it scares the hell out of me. I need every single part of our bodies to be touching to make sure he's OK and that we're OK, and I need it right now, but I don't know how to ask for it. I've never initiated any serious physical contact, feeling shy and inexperienced next to Alex. It has always been Alex who would hold my hand, stroke my cheek or kiss me.

'Please stop,' I implore.

He slowly turns around, the steaming tea abandoned on the counter.

'What? You don't want tea?' He's still using that impassive tone, and I don't know how to snap him out of it. I'm desperate.

I gather my nerves and walk towards him. I grab his face and press my lips against his, my body coming flush with his. Toes to toes, thighs to thighs, stomach to stomach. His heart is beating fast against my chest, in synchrony with mine. I've never touched a boy like this before. I know I'm being a bit clumsy, but now that I've touched Alex, I can't stop or even consider the possibility of ever wanting to touch another human being who is not Alex.

At first, Alex doesn't do anything. Then, as if a switch was turned on, he opens up to me and our tongues connect, the sensation electrifying the insides of my mouth and sending tingling numbness down my spine. He slides his hands down my back and to my backside, squeezing with urgency. The combination of his slick tongue, the cool sting of his piercing against my bottom lip and his hands on my bum is indescribable. We've kissed and touched before, and it has always been amazing, but I've never thought it could be like this. My core has turned hot and liquid like lava and I need Alex to do something, but I'm not sure exactly what.

Everything inside me clenches as he presses me against him. I can feel him hard against my leg, and the proof of him wanting me as much as I want him makes me moan. I need to feel every part of him, but I'm too shy to really touch him where I want to the most, so I settle on his shoulders. But I'm restless and impatient and move to his waist, my fingers dipping under his T-shirt where his skin is the softest. He pulls it off and over his head and then disposes of my hoodie.

Not breaking the kiss, he guides me towards the sofa, and we sort of fall, tumble, with Alex's weight pressing down on me. He is heavy, but the solidness of his body against mine feels delicious, and my bones crave him. I feel vulnerable and fragile, about to disintegrate under his touch. A pang of panic speeds up my pulse, but I don't want to stop or slow down to overthink what's happening between us.

He pushes my thigh up and hooks it over his hip, spreading my legs enough for him to settle between them. The position makes us even closer. Hands searching, I explore his lean back, and my nails rake down his body from shoulders to waist. He groans and arches against me, and the reaction sends my head back, slamming against the armrest.

He moves his hand between our bodies. Even through the jeans, his touch is everything, and the heat between my legs quadruples. I can't think and my eyes close to process the strong feeling. All I think is that I've never wanted anybody so much in my life and that I need him to do things I've never thought

I would want another being to do to me. I want them all with Alex.

He shifts his focus to the waist of my jeans, his fingers delving under the waistband towards the place I want him to touch me. Some vestige of nervousness comes back, and I jerk under his advances. As if pulled from a trance, he shrinks back and sits up against the opposite corner of the sofa. His cheeks are flushed, his red hair tousled.

'No,' he forces through his gritted teeth. A hard lump forms in my throat and threatens to choke me.

'Was I that bad? I've never…' I don't know how to finish the sentence without crying.

Alex gathers his T-shirt and pulls it on. As he stands, he mumbles, 'I'm not your rebel boy to piss off your daddy.'

Is that what this is about? I'm hurt that he thinks so little of me, but when I replay his words, all I hear is vulnerability, and I can't stay cross at him. He always seems so composed and confident. I have never thought that he might not feel that way. I have never given him the benefit of the doubt.

I stand and put my hand on his arm, but he shakes it off.

'It's not what this is.' I try to speak calmly but fail halfway through.

'I shouldn't have touched you like that, I'm sorry. I think you should go.' He turns around and starts pouring the undrunk cups of tea into the sink without looking at me.

I consider just leaving and being angry at him for being stupid, but then I get defeated and instead whisper, 'I'm in love with you.'

He freezes, the water running loudly in the sudden silence. The cups clank in the sink. His shoulders stiffen, but he's frozen otherwise, like what I've just said bears no weight. A tear escapes my eye and leaks over my flushed cheek. I brush it off, not wanting him to see my shame. Not knowing what to say, I say the lamest thing I can think of, 'I'll see you at school.'

I'm almost at the door when he envelops me in his arms, pressing me against him with an urgency that nearly chokes me. His heart is pounding what feels like a thousand beats per minute against my chest.

'I'm such an idiot. I'm so sorry,' he mutters into my hair. 'I thought… it's stupid. It doesn't matter.' When he pushes away, his face is shattered and devastatingly handsome. His eyes don't leave mine when he says, 'I'm in love with you, too.'

Knee-trembling relief floods through my system. He wraps both his arms around me again but then pauses, his nostrils flaring.

'Have you used my deodorant?'

I can't help but grin. I don't think I've ever been this happy.

16

I'm brought back to the present and wonder how much I've ever actually known Alex.

Oblivious to my bittersweet trip down memory lane, Alex takes a slow sip of his coffee. 'They're coming.'

I follow his lead and start drinking my beverage. The sweetness tastes almost bitter on my tongue and I *hmmm* in approval.

Registering the approaching footsteps, I can't stop my body from tensing.

'By the way, I strongly approve of your band choice.'

I splutter into my cup. I hoped he hadn't noticed my T-shirt.

'Holly. I thought it was you,' Aaron greets me as soon as he stops by our table.

I recognise the doll-like brunette next to him, even though the last time we met she had less clothing on and was significantly more flushed. Aaron towers over her, and I bet he loves it; he always hated I was a bit taller.

The woman, Eva, smiles at me good-naturedly, like we're friends and not like she's a dirty homewrecker who derailed my life. I hate everything about her, so I ignore her and focus on the spawn of Satan in front of me. I don't understand why he's come over to say hi in the first place, especially with the truncated conversation about repayment hanging over our heads. If I were him, I'd avoid me. If I were him, I'd dig myself a very deep hole, cover it with heavy rocks and finish it off with a layer of concrete. I'd stay there, marinating in my own guilt and shame and contemplate what a bad person I was until I ran out of oxygen.

'Aaron.' I'm pleased with myself because I sound almost dignified. As dignified as somebody can be wearing a faded Spice Girls top.

Aaron scans the table and ends at the emptied sachets of sugar in front of Alex, knowing full well how I drink my coffee. Then his face scrunches up and I'm forced to find the source of offence. Alex's hand has ended up casually resting next to mine on the table. To a stranger, it might seem Alex and I are a couple, as preposterous as it sounds. I feel wounded that Aaron should be this aghast at me having a male companion.

Judging by his rigid posture, Aaron's waiting for me to introduce Alex or for Alex to introduce himself, but neither of us makes a move. It's like we've rehearsed this. Mirth makes my lip twitch, and my nausea retreats.

Unable to stand the tension, Eva smiles at Alex, but he's doing his Lord Sugar impression, staring at her in that intimidatingly passive way he used to at me at school. With that performance, I'll have to buy him a life-long supply of coffee and pastries.

'How have you been?' Aaron loses the game. He's always been a people pleaser and could never stand the idea of people disapproving of him.

'Great actually.' I don't elaborate, and I don't ask him how he's been. I hope he's had the worst time ever.

'Aaron has just been promoted.' Eva pulls herself up to her full hobbit height. Aaron's cheeks gain a subtle pink sheen, and he adjusts his watch; he's embarrassed. Good.

'Good for you.' I take another sip of my coffee.

Eva rubs her rounded belly pressing against the blue cashmere jumper. I've tried studiously ignoring that part of her body for the last two minutes but failed. 'Oh, dear. I have to pee. It's the baby,' she says jovially to Alex who remains stone-faced. Who says *oh dear*? She pecks Aaron on the cheek before she strides towards the toilets at the back of the café. One of Aaron's past comments rings in my head. He used to complain that I never kissed him in public. I guess he's gotten everything he's ever wanted.

Alex's phone starts ringing. For a nanosecond, his brow furrows, the old Alex glimpsing through that gesture. He used to have that exact expression whenever his phone rang, always anticipating a catastrophe, but I guess Alex had to turn into a fatalist. When he pulls it out of his pocket, *Jane* lights up the screen.

'Take it. It might be important,' I say calmly, but on the inside, I'm screaming *don't leave me*. I hate to admit it, but Alex's presence has steadied me.

He weaves through the crowd that has just strode through the door and heads outside, disappearing from view.

Once Alex is gone, Aaron drops the pretence. 'Can't you be more civil? It's not like we're at war. We split up. That's not the end of the world.' He scolds me like we're still together. 'And what's up with that?' He points towards Alex's vacated seat.

It takes me a while to process his words because a part of me still thinks he's not being serious, but his expression and body language say otherwise. How had I missed seeing what a colossal arsehat he is?

'How would you like me to be? Friendlier?' My voice drips with sarcasm.

He scowls at my tone. 'Eva has nothing to do with this.'

I don't deign to react to his stupid comment because, of course, Eva has everything to do with this. 'I've messaged you,' I say to change the topic. The power balance has tipped slightly in my favour.

'I've been busy.' He rakes his hand through his hair, making the top stand up. That's when I notice the subtle changes about him. His hair, usually immaculately styled, looks messy, and his T-shirt is creased. His stubble has also seen better days. I wonder how he's been enjoying his new life, but I'm not petty enough to ask him that and give him the satisfaction of making me the villain.

He exhales loudly and sits in Alex's seat. A breath whooshes out of me. Have I given him the wrong impression?

He leans over the table, moving the coffee cups to one side. He invades my space by parking his arms so close I have to move my hands to my lap. It feels almost like the old times, when he says, 'Let's not fight. It's the promotion and all the baby stuff. It's exhausting. It's a scan here, a pre-natal course there.' He rubs his stubble and waits for my reaction.

I've never realised it until now, but Aaron is an emotional vampire. He drains but doesn't give in return. We were never a good match.

I press my lips together until they feel numb. 'What does that have to do with my money?'

A sullen expression forces itself onto his features. Did he really expect sympathy from me? He sits up in his seat, his back ramrod straight.

'We can't afford it right now. Maybe we can revisit this discussion next year?' He sounds a degree less assured.

'That's not acceptable.' His posture changes with my answer. He pulls himself to his feet, playing the height game, but I'm not going to stoop so low as to stand up.

'I liked Eva's cashmere jumper and her Timberland boots.'

He glowers at me. 'You've always been mean-spirited. I shouldn't have expected sympathy from you.' He inhales deeply. 'You always look down on people, thinking you're better than everyone else.' I try to interject because that's not true, but he doesn't give me a chance. 'Finally, you're showing your true colours. Casually drinking your coffee with some bloke you probably found and shagged five minutes after we split up. You are your daddy's girl, after all.'

That is the lowest blow he could have dished out and it lands right smack in the middle of my chest. I go light-headed, and my vision starts swimming. The inside of my mouth feels like sandpaper. I feel so exhausted I can't muster a single word.

Judging by the determined glint in his eyes, Aaron's ready to give me some more.

'I would be very careful about what you say next,' Alex warns coolly, managing to loom over Aaron. He crosses his long arms in front of him in a casual stance, but his face is impregnable permafrost. My mind goes completely blank.

'Who are you to be telling me what to do?' Aaron barks. Either he's brave or he's an idiot. I would bet on the second.

Alex is nothing but calm when he answers, 'That's none of your business.'

Aaron measures his options but comes up short because Alex gives out raw male energy whereas Aaron just looks pathetic.

Alex finishes with a carefully enunciated, 'Now, you're standing in my way. I suggest that you move and take your bimbo with you.'

I cough in surprise at his wording, so unlike Alex.

Before Aaron flips his lid, I implore, 'Just go.' I hate the defeated tone in my voice, but it propels Aaron to spin on his heel and leave.

From the corner of my eye, I see my ex walking towards Eva who has just come out of the toilets. He whispers something in her ear at which she grimaces, and they both exit the café without a single backwards glance.

I slump in my seat, feeling drained, like I've just finished a double Les Mills session. My head is swirling with a myriad of emotions firing into each other, causing a chemical reaction similar to Mentos mixed with cola.

Alex seats himself opposite me with deep indignation in his usually stoic expression. Looking like golden dust, all his freckles stand out against the paleness of his complexion. I take a gulp of coffee to ease my swollen throat.

For a long moment, we sit there in silence, neither of us feeling the need to fill it with small talk. Even though I do feel the need to fill it with profanities. I have an inkling that Alex is giving me space to process what has just happened. I'm starting to gather that despite the thick layer of ice and hostility, Alex is actually a decent human being underneath. Then the past floods in and sweeps over my newly acquired idea of Alex, and his image warps and tarnishes like silver in humidity.

Unaware of my emotional turmoil, Alex curses, 'What a scumbag.' Abandoning his coffee, he studies me solemnly. 'I'm sorry. That was very inconsiderate of me.'

'But apt – that was a very accurate assessment of Aaron's character.' Something gave in within me after his offer of truce yesterday and now I cannot rebuild the walls I so carefully put up around myself. 'Shame I didn't reach the same conclusion when I met him five years ago.'

He looks nonplussed at my forthcoming comment, but my openness must unlock something within him, too, because he says, 'I presume he's the reason why your current address didn't match the original paperwork?' I nod.

He considers this before he's ready to continue. 'I want you to know that what I am going to say next is meant in good faith, not condescending or dismissive as it will probably come out as. I know that we don't exactly have a good track record of communicating effectively or understanding what the other person is trying to say.' That's a mild way of putting it, I think to myself. 'He did you a favour by doing what I think he did and you discovering the truth because otherwise you'd still be stuck with him and not know any better.'

Alex has always been pragmatic and said things how

they were. The past and present merge together and become entwined and blurred.

Something that got broken inside me with Aaron cheating has been mended over the past two months without me noticing. I feel brand-new, reborn and raw at the same time, whole but ready to be hurt all over again. I'm a kintsugi vessel, all the broken fragments of me fused together with veins of gold. Looking at the man in front of me, unbearable vulnerability hijacks my entire being.

A peculiar fragile sensation balloons in my chest. I could fall apart with a single word. With paralysing fear, I realise I want this version of Alex to be the real Alex. I get a sudden need to run, to escape him and then run some more to dodge my crashing epiphany.

Exasperation lances my insides at being caught in Alex's trap once again, and the last thing I want right now is his pity. Before I say something I might regret, I start gathering my things.

'I need to go.' I'm a trapped animal.

'What?' He looks genuinely puzzled at my sudden one-eighty turn. He follows my movements as I zip up my bag and slide it over my shoulder.

'Whoa. What have I done?' He stands up abruptly, making the chair scrape in his wake. I don't see what he does next because self-preservation makes me storm out of the café.

I take a shortcut through the high street and cut across the car park behind the main row of shops. The temperature has unexpectedly dropped, and gravel mixed with mulchy leaves crunch and squish under my boots as I gain distance from Alex. The car park is brimming with cars, but there's not a soul in sight. Steps sound behind me, and when I realise who it is, my heart jolts in my ribcage and then starts racing.

He must have run here because Alex's cheeks are flushed, his chest heaving, and his eyebrows drawn together in an angry line. He's standing so close yellow specks are glinting in his green eyes. 'You forgot your purse.' He shoves the familiar polka-dotted item in my hand. I deserved it.

'See you later.' He's about to turn but changes his mind at the last minute and halts. 'Actually, a *thank you* would do before I go.' He carries on, 'I thought we agreed on a truce. You asked me to help, and I did. I don't understand you.' He takes a gulp of air, all pretended composure wiped off his face and replaced by exasperation. 'Are you angry with me?'

'I'm not angry with you. I'm angry...' I half-shout, echoing his words at the farm, but then my voice falters.

He becomes still, waiting for me to finish the sentence, but I can't do that without compromising myself.

I take a step back to gain some composure, but he immediately takes a step forward. It's like we're dancing the waltz. 'Why are you angry?' His words come out as a gruff whisper. Familiar restless energy takes over my limbs and empties my head of any thoughts other than Alex and his closeness.

I'm done fighting. 'I'm angry with myself because I don't know whether this is real. And I'm angry because I still get affected by you like this.' Stunned by my confession, he shrinks back, but I don't stop now. 'I don't know which one is the real you. Is it the Alex who puts me down in front of a class or the one who asks me for a truce and admits he was wrong? Is it the one who tells me I'm a mess or the one who stands up for me against my cheating ex-boyfriend?' I land the final blow. 'Is it the considerate and caring teenager who seemed to like me or the boy who got bored of me and found another toy to play with five minutes after we were finished? You can't have it both ways, Alex. You can either be an arsehole or not. I find you and your motives conflicting and confusing. The most confusing thing is that I don't know what you want from me.'

His shoulders lift when a breath whooshes out of him at my confession. I don't know what possesses me next, but I breach the space between us, stand on my tiptoes and draw him to me.

Then I bring my lips to his. I don't give him a chance to push me away or pull me close, because either reaction would shatter something inside me. I press my lips to his, masochistically waiting for the electric current to singe them and when it does, I pull away.

Alex's face acquires a strange expression, dark storms stirring behind his eyes. He makes a move, but I turn around before he decides what to do and leave him standing there, dishevelled and confused.

17

The following week is spent with Lydia, hitting all the bottomless brunch places across the town using her work benefits card, and with Catherine, day-tripping to *Peppa Pig World* and *Adventure Wonderland*. On Wednesday, I go for an afternoon tea with my mother in M&S and spend the whole afternoon watching her buy a single pair of gloves.

It's not until Friday afternoon I start thinking about Alex and what I'm going to do when I see him tonight at Becky's birthday party.

I keep rethinking my decision to go because I can't stand the idea of Alex pretending that I didn't kiss him, or worse, acknowledging I did. It's wrong on so many levels, not to mention he's my ECT mentor.

I get changed five times until I finally settle on a strappy blood-red dress flaring into an A-line skirt. It barely reaches my mid-thighs, and I ponder on the appropriateness of it. To dress it down, I complement it with a white shirt underneath and black-and-grey tights. I put on red lipstick but only brush my lashes with mascara that turns my muddy-brown eyes hazel. If I squint, I look like a slightly more mousy-haired version of Emma Roberts.

I drink half a glass of white wine I find at the back of the kitchen cupboard. I definitely don't remember buying it, but I need to quieten my nerves. The label is so washed out I can barely read what it says, and the cap is slightly crusty when I unscrew it. The contents aren't much better and smell like malted vinegar. When I take a swig, it reminds me of something you would use to scrub windows with if you ran out of Mr Muscle. It's acidic, and I can feel a literal hole being burnt into my stomach wall, so I drain the rest down the sink. I watch the liquid glug lazily for a few moments.

I should have someone to unblock the drain, but I'm concerned about what blockage they might discover down the pipe. A rat? A dead man's finger? A human scalp? Anything is possible in this flat.

By the time the taxi arrives, I'm ready to go despite my stomach feeling bruised from the acidic aperitive and apprehension.

Liberté Lounge, a French bistro slash cocktail bar, is packed to the brim. As soon as I enter, a waft of stale air and overcooked chicken smelling of fancy herbs hits my nose.

I find our table easily because it's the loudest table by far. It's also covered in confetti and scattered with half-unwrapped presents. Immediately, I notice the informal sections it's divided into. It's like sixth form all over again. To my left, it's the boisterous centre of the party. John, Danielle, Rob and a few younger members of staff I rarely socialise with occupy the left wing. I catch Danny lobbing a French fry at John who attempts to catch it with his mouth.

To my right, it's the more conservative table that's occupied by Ellie, Tom, and Jane who is politely sipping on a glass of red wine, her purple glasses reflecting the buttery light escaping from under the shaded lamps scattered around. Next to Jane and positioned at the end of the table is Alex. I ignore the way my stomach keels over in my belly at the sight of him. If it wasn't for Alex, I would park myself there for the night.

Nobody registers my entrance, and I hang my parka on a coat stand in the corner, stalling for time to decide where to sit.

I feel a bit exposed, but it's too late to go home and get changed. Maybe I should have put on something longer and less... I try to think of the right word but only come up with... *red*.

Becky, who's sitting in the middle of the long table, the neutral territory, spots me and shouts excitedly, 'Holly.'

I stop myself from adjusting my collar when everyone looks up from their respective drinks and plates of food. John mouths *hot* while pretending his fingers have turned into claws. Judging by the gesture, he's had a few drinks already. Danielle gives me a forced smile, but I'm OK with that after our interaction at the farm. We were never destined to be friends.

I wave noncommittally at everyone because I've always hated being the centre of attention. But then I register Alex and my heart turns into a timpani, each beat sending vibrations through my entire body. He scans every centimetre of my body, settling on my shoes. My new vintage red ballroom shoes that were delivered just a couple of days ago. When his attention rounds off to my face, we lock eyes. A strange tingle washes over my body. I muster all the restraint within and drag my gaze away.

There's an empty seat next to Jane, but I'd rather sit on a bed of nails. I'm grateful when John makes room between him and Becky that I just about fit in. Settling in my seat, I catch Jane whispering in Alex's ear. Immediately, they both stand and head to the bar. I try not to feel disappointed that Alex disappears at the first sight of me. Was the kiss that disgusting to him? I cringe at the possibility of Jane knowing about it.

When nobody pays us attention, John leans in. 'You look amazing.' He smells of booze, but it's nice of him to compliment me. He's messaged me a few times over the week, and all the messages were friendly, asking me what I've been up to. I feel a little bad because I've only replied to half of them.

I turn to Becky. 'Happy birthday.' I induce some cheer into my voice and immediately jerk when John's thigh presses against mine; I forgot about John's manspreading. I cross my legs to make myself smaller, but it's uncomfortable, so I just give up and try to filter it out.

I refocus on Becky. I pass her a small bag that contains a vintage brooch in the shape of a scarab because I know she's fascinated by them and a voucher for an afternoon tea with alpacas. I remember she mentioned she loved animals and always wanted to have a farm. She flushes at my gift and hugs me.

'That's so generous and thoughtful, Holly,' she mumbles into my hair with self-consciousness.

'I thought you might not want another scented candle or a box of chocolates.' I scan all the presents around me.

She checks that nobody is listening and whispers, 'Don't get me wrong. I love the gifts, but I'm also allergic to anything scented. It makes me sneeze.'

'I guess you can always pull a Rachel,' I suggest, and she laughs. I know she's a *Friends* fan.

We end up talking about mid-2000s TV shows and spend a solid forty minutes discussing *Pushing Daises* because Chuck is the most iconic undead character that has ever *lived*, and her fashion choices are the thing of dreams to which Becky readily agrees. I sip my glass of wine slowly because I'm worried about what drunk Holly might do or say. After my third glass, Becky and I share a bowl of fries and pepper-stuffed olives.

'I must admit I've always had a crush on Ned. There's something about brooding, emotionally detached men.' Becky titters; she's passed the tipsy mark by about a mile. She searches the bar with her eyes, stopping at Alex who's spent the last twenty minutes there, drinking and talking to the barmaid despite Jane leaving a while ago. No doubt avoiding me. A few people have a friendly chat with him despite professing at work he's the bane of their existence. But Danielle sticks the longest, involving Alex in what is obviously a one-sided conversation. Eventually, she returns to her side of the table, crestfallen. Despite Alex being on the opposite end of the room, I sense his eyes watching me.

Half an hour later, the party takes a wilder turn. I've had two piña coladas, and my body feels light as a feather. I'm convinced that if I lift my feet off the floor, I'd instantly go up in the air like a helium-filled balloon.

Alex eventually returns to our table, drinking his fourth gin. Not that I'm counting. I notice he never finishes a glass but don't think much of it.

Around half ten, a few tables are pushed to the sides and some people start dancing on the makeshift dancefloor, Danny and Danielle among them.

John keeps flitting between different people, but like a yoyo, keeps coming back to his seat to speak to me. Every time he does, he leans a little closer despite me sending a clear message I'm not into him. When he does that the fourth time, his fingers rest on the area where the collar meets my bare skin. It's an overfamiliar gesture that draws attention. I squirm, but he doesn't register my reaction. My attention snaps to Alex whose gaze is Velcroed to the place where John is touching me. What must he think of me? First, I kiss him, and now I let John manhandle me in front of everyone. I pull away from under John's octopus-like touch once again, making a vague excuse of going to the toilet.

For someone so shy, Becky gives it her all. She gets so drunk she ends up what can only be described as hollering along to Rihanna's *Only Girl*, but because she doesn't remember most of the words, everyone's in stitches. It doesn't stop her from trying. Eventually, Joanna takes her to the bar to ply her with some coffee to sober up so she can carry on in her rendition of Shakira that's to play at her request later on.

By that point, I'm ready to go home, so I push through the dancefloor to say my goodbyes to Becky, but the small crowd is denser than I expected, and I have to elbow my way through.

'Aha. Our sexy femme fatale.' John appears out of nowhere and grabs my waist, forcing me to his side. He's sweaty and drunk as a lord. I push against him when he attempts to sloppily slide his hand below my waist while still holding a drink in the other. By the smell of it, it's rum and coke.

'Ha, ha,' I say without humour and try to pull out of his icky grip once more. I'm close to committing second-degree murder if he doesn't release me soon. 'Let go,' I command him, but he either ignores it or doesn't hear my order.

I'm ready to give him my first-ever hammer fist punch on the jaw that I learnt from a YouTube tutorial when he dips his head to the crook of my neck, but immediately he's plucked off me before I spur into action, his falling drink narrowly missing my shiny shoes.

'Get your hands off her,' a male voice grinds out from behind me. I swipe my head to the side to catch Alex glowering at John who, suddenly, almost sobers up. Alex's fists are tightened, his knuckles white, ready to squash John with his big hands until he's the size of a pocket Rubik's Cube. I've never seen him this incandescent. I fear that if I don't do something, he'll rip John's head off. Not that John wouldn't deserve it for being a gargantuan sleazebag. Heedless of the attention he's attracting, John wobbles on his feet, and his smile turns into a laugh.

'I knew it,' John roars victoriously. A few people whisper curiously while still pretending to dance. I hate making a scene and think of a quick and quiet escape.

'You're shagging, aren't you?' John spins drunkenly to pin me with a disgusted look. 'I thought you had better taste than that.'

My mind whirls. I see the situation play out in front of me in slow motion. Alex's eyes flare with the rage of a thousand volcanic eruptions. His body sets into motion, his fist ready to wipe the smirk off John's face. Before it lands, I jump between them and splay my palms against Alex's chest and push. It feels like trying to budge a wall, but it stops him in his tracks.

'Alex, don't. He's drunk,' I croak, barely audible over the blaring music.

When he registers my hands on him, he slumps. His expression softens before it steels again. We're almost the same height, but I feel fragile next to his powerful body. All I feel is lean muscles under my hands, and his heart, pounding almost painfully against my skin.

'Sleep it off, jackass,' Alex spits at John who salutes before he swivels around with a wobble like a clumsily twisted spinning top and buggers off the dancefloor.

I rear back when I realise I'm still latched onto Alex. As soon as I break contact, I feel strangely bereft.

Alex turns unapproachable once again. 'We need to get some things straight.' I nod nervously, for once in agreement with him.

We walk to the edge of the dancefloor. When he checks everyone is immersed in Bruno Mars, he takes my hand and leads me away from the main area of the lounge. His grip sends shivers up my arm, but I try to focus on where we're going instead. My forehead puckers when he weaves through the crowd to the back of the lounge where an unused private room is. The sign on the wooden door says *not in use*, but Alex pushes through the door anyway.

When he's happy we're alone and the music becomes muffled behind the solid door closing shut, he lets go and rotates to face me. I look around the room and inhale shakily. It's mostly empty save for a few pieces of furniture covered in off-white dust sheets. The only window in the room is draped in purple curtains that hang shapelessly against the wood-panelled wall and drag on the tiled floor. The room is bathed in semi-darkness, and a hideous tulip-shaped light casts shadows across the room and Alex's expression in an almost ominous way.

His usually pink lips are the colour of raspberries in the dim light. His hair, usually short, has grown since September and now is almost messy around his delicate cheekbones. He looks more like the Alex I knew.

He stares at me with those bottomless green eyes. I want to look away or step back, but I don't do either and just stand there, feeling more and more fidgety under his scrutiny.

He bites the corner of his bottom lip, an old habit from where his piercing used to be. There's a tiny scar that mars the otherwise soft skin. X marks the spot, that's where Alex should be kissed. As soon as the errant thought materialises in my head, I try to force it out, but it clings to me with its tenacious limbs. The force of the emotion makes me sway. When he reads my body's reaction, he inhales deeply.

'I can't think when you look at me like that,' he exclaims at the same time I say, 'I know what you're going to say.' My thoughts scramble when I process his words.

'I doubt that.' His voice comes out hoarse.

To my shock, he places both his hands on my waist and pulls me to him until we're as close as we can be without touching. Heat radiates off his body in waves. I don't dare to breathe. When I don't protest, he pulls me even closer, until there's no space at all. That's when he smashes his lips against mine.

His kiss is not gentle, far from the subdued peck I gave him on Sunday. This is something else because he's a hundred per cent in this kiss. My hands automatically shoot out to grab him by his shoulders to hold him as close as physically possible. When he notices my reaction, he deepens the kiss, tracing the seam of my lips with his tongue until I open up to him fully. His tongue meets mine in an electric storm. A moan escapes my lips as soon as it happens, and he digs his fingers into my sides. My heart is a galloping horse, an industrial sewing machine thrumming out sixteen hundred stitches per minute, a steam turbine propelling a submarine, not a mere organ pumping blood around my body.

Footsteps approaching on the other side of the door make us jump away like a pair of teenagers. Thinking on my feet, I drag Alex behind the curtained window that, to my surprise, shelters an old full-length mirror. I place a finger on my lips as I tuck myself into the farthest corner of the window. It's so cramped Alex ends up pressed against me, his hip digging into my stomach and my boob squeezing against his shoulder. It reminds me of the sardines game, except that this isn't an old mansion, and if we get discovered, there are much worse consequences than becoming *it* in the next round or doing a dare.

'Holly. Are you here?' John loud whispers.

I don't dare to move and anxiously watch Alex in the semi-darkness. Face tilted away, his stormy eyes are looking towards where invisible John is, solely focused on the noises on the opposite side of the curtain. He smells faintly of gin and his customary woody smell. Without meaning to, I lean in and inhale. He swings his head sharply in my direction.

After a few more attempts at calling me, John gives up and his receding steps plunge us back into silence. However, it's like we're on a halt, like the kiss has never happened. Neither of us wants to make the next move because it would mean something. For now, we're even. A kiss for a kiss.

I need to find my footing. 'What is it that you wanted to get straight?' My lips are swollen, but I push the words through them anyway.

He steps away, his back brushing against the heavy curtain. His eyes narrow at something over my shoulder. I turn my head and catch our reflection in the mirror. My dress has ridden up and exposed the back of my thighs; the lacy tops of my stockings now peek from under the skirt.

I watch him watch me in the mirror. His cheeks are flushed, and his lips are pursed in what I used to think was disapproval, but now I'm not sure. He reaches behind me and grips my thigh where the lace meets my skin. The sight of his hand on me in the mirror is arousing and immediately heat pools between my legs.

'Your lacy collars and shiny buttons…' He breaks off, and I don't comprehend why, out of all moments, he chooses to discuss my fashion sense. He forces me back until I'm against the ledge of the window as he growls, 'They drive me insane. I can't seem to…'

Energy crackles between us until the air is so charged I expect the fire alarm to go off. He braces himself on either side of me against the ledge, trapping me in the cage of his arms. I hang on his lips, unable to move until he finishes the sentence.

His words split the moment in two. 'I can't seem to think whenever you're around. All I can think about is how I want to watch you come undone with my mouth and my hands. What have you done to me?'

Air rushes out of me and then our bodies crash against each other like tidal waves. His hands anchor on my buttocks without hesitation. Unable to last any longer, I meet his mouth. He's ready for me and immediately opens up, his tongue exploring and tasting mine while his hand is kneading my backside in the most exquisite way that makes me groan.

I slide my hand to his neck where the hair touches his nape. I used to pull at the hair there when we were teenagers, and it used to drive him crazy. As if he remembers, he moans into my mouth, and I can't help but rub against his body. I can feel how much he wants me, his hardness pressing insistently against my belly.

He grabs the back of my thighs and hoists me up onto the ledge, making me yelp in surprise. My legs automatically wrap around his waist to steady myself and to be even closer to him. I reach between our bodies and move my hand down his belly, but he doesn't let me touch him, and I growl in frustration. Instead, he propels us around and deposits me in front of the mirror, positioning himself behind me. He slides his hand down my belly and towards the edge of my dress, ending up under my skirt and deliciously circling my core through my underwear. The entire time his eyes are on me in the mirror. I grab onto the mirror with one hand and the windowsill with the other as he slips his fingers under the seam of my underwear and obliterates any remaining doubt.

His hand is warm, his fingers torturing before they finally sink inside me and my mind scrambles. He's never touched me like this, but it feels like he was made to touch me. People always say that if you have wanted something for a long time, the actual thing is pale against your previous imagining, but this isn't the case. It shatters my expectations.

He sinks another finger inside me, making me gasp at the fullness, and yet, feeling like it's not enough. I start moving against his hand. My head lolls back against his shoulder as I try to stop myself from falling apart because the idea of Alex watching me come makes me vulnerable. Once again, I try to reach the space between us, but he presses harder against me, preventing me from touching him the way I want to. The way I need to.

He must sense my thoughts because his voice rumbles in my ear, 'It's my turn to touch you. I want to watch you.' He moves his hand faster, and all I can do is stare at him pleasuring me in the mirror, memorising every second of his hand between my legs while his green eyes threaten to devour me. He presses his other hand against my belly, holding me in place as I give myself to him.

The feeling builds up in my stomach, and I start trembling in his arms. I must whisper his name because his body stiffens.

He sinks his lips into my hair and his hot breath hits the shell of my ear. 'Say my name again.'

I shake my head, fighting against the need.

'Say it,' he urges as he continues torturing me, systematically undoing me. 'I need to hear it. I need this. This is the only way I will get you out of my system.'

Before his words register fully, I fall apart so hard my eyes close. He strokes me through the last moments.

When I plummet down from my high, I replay his words in my head and my body is plunged into icy water. Immediately, I step out of his arms. Disgust with myself and my stupidity hit me so hard it's like an uppercut punch to my gut. I can't stand the sight of myself in the mirror. Shiny eyes, red cheeks, tousled hair. I look like a mess.

Is this what this is for him? Am I to be used as a tool to get him over wanting me? An outstanding list from the sixth form to massage his ego? Sleep with Holly. Tick.

He takes a step towards me to help me pull my dress down, but I shrink back. I feel cheap and dirty. The logical part of me knows that I wanted this and he did nothing wrong because from the start he said he wanted my body, especially after I kissed him first. But the illogical part is screaming at him because, even after ten years, he's the only person in the world I can't bear to hear those words from.

Something akin to hurt passes across his face, but I'm sure I'm reading him wrong. I'm almost glad my phone rings even though it's my mother. I dismiss him by pushing the curtain out of my way and walking to the opposite side of the room without looking back. I know if I do, I'll cry, and I don't want to give him the satisfaction.

'Yes, Mother?' I inject some cheer into my voice when I pick up, even though on the inside I'm an empty eggshell about to crack. The door behind me opens and closes.

Only when Alex has gone do I let my tears fall.

Why do all the men in my life hurt me?

18

I wake up in my old bedroom with the beginnings of a headache pressing against my temples. It's like someone has trapped me in a time capsule. Apart from the ironing pile and my mother's Peloton in the corner, everything looks the same to the smallest detail. I wonder why she's ditched the bike here, having three more bedrooms at her disposal.

One of the walls is solely covered with posters of the Spice Girls and Backstreet Boys because I was going through a '90s bands phase in my teens, while the other has a noticeboard stuck to it with old photos. There are a few photos of Catherine, but it's mostly filled with Vicky pouting her lips at the camera and an occasional flash of me. The corner of my face here, a lock of hair there. I pad barefoot towards the board, knowing what I'm searching for. As soon as I find the incriminating photo, I pluck it off the board mercilessly. In the picture, I'm standing next to Catherine at one of the rare parties we attended, neither of us being much of a party animal. We're both dressed in collared shirts, but where mine is ditsy floral, hers is burgundy.

But it's not our dismal fashion sense or the terrible haircuts we're sporting in the photo that enrages me. In the corner of the picture stands a boy with ginger hair, looking at me with an unreadable expression. He resembles the Alex I know now more than ever. My grip around the photo hardens. For the first time, I spot another person in the photo I've never noticed.

Vicky is standing a little distance away in the crowd, sipping a drink and watching Alex with hooded eyes. I study her strange expression for a moment.

Alex is the sole reason for what I do next. Hot tears leaking down my cheeks, I rip it into confetti-sized pieces and chuck it in the bin. Without another glance, I pad back to the warm bed and barricade myself with my pillows and duvet.

Last night when I cried on the phone to my mother, she insisted that I stay overnight at their place, and for once, I had no strength to refuse. I tried to play the sad drunk card, but I don't think she bought it because I haven't cried in front of her since I was a child.

I lie lethargically in my childhood bed for long moments, staring helplessly at the ceiling covered in fluorescent stars that my dad stuck on when I was fourteen. I remember he gave himself back pain for a week, never having been one for physical labour. I cherished them because I knew he had gone out of his way to make me happy. A fresh wave of searing tears covers my face, soaking into the lavender-smelling pink bedding.

My mood shifts from crushed to irate; I need to scream or smash something so badly my hands are shaking. I've suppressed this part of me for the last ten years, convincing myself that all those broken parts had healed over, but the truth is, I'd just pushed them deeper and fragmented them into even smaller, much sharper, pieces.

Eventually, I make myself move and take a shower. I find some old clothes in the wardrobe that are freshly laundered and pressed. The wardrobe, too, is a time capture of an eighteen-year-old Holly, so I choose the least offensive garments to put on. Embarrassingly, both the flared corduroy trousers and the purple polo-neck top still fit. When I look at myself in the mirror, I resemble an older version of Sabrina Spellman. I wash my face but don't bother with make-up. I feel marginally better but still fragile.

I head downstairs and find the kitchen abandoned. I pour myself some coffee from the cafetière sitting next to the fancy-looking bread bin and douse it with five heaped spoons of brown sugar. It's still warm and bitter, and it's exactly what I need. I head to the lounge with it and park myself on the largest sofa, pulling my legs up. Feeling exhausted from all the emotions, I drop my head to my knees.

'Hangover?' My dad asks jovially from the doorway. His tone is a little too cheery to be genuine.

Everything tenses in me. It's a reflex that I haven't learnt to override for the last ten years.

'Sorry for crashing here last night,' I say automatically.

'You're always welcome here. Your mother was so excited she went to the bakery to buy some fresh pastries for breakfast.' I nod because I don't know what else to say. I don't remember the last time we were alone like this. His expression is uneasy, he's fighting with something. He says carefully, 'It's been too long since you've stayed overnight.'

I guess he never understood why, last minute, I chose a university all the way in Wales when all along I planned to go to a local university. I haven't lived at home since I was eighteen, and yet, I still feel like a little girl in this room with him. Surrounded by cream chenille sofas and potpourri in various silver and bronze bowls placed around the room, I feel more like the old Holly than ever, and it chafes like polyester against sensitive skin.

I can't stand to look at him, the good old dad. The benevolent father figure he's pretended to be for so long, and I've let him maintain that image by keeping quiet.

He sits on the sofa opposite me and sips his coffee. He's wearing one of his many almost identical chequered M&S shirts. This one is blue, red and white, and presses tightly around his pot belly when he leans against the back support of the sofa.

I'm reminded of how comfortable our silences used to be. It was me and my dad against the world. I remember the times we would affectionately mock Mother for her tomfoolery, but that turned sour a long time ago. I pretend to check my phone, but what I'm really doing is trying to find something to do with my hands and eyes.

'You worry your mother.' He breaks the silence and then takes another loud sip of his coffee. He's studying me over the rim of his old-fashioned glasses.

I wish he'd leave it there, but he doesn't. 'Did yesterday have something to do with Aaron?'

He's never been the prying type, so at first, I think I haven't heard him correctly.

'Whatever happened between you two, you should have given it a second chance. Instead of giving up.'

I place my mug on the coffee table, my body tensing all over. Out of all days, he had to choose to have this conversation this very morning. It reminds me why I have avoided being with him alone. The lecturing.

'That was my choice to make, and as such, it's none of your business,' I snap and flinch at my own words. I've never snapped at my dad, apart from that one time ten years ago. Everything floods back in a hot, overwhelming wave that carries so much anger it surprises me.

'Pardon?' he exclaims, but it sounds anything but apologetic. He sits up, emanating disapproval. 'It's got everything to do with me because it upsets your mother. She has worried about you ever since you broke up with Aaron. See it from our perspective. One minute you are happy, buy a bungalow with that boy and all seems well. Next, you quit your job, break up with Aaron and move to a shoddy bed-sit. We both liked him. He was a decent man.'

I pull myself to my feet, ready to get my stuff and go without another word. Think me a coward, but I'm not good at confrontation. Then everything quietens inside me and hones into a single argument. Why should I keep quiet? I've had enough of deceptive men in my life.

'No. He was a piece of shit, *Dad*.' I say *dad* like it's an insult. 'And I didn't quit my job. I was made redundant.'

His chin wobbles at my foul language.

'Young lady,' he tries to interrupt.

'You can shove your *young lady* deep down where the sun doesn't shine. He was a scumbag who cheated on me in our own home.' My dad's eyes widen behind his glasses, and his hand, still holding the mug, shakes. 'I found out by walking in on them because he didn't have the decency to tell me himself, so stop singing the praises of that man because he doesn't deserve that. Unless you think that cheating on someone who you made a commitment to should be condoned.' I pause for a moment. His lips are slack; I've shocked him. The immature, angry Holly inside me is pleased.

'To top it, he's expecting a baby with her. What do you say now? Do you still like him that much? Maybe you should give him a chance yourself. It's not like being *married* has stopped you before.' I don't know what has got into me, but a dam has burst, and all the feelings and memories spill out.

*

The street is abandoned, and I check my phone to find that I've passed my curfew by twenty-two minutes. If my mother catches me, I'm dead, literally coffin material. Alex and I lost track of time. It's been happening whenever we touch. It's overwhelming and exhilarating. All I can think about is him and all the places he hasn't touched me yet.

A flash of movement catches the corner of my eye. At the sight of the man, I still. My dad gets out of his car, and I wonder why he's parked two streets from our house. I watch him walk to the opposite side of the car and open the door. He steps to the side and a familiar woman gets out, tugging at her fluffy pink coat to adjust the sleeves.

My eyes narrow as he leans towards her. Then my mouth shoots open. I watch as he kisses her on the lips, and after scanning the street, pulls her to him flush against his body.

When they separate, they both giggle like a pair of teenagers. Bile rises in my throat. I'm surprised that I don't puke in the bushes. Somehow, I make it home and shut myself in my room. I don't come out for two days, pretending I've got the flu.

*

'I'm sorry that that's what happened between you and Aaron, but I don't appreciate your rudeness.' His wrinkled forehead puckers. He pulls himself to his feet.

'Stop pretending. I know,' I shout at him, and it stops him in his tracks. His face crumples. 'I know that you're a cheating bastard. Just like Aaron. Just like every other man in my life. That day ten years ago when I caught you in that café, there were no consultations, were there?' I wait for him to deny it, still carrying a minuscule spark of hope, but his shattered look is my answer. 'How could you?'

'Holly.' He stretches his arm in an attempt to placate me, but I won't be so easily silenced any more.

'No. Don't bother.' I put my hands up. 'I have nothing to say to you. I've kept the secret to myself for the last ten years, but I'm done carrying your burden. I'm done with your bad decisions impacting my life and my life choices.' I realise that as soon as the words are out they are true. My relationships with Alex, and even Aaron, were affected by my dad's treachery. 'Why do you think I went to a university so far away from here? Or moved out at the age of eighteen? You're not on my pedestal any more, Dad.'

I turn around about to storm out when a figure in the doorway halts my steps. My mother's hand is planted firmly over her mouth. She's deadly pale.

By the time I arrive at my flat, I have four missed calls from my mother and two from my dad, but I'm too terrified to answer. I can't lie to my mother any more, so I stay silent.

I spend the rest of the day feeling like a geyser about to spout out boiling water. The next day, I join Catherine and Lydia for our monthly roast dinner that Richard cooks for us. If there were medals for number-one husbands, Richard would get one at least once a week.

His hulking figure is currently moving between various pots bubbling on the stove and chopping carrots on the breakfast bar while checking on the pork joint in the oven. His beard, which is usually his pride and joy, is sprinkled with gravy granules and what looks like a single frozen sweetcorn kernel.

Gabby is working on a Moana colouring sheet with felt tips scattered across the dining table and the floor. I love how self-sufficient she can be at times. She ignores all the outlines and chooses to colour Moana's face green and her hair purple. The set-up in the kitchen gives Lydia, Catherine and me some needed alone time, and so we spend it in the lounge chatting.

We spread out on the large grey settee with a Long Island Iced Tea, non-alcoholic for me after Friday's debacle, our Sunday roast tradition.

Catherine takes a gulp of her drink and hums in contentment. She's wearing a purple Oodie adorned with avocadoes with cute winky eyes. It's the most bizarre outfit I've seen on her so far, but the rules of Sunday roast gatherings are strict. No denim, no zips, no buttons and no regrets. I'm wearing Christmas leggings, stripy leg warmers and an oversized hoodie, whereas Lydia is sporting a feline onesie.

'When are you going to tell us about Ted?' Catherine peeks from under her overlarge hood at Lydia with interest.

Lydia waves her hand in dismissal. 'Nothing to tell. Let's say Ted and I aren't compatible. By that, I mean he talks too much, and what he has to say is boring as hell. But most importantly, he's an awful kisser. At first, I thought he had the geek thing going for him and that he might be dirty in bed, but it turned out Ted is boring regardless of the place.' Poor Ted is decimated by Lydia. 'Now, your turn.' Lydia turns to me like this is circle time at an AA meeting.

I close my eyes for a moment to brace myself. When I'm ready, I retell Friday's events, finishing with my mother calling. I'm saving the retelling of Saturday for dessert.

Throughout the story, Lydia shouts, 'Shut up,' a few times while Catherine gawks at me like I've just said that dinosaurs were a social construct.

Catherine shoots Lydia a look at her swearing, her dark eyes locking for a moment on little Gabby who's totally oblivious to our conversation. Lydia clamps her mouth with her well-manicured hand and then mouths sorry. I study my chipped nails and feel disgusted with myself. I always hoped that by the age of twenty-seven, I'd have my shit together, but I've never been further from that than at this very moment.

When I get to the part where Alex told me he just wanted to get me out of his system, a lump the size of a golf ball lodges in my throat, and I pause.

'That guy is full of crap, Hols.' Lydia adjusts her cat tail over her knee.

'You don't even know him,' I protest.

'On this one, I agree with Lydia,' Catherine chimes. I notice her glass is empty, and I have no idea when she had the time to finish it. I suspect it's got nothing to do with my story but everything to do with the fact that having a child, one needs to do everything double speed.

'Yes, he's behaved like a dick to you since September, but all he's really done is stop everyone gossiping about you, bought you lunch and apologised when he was awful to you. He also saved you from sleazy-easy John by the sounds of it. Not to forget he's given you the best orgasm of your life,' Lydia explains like this is plain old logic to everyone.

'His actions speak louder than his words.' Catherine is full of wisdom. 'On the other hand, it doesn't justify him being so hostile to you.'

'I agree with Cat, but having a little romp wouldn't hurt either of you, would it? It's not like feelings are involved anyway, are there?' Lydia's sole attention narrows on me.

'No.' I sound almost convincing to my ears. The truth is, I'm not so sure any more. 'Don't you think I'm pathetic? It's like I didn't learn my lesson ten years ago. But equally, it was the hottest experience of my life. There was a mirror and a heavy curtain.' I break off at the size of Lydia's eyes. She's itching to ask, but Catherine jumps in first.

'Better than ten years ago?' Catherine winks, and there's a cheeky spark in her eyes.

I nod. 'This was…' I keep coming up short of words like I'm a printer running out of ink. 'It was so carnal. So…' I get frustrated with myself at the lack of eloquence and my stupidity at repeating the same mistakes.

Lydia looks like she's ready to pat my shoulder, completely discounting my previous comment while Catherine is grinning from ear to ear.

I *grrr* at their simpering reactions. 'You're my best friends. You should be telling me it's a really bad idea. So why do I get the feeling the opposite is happening here?' My mouth shapes into an involuntary smirk. I can't help but whisper, 'He said that he finds my clothes disturbingly sexy.' Maybe they're right. Why don't I do the same and try to get Alex out of my system?

Catherine makes a surprised gurgle slash snort. 'I miss this. Being a mum sucks. Most erotica happens when I manage to get an evening on Netflix and watch *Fifty Shades of Grey*.'

'Aaron used to hate how I dressed.' I'm still stuck on the same thought. I can't stop comparing the two men. 'We never clicked sexually.' I know I've lost this game because I'm making excuses to myself.

'Alex seems like a more well-adjusted man who doesn't seem to need to play at being a man.'

Alex hasn't done anything bad per se. He said he wanted me, but he never said anything about feelings and definitely didn't promise me anything.

'What are you going to do when you go back to work tomorrow?' Catherine asks after a few beats of silence.

'I guess like any functioning adult, I'm going to pretend nothing happened but secretly wait for his reaction first and hope he still wants to take me to bed.'

At that, they both burst out laughing, and I can't help but follow. I guess I've made my decision. The idea of Alex in my bed starts palpitations in my chest, and I need to swallow a few times because I'm suddenly parched.

'Dinner's ready,' Richard's voice booms from the kitchen.

'Good old Rich. I'm ravenous,' Lydia says suggestively. Catherine only shakes her head.

19

On Monday, I go back to work, feeling apprehensive about the onslaught of gossip that's bound to hit me after Friday, but it's surprisingly quiet. John barely looks my way, and Danielle doesn't even say good morning to me when she passes me in the corridor. They don't come to see me during lunch, nor do they stop to chat at the end of the day. I think our pretend friendship is truly over, but I can't find it in myself to feel disappointed.

Alex is visiting another school in the trust, and a part of me that is a tad self-centred is taking it personally. Is he avoiding me? My suspicion grows when the next day, Alex works from home. For the first time, doubt creeps in. Maybe I shouldn't have ignored him the way I did after he had his hand down my knickers.

Vicky messages me and asks how things are at work. I don't have the strength to tell her what happened, so I keep my answers vague. It's strange how she's been in touch more since I told her about Alex.

At the end of Tuesday, Jane calls me to her office. When I walk in, she's speedily tapping away on her laptop, her plum nails clicking away like she's an automaton. She's always efficient and professional, but she's also kind of nice. Last month, when I couldn't meet a deadline because I was getting the trip plans together, she put it back by two weeks.

She pushes the laptop to the side and motions for me to sit on the padded blue seat opposite her desk.

'How are you settling in?' she enquires once I'm seated.

'OK,' I say with hesitation. Is this the point where she informs me that I have to find a new position and finish my ECT somewhere else? Has Alex filled her ears with poison after Friday? Feeling nervous, I cross my legs.

'I hear from Alex you've been an exceptional addition to our staff,' Jane shares, clasping her hands on the polished desk.

'Is that so?' I scoff in disbelief before I manage to stop myself. I feel like the villain here.

At my doubtful look, her lip twitches. 'I know. Alex has always been…' She searches for an accurate, and no doubt politically correct, word. '…austere with praise, but he means well. He said you've been the most dedicated mentee he's had and that you have a great relationship with your pupils.'

When she delivers this, I have to school my expression to keep a modicum of professionalism. I think that once again I've gotten him wrong. I nod because I'm not sure what to say to this.

The strangest expression flits across her features. Her eyes framed by dark lashes turn almost soft behind her glasses.

She sweeps her hands to her lap and leans towards me. 'Can I be direct with you please?' She doesn't give me a chance to respond and continues, 'I want to give you my assurances.' She measures her next words. I've never seen her this careful, and it's making me agitated. 'If for whatever reason Alex being your mentor isn't viable anymore, I can assign you a different mentor. If you're concerned about your position here, you shouldn't be.'

Is she saying that I haven't been as professional as I thought I had been where Alex is concerned? Mortification shrinks my internal organs to raisins. Or worse, has Alex suggested this? A small part of me considers her offer, but I can't imagine going through another mentor. I must reluctantly admit, as mentors go, Alex has been a good one.

'No, why? Has Alex said something?'

'Alex, confiding in me on matters that aren't strictly professional without duress?' She snorts, which makes me startle. I didn't think she was capable of snorting. However, she has summed up Alex accurately.

'Anyway.' She checks her watch. 'If there's ever anything you want to talk about, I'm here.' She gives me one of her X-ray looks before I'm released.

The rest of the day is uneventful and almost boring without the constant threat of Alex walking into my classroom or the prospect of bumping into him in the corridor.

On Wednesday, I know Alex is around, and my suspicions that he's avoiding me are confirmed. Usually, he pops into my class at least once a day. When he's not randomly visiting my class, he's outside during the afternoon break, but he's nowhere to be seen.

Developing stalker tendencies, I walk past his office a few times and peer through the glass slit that decorates the middle of the door, but his chair is empty.

At the end of the day, his car is the first one gone from the car park despite Alex usually working until six like me. My nerves are tattered.

I go home early because I'm going for dinner with Lydia to check out a new Thai restaurant she got vouchers for at work that are about to expire. I spend the early evening attempting to make my place look more agreeable by strategically placing potted plants that I salvaged from the bungalow to hide some of the worst carpet stains. But it seems that the place will forever defy feng shui.

I get vexed all over again when I remember the nice hessian rug that I laid in the hallway of the bungalow. It took me weeks to find the right colour, and I got it for a good price. It would look perfect here. Determined for once to get what I want, I message Aaron. *I want the hessian rug and the matching rattan mats. I'm picking them up in 30 minutes.*

As soon as the message is sent, it feels like there's nothing as important as getting the stupid rug. Replaying our last conversation in the café makes me crave victory over Aaron in any way I can get it. I'm done with him walking all over me.

I put mascara and red lipstick on and smooth my bob. I finish my look with a white shirt and tight jeans with black cowboy boots, channelling Mia from *Pulp Fiction*.

I book a taxi with a stopover at the bungalow before I chicken out. A message that my driver, Rocher, is here pings on my phone ten minutes later.

Rocher turns out to be a very chatty middle-aged woman who talks incessantly about her dog, a mixed breed of long-haired chihuahua and Jack Russell whose picture has a prime spot on her dashboard.

I text my mother that I will meet her on Saturday for a coffee at M&S because I refuse to go home and confront my dad, but it's not fair to avoid her because she hasn't done anything wrong. She only replies, *OK, darling* which is very tight-lipped of her, but I guess she's shell-shocked. I've never considered how she would feel when she found out that I knew all along. My heart is laden with guilt, which makes me hate my dad even more.

Rocher stops by a curb in front of the familiar bungalow and lets the car rev.

I knock impatiently on the door, however, it's not Aaron who opens it, but Eva dressed in ugly pyjamas with ice cream cones on, stuffing herself with a chocolate biscuit. Her hair is sloppily piled up on top of her head and when my gaze travels down her body, her belly is even more rounded than the last time I saw her. I tighten my hands into fists. I've got this.

She shifts her weight from foot to foot before she fleetingly scans the street over my shoulder like she's expecting me to make a scene. I wonder what Aaron has told her about me. I wouldn't be surprised if he painted me as a villain of the Grand High Witch calibre, anything to ease his consciousness.

'I'm here to pick up a rug and a couple of mats,' I inform her coolly. I straighten my back and end up almost a head taller than her. She brushes crumbs off her pyjama top. I can tell from the submissive angle of her shoulders she's not a confrontational person, but for the first time in my life, I don't care how my actions make her feel because I'm done accommodating other people's feelings and suppressing mine in the process.

'Aaron didn't tell me anything about you stopping by. He's on the phone in the bedroom.' She seems a little unsure, her eyes flying towards where the bedroom is.

'He's never been exactly organised. My taxi is waiting so I would appreciate it if you got a move on.' I wave towards the bored-looking taxi driver. I don't think I've ever been this hostile to anybody, but it's been a trying couple of weeks.

I've worked her out right because she disappears behind the door. I wait long moments until I hear shuffling and some strained breathing. Doubt creeps in. Maybe I should have thought this through. Am I so hateful to let a pregnant woman heft a heavy rug? Also, how am I going to stuff it in the taxi anyway? I guess that's a problem for future Holly. Determination forges my body into a rod of steel. Even if I have to walk to the Thai place, I will have the rug.

Strained voices from behind the door travel to my ear, and when the door opens again, an enraged Aaron is standing in the doorway, dressed in sweatpants. I guess the standards are really slipping. He refused to wear anything classed as *loungewear* when we were together. He's looking more tired than the last time I saw him.

'This is highly inappropriate. You could have at least waited for my reply,' he complains. Eva is peeking from behind his shoulder.

'Honey, we don't like the rug anyway,' she starts, but he interjects, 'If you think you can barge in here anytime, you're wrong.'

I put my hands up, and he surprisingly shuts up.

'Stop talking,' I command forcefully, bolstered by confidence I have no clue where I've found.

'I've had enough of you interrupting me. And I've had enough of your bullshit. I refuse to suffer the consequences of you being a shitty person.'

He's completely gobsmacked. After all, I've never spoken to him like this. I've always been easy-going. He's about to speak, but I take a step towards him, and he backs off. I don't know what has possessed me, but it feels good. 'I'm speaking and you're listening. I can see that you haven't changed. Still bossy and insensitive and selfish. Do you know why I never gave you all that you needed? Because you're not a child, you're a man. Stop looking for somebody to be your mother and a girlfriend. It's pathetic.'

He turns tomato red, and his cheeks puff up like a hamster's.

'Now, my solicitor will be in touch with you to sort out my money because you haven't had the initiative or decency to do so yourself.'

Aaron slouches. He knows he doesn't stand a chance. I've won.

I train my eyes on Eva. 'I want my rug. I could ask for half of the kitchen cabinets, the bed or the cooker that I paid for but I'm not that petty.'

Aaron looks torn, his lip cinched between his teeth. He's calculating whether he can leave me alone with Eva.

'I'm not going to bite her head off,' I bark at him. He scowls, but nevertheless, leaves to fetch my rug.

We wait, Eva fidgeting with the hem of her sleeve. I make her nervous. Despite my poker face, my insides are in ribbons, and at any moment I could vomit out my lunch.

I just about catch her whispered words. 'I know what Aaron meant about the ice-queen act.' I see red.

'Fuck you,' I cry out, and she shudders at the volume of my voice. 'You should be ashamed of yourself. Sleeping with a man who isn't single and ruining somebody's life like that. What stops him from doing it to you? Anyway, good luck with that.' Her eyes glisten with tears.

'I think we threw the mats away,' Aaron says contritely when he comes back, passing me the heavy rug. I don't blame him. I'm feeling very unpredictable, some would say unstable.

'Goodbye, Aaron,' I say with a flare and turn around. We are done.

I stuff the rug in the boot of the taxi, sweating and heaving with the effort, but the taxi driver only shrugs at my newly acquired baggage. I feel proud of myself. That is until I arrive at the restaurant laden with a massive rug and nowhere to put it.

Still pumped up on adrenalin, I give the waitress standing by a *please wait to be seated* sign an honest explanation when her eyes home in on the interior accessory. 'I don't normally go to restaurants with rugs, but I had to pick it up from my ex-boyfriend who after we purchased a bungalow together cheated on me and then refused to give me my share. I almost made his pregnant girlfriend heft the rug across the bungalow and threatened them both with a solicitor if they didn't pay up because I can barely afford to pay rent. Think me a terrible person, but I had to get my rug back because I really really like it.' My words turn a little loud, and I have to dial my voice down. The auburn-haired waitress sniffs inconspicuously during my story, and I end up passing her a tissue.

'It's a nice rug. Good for you,' is all she says and lets me store it in the staffroom. My belief in good people is restored.

Regaining some dignity, I announce with pretended composure, 'I'm meeting a friend. She booked a table for two. Lydia Dean?'

'This way,' she says gruffly, and I follow.

The restaurant is busy. Every square table decorated with candles in intricate bronze holders emanating a buttery glow is taken up. The restaurant is mostly filled with couples, and the intimate atmosphere of dark mahogany furniture, bronze table dividers and tall bamboo plants is perfect for a romantic evening. But my mood is miles away from romantic endeavours and much closer to planning a homicide.

I feel a little over-dressed, and my lipstick feels tar-thick on my lips. I make a movement to wipe it discreetly but stop in my tracks at the sight of a solitary figure sitting by the bar. Automatically, my pulse picks up like I've run up a flight of stairs and then another. I frown as he checks his watch like he's waiting for someone and the thought of witnessing Alex on a date sends me spiralling, a feeling similar to sliding down a helter-skelter at forty miles per hour. As if he's heard my mental processes, his ginger head swipes in my direction. When he spots me, his gaze narrows. To my dismay, he turns around to face the bar without acknowledging me.

Has Alex just given me the cold shoulder?

20

I'm surprised I manage to walk to Lydia's table without a stumble. The waitress squeezes my shoulder before she leaves us, and Lydia eyes the gesture with interest.

I sit woodenly opposite, and a confused Lydia retraces my steps to the bar. Her pupils turn to pinpoints and she mouths *fuck*. 'I get why you get so flustered. He's even hotter in person. And he was sex on legs in the photos.' She cranes her neck to see better.

'Don't. How is it that, until this year, I hadn't seen him for ten years and now he seems to be everywhere I go?' I vent. I don't tell her he gave me the cut when I walked past him because I'm embarrassed, and a part of me naively hopes that maybe he didn't see me. I peruse the drinks menu to busy myself, pretending to be as engrossed in it as if it was the next book by Colleen Hoover. The satisfied feeling of victory over Aaron is gone.

'Serendipity?' Lydia offers.

'Bad fortune more like it,' I reply sourly.

'I do have to say you've got good taste. I would have cowboy dreams about that bad boy any night.'

A waiter comes to take our order and clears their throat awkwardly. I think the ship called *Dignity* has long sailed away with the rug.

I order some fancy-sounding fruity cocktail, and together we pick a few starters before we choose mains.

'Is now the time to tell me why you've lugged a rug to the restaurant? I thought I'd give you a minute to catch your breath.' She's so unaffected when she says this, like this is totally normal behaviour, that I burst out laughing, and Lydia follows. She shakes her head. 'Seriously, only you.' Her words bring on another bout of laughter. I think I'm turning hysterical.

In between heaving, I confess, 'I went to Aaron's and threatened him with a solicitor if he didn't pay me back.'

Her hand raises to fist bump me, and only because it's Lydia, I raise my fist to meet with hers. 'Good for you, girl.' Pride warms up my belly once again.

'Did everyone see me with the rug?' I scan my surroundings self-consciously and end up on Alex who's on the phone, smiling. I freeze. I've never seen him looking this carefree and wonder, with a pang of jealousy, who's transformed his face like that.

'Nah. Only about half of the people here.' She waves her hand in dismissal; she's never cared about what people think.

When I ask her about how things are going in the love department, she surprises me by telling me about having TED Talk Ted over on Monday.

I must look confused because she explains, 'I have my needs. There's no big love written in the stars for me anyway, so I might as well enjoy some mediocre sex.' She takes a sip from her glass of water before she elaborates, 'We both know I'm not the sort of person who can ever completely fall head over heels or even be able to trust somebody on that level.' Her tone is subdued, almost mournful.

'That's news to me. Are you suggesting that only a certain type of people fall in love because of their proclivity to trust?' It's a very sad outlook on life but sums up Lydia to the point.

Our conversation is interrupted by the waiter bringing our food and drinks. Everything smells divine, and the air around us fills with the scent of chillies and coriander. We tuck in, silent for a few moments.

'I think it's about the level of vulnerability you're able to extend to the other person and your ability to trust.' Lydia's statement drips with resignation. She always seems like she's above it all, but I wonder whether that's not the case this time. 'I've never been able to let go to the degree of giving it all.'

'Would you like to be that person who gives it all?'

'Maybe?' She sounds uncertain for the first time. 'I'm just tired of being alone, Hols. It would be nice, for once, to have someone to take care of me.' I reach for her hand on the table, and she squeezes mine. Affection curls the corners of her lips upwards.

'Then we'll stay alone together.' I assure her.

'You know that Aaron was talking out of his arse when he called you an ice queen?' Lydia says between two mouthfuls like she can read my mind.

She moves on to the sticky skewer starter as she nonchalantly finishes with, 'You'll find someone someday.' With a suggestive wink, she tosses her head towards the bar.

I shake my head violently. 'No way. He doesn't feel like that, and I don't feel like that, and anyway, there's too much bad history between us.'

She sips slowly the margarita that she's been working on since I got here. 'So why does he keep looking in your direction every two minutes if he doesn't feel like that?' I flush at her comment. 'Hols, you were teenagers. I did some bad shit when I was seventeen; everyone did. Not that I'm excusing him of the shit he did, but maybe he's a different person now.'

I consider her words. 'It wouldn't matter anyway at this point. I think he's angry with me because I basically ignored him after he gave me a mind-blowing orgasm.' I change my mind. Again. I can't keep up with my mental gymnastics these days. 'But maybe I should listen to you and Catherine. Maybe I should apologise and just enjoy his company while it lasts at least,' I babble on.

Before Lydia has a chance to really process my words, she gets distracted and gestures towards the bar. 'New developments.'

Alex is joined by Jane, all prim and sexy in her burgundy dress and pointy glasses. Immediately, she gives him a hug and a kiss on the cheek. If I didn't like Jane, I would wish her a slow, torturous death right now and the newborn propensity to violence shocks me to the core.

'That's Jane Trainer. The principal,' I say tightly, all the bad thoughts swirling in my head like a solitary olive at the bottom of a dirty martini.

'The principal he's sleeping with according to the gossip?' Lydia's perfect eyebrows rise in question. She studies Jane as she leans over the counter and says something to the barmaid at which the black-haired female laughs. 'They're not sleeping together,' Lydia announces enigmatically.

'How do you know? Do you have a radar for that kind of thing?' I shake my head. 'Actually, don't answer that. I don't want to know.' She smirks, but then her expression is wiped clean.

'They're heading our way,' Lydia grinds out through her teeth.

Off its own accord, my leg starts jiggling up and down when I connect the empty table next to us with their approaching figures. Alex is distinctly grey, his eyes glancing my way a few times before they settle on the ground.

'Check out those posh shoes,' Lydia exclaims.

'She's actually a nice person so please behave,' I hiss.

She doesn't acknowledge my words and carries on, 'God, he's not very happy to see you, is he? I sense pent-up resentment. What did you do to him on Friday?' Lydia is right; he's put off without a doubt. 'Oh. It must be the whole you-ignoring-him-after-he-gave-you-a-good-ride-on-his-hand thing.' My cheeks heat at her words.

Before I can compose myself, they're upon us.

Jane is genuinely beaming at me while Alex looks like he's just had all his wisdom teeth removed and was told that all his molars will have to go, too, but there's no anaesthetic left.

'Hi, Holly. So nice to see you here,' Jane says kindly when they reach the table. She sends Alex a loaded look that he ignores. He nods our way, always the conversationalist.

It doesn't escape me how his gaze snags on my red lips, and a wave of heat sweeps over me.

'Should we get rid of the divider?' Jane offers with cheer unusual for her, and Lydia agrees with an eagerness that is equally out of character. She's enjoying this way too much. Alex's expression turns so sour I almost laugh out loud. Jane snorts. 'Don't be a killjoy, Alex. The more the merrier.'

I'm gobsmacked because I've never seen anybody speak so frankly to him. I think Alex grumbles *the fewer the better fare* under his breath, but maybe I've imagined it. It doesn't escape me that Lydia studies Jane with a new-found interest.

Once we push the divider out of the way, join our tables together and get seated, I introduce Lydia. 'This is Lydia, my best friend. Lydia, this is Jane, the principal at my school, and Alex, my...' My words fail for the shortest second, but Alex spots it as I finish, 'my ECT mentor and vice head.'

'So formal, Holly.' Jane laughs. 'Nice to meet you, Lydia,' she says with warmth in her tone, and Lydia smirks like she knows something I don't. They shake hands, and Lydia's hand lingers a second too long.

The waiter from earlier comes to take their orders, and when Jane orders herself a margarita, Alex goes for green tea. Silence settles over the table; it's going to be a long evening.

Sensing the tense atmosphere, Jane starts asking Lydia questions about her job. I end up tuning in and out of their conversation as they seem to entertain each other while I'm surreptitiously watching Alex, who radiates discomfort with the intensity of a subatomic particle. Where I join in a few times as they talk, Alex doesn't speak at all.

'I've heard about your trip to the farm.' Jane tries to lighten up the atmosphere. I blink in horror.

I cannot stop myself from throwing daggers in Alex's direction, and for a moment, there's a fragment of amusement on his face, but it's gone in a second.

'Which part have you heard about?'

'Don't worry. I didn't tell her about a pig licking your calf. I left that for the next inset day.' He speaks for the first time. His tone is so deadpan I choke on my curry. Lydia openly cackles, delighted.

'Have we all finished amusing ourselves with Holly's animal-themed disasters?' I ask, but I'm suppressing a laugh.

The conversation steers to neutral topics after that, and Alex even occasionally contributes. It's marginally less awkward, but we reach a natural pause after Lydia and I have finished our dishes.

Jane excuses herself to visit the ladies, and Alex offers to order her another drink at the bar. It's his move to avoid staying alone with us, and I can't blame him.

When we're alone at the table, I lean into Lydia. 'Can we please go now?'

'If that's what you want.' I nod.

I hesitate as I get to my feet. 'Wait. I think I'll go to the bar first and talk to Alex.' I promised myself that I'd be brave from now on. I'm a big girl, and I can admit when I owe an apology to someone. Lydia nods in understanding.

But when I weave through the tables heading towards Alex, I hear two raised voices.

'Why are you being like that?' Jane asks sternly, her lips pursed in disagreement.

'Like what?' Alex grates and leans against the wooden counter, pretending to look relaxed, but his stiff back says otherwise.

'Unreasonable. Talk to her. There's clearly something going on between you. You can't carry on pretending like you don't care.' Jane's tone turns insistent.

I shift nervously, torn between making myself known and waiting for what they're going to say next. My curiosity wins, and I hide behind a potted palm.

'There's nothing to be said.' Jane's eyes turn sceptical, and she reaches for his hand. He shakes her off and pushes away from the bar. 'I don't care. She's nothing to me and there's nothing between us. I don't want to have anything to do with her. She's bad news. A walking disaster. Once she passes her ECT time, we don't need to talk to each other ever again and good riddance to that.'

My breath snags in my lungs, and I must make a sound because they both spin on their heel. Alex's cheeks drain of colour, and Jane's mouth falls open.

I turn around and head woodenly towards Lydia who is chatting to a male couple she must know.

'Hey, Lydia. I'm ready to go home. I don't mind if you want to stay.' I eye the two guys, and they both nod to me in hello. I return the gesture stiffly because inside I'm boiling, unsure how long I can keep pretending I'm calm.

'You're OK? I promised to share a taxi with you.' Lydia sounds uncertain like she can read me.

'That's alright. I'll take a bus; I'm just feeling really tired.' I dismiss her worried look. 'I'll see you next week, OK?' She nods, and after we embrace, I collect the rug and leave without a backwards glance.

I walk to the closest bus stop a street away from the restaurant. On my way, a few onlookers gawk at my load, but I scowl at them.

'Why did you bring a rug with you?' Alex asks from behind me. I close my eyes for a brief moment, trying to compose myself without success. He's got some nerve.

'I didn't *bring* a rug with me. I picked it up to take home,' I say lamely.

He pauses next to me, but I still don't look at him, scanning the road for the bus instead. 'I'm sorry about what I said. I was harsh.' He puts his hands in the pockets of his jacket.

'I guess I can't stop you from speaking your mind,' I say, teeth chattering in the cold. I detect an edge to my words that I don't quite manage to tame.

'I was cross with you, so I said some things I didn't mean, but what I don't understand is why you're cross. You're the one ignoring me five seconds after I had my hand under your skirt.' His tone turns exasperated.

I turn around, and the rug slips in my hands, almost making me topple. I laugh humourlessly. 'That's why I went to the bar. To apologise – I overreacted.' My knees feel weak under the weight of the rug and this conversation, and I don't know how long I can carry on standing. 'But I have to admit that I found it a little hard to digest your passing words after you, as you put it, had your hand under my skirt. One never knows how to react when someone says they want you to only get you out of their system like some tool to be used. That doesn't exactly give one a post-orgasmic glow. But I understand now, we never promised each other anything and you don't owe me anything. We are two consenting adults…' He grimaces at my words.

'Stop.' Understanding dawns on him and his cheeks turn pale. 'That's not what…' He trails off.

'That's not what you meant?' He looks unsure. 'What did you mean then? And what did you mean just now when you professed I'm nothing to you? Because you can't have it both ways, Alex. Either you want me or not. And if you hate yourself for wanting me, which seems like the case, that's your answer.' By the end of my tirade, air whooshes out of me like I've just climbed Kilimanjaro. My cheeks twitch in exhaustion. I can't keep doing this hot and cold thing.

He stays silent, his eyes searching my face like the answer is written there. His obvious mistrust of my character vexes me even more.

My bus rounds the bend, and my shoulders drop in relief. Finally. The last two minutes have felt like an hour.

'What do you want?' I turn on him, raising my voice in exasperation as the bus approaches the stop. I wave at the driver to signal for him to stop.

Knowing he's running out of time, Alex throws a desperate look towards the bus. 'I don't know what I want,' he growls and combs through his hair jerkily.

I heft the rug over my shoulder. 'Let me make it easy for you.' My words turn determined. 'Leave me be, OK? I don't want to have anything to do with you.'

21

The next day I feel like I've contracted the flu or a bulldozer has run over me a couple of times. My entire body aches, my stomach is in tight knots, and an overwhelming sense of sorrow has settled over my bones like a layer of tar, making every move cumbersome. I recognise the symptoms and guess at the cause. But this time, I'm not willing to let my heart be shattered into pieces by someone who doesn't seem to understand me or want me.

I ward myself mentally. I'm not going to let this happen again; I need to take control. I go to Jane's office and ask to be assigned to a different mentor. She doesn't ask me any questions, only nods in acknowledgement. After, I feel like a weight has lifted off my shoulders, and I can finally breathe.

I know I can't avoid him in school completely, but outside of school, I can forget that Alex has ever existed.

My phone in my bag keeps buzzing, but I studiously ignore it because I don't want to risk getting another pathetic excuse from my dad which I've been getting since yesterday. I can't pretend like nothing is amiss any more, but I also don't know how to move forward yet. I never expected all the men in my life would turn into adulterers, but here we are.

Halfway through the science lesson, somebody knocks on the door and abruptly truncates my thoughts. The children are creating electrical circuits and are so engrossed in the task that they're oblivious to the intrusion at first. Alex's sombre expression peeks through the glass, and something in me flinches. My body gets stuck in a freeze response. He walks in stiffly, and his presence fills the room the way only his presence does. The children halt, and their heads lift like a mob of meerkats, immediately picking up on the change of atmosphere. Their curious looks flicker between me and Alex like they're watching a tennis match.

My feet start working again, and I take a hesitant step towards him. 'Yes, Mr Bennet?' I try to speak as calmly as I can, but I know something is fundamentally wrong, even though I'm not sure what exactly. All my resentment is forgotten at seeing his strange expression.

'Apologies, Miss Collins. Do you have a minute?' he says overly politely, his posture more rigid than an ironing board.

I nod and motion for the children to carry on. Only half of them follow my instruction. I take a sweeping look across the classroom, and soon, all heads are down. At least they have the decency to pretend to carry on with their learning.

When I trail behind Alex, my muscles tense at the sight of Danielle who is hovering behind him in the corridor. She's supposed to be on her non-contact time, so I can't fathom what she's doing here.

'While we're speaking, Miss Davies will step in,' Alex informs me, and Danielle passes me with a not-quite-convincing neutral expression. It's obvious she's more puzzled than I am. I get this strange gut feeling like the other shoe is about to drop. Surely this is not about me asking for a different mentor. Whatever this is, it's more serious.

My dread is confirmed when he continues, 'Let's step into the outreach office.' He heads towards the only place that doesn't have a glass panel in the door, and henceforth, the only private room in the whole school.

The office is empty and meticulously tidy. With dread, I watch grey clouds gather behind the only window in the room before I make myself look at Alex.

He offers me a seat on a blue sofa, but I shake my head; I'd rather be standing if I'm being fired, but he shocks me with a completely different kind of message.

'The reception had a phone call from your mother. She's been trying to reach you the whole morning.' His tone is forcibly calm, and it loosens something inside me, something that is now rattling like a loose cog in a broken watch. 'Your father is in hospital. He's had a heart attack.'

My ears fill with white noise. I know his words are simple, but they don't make sense strung together. My mouth opens, but no words come out. Somebody makes this strange, whimpering sound, and because there's nobody else in the room, it must have been me. He squeezes my arm, and I nod helplessly because I'm certain that if I try to speak, I'll vomit.

His voice softens. 'Do you want me to wait outside while you call her?' If anybody else suggested this, I'd feel offended, but from Alex, it sounds kind and considerate. I want him to stay here and hold my hand and tell me that everything will be fine, but I don't let myself imagine this fantasy because it's damaging. Instead, I just nod again. I feel like one of those car nodding figurines because it's all I'm capable of. He looks almost relieved, as if he was worried I might say no.

The door closes behind him with a soft click and immediately a myriad of emotions floods my system and sends it into overdrive. Fear, dread, anxiety and helplessness followed by guilt and shame, but also, unexpected gratefulness that it was Alex who delivered the news and knew exactly what I needed when I didn't know myself.

With shaking hands, I dial my mother's number, and she picks up after the first beep. But it's worse than I thought because all I hear on the other end of the line are her sobs as she's trying to speak but is unable to utter a single word. My always perfect, stiff-upper-lip mother is barren of words.

'Mum?' I pull myself together, trying to sound like I'm in

control, but I'm not fooling anybody here. I can't remember the last time I called her mum, but she doesn't notice. Things must be really bad.

'How is Dad?' My breathing slows right down as if somebody has hit a pause button. I'm suspended in the air like when you jump and there is a moment of nauseating weightlessness before gravity catches up with your body.

'He...' she manages to say between sobs. My fingers tighten around the receiver in a deathly grip while I'm waiting for her to finish the most important sentence of our lives. '...he was in a critical state the whole morning but is now stable.'

Air whooshes out of me so forcefully I sound like an extractor fan. My body slumps, and I end up half sitting on the desk.

The thought of my dad being stable – whatever that means – makes my tongue swell up until it feels alien in my mouth. Stable is such a stupid word. Does it mean he was at the brink of death, but he's not any more or that he's completely fine and there's a full recovery ahead?

My mother's muffled crying rattles me. 'He was in a bad way, Holly. We were just bickering about some nonsense or other, something that he found in the newspaper earlier in the morning. I told him he should go paperless and be more conscious of the environment. He said his usual old-man nonsense about being interested only in a proper piece of news that can't be found in the digital trash that shares every celebrity break-up and dieting trend. Your father can sometimes be so dense and stubborn.' She hiccups a little. 'All of a sudden, he clutched his arm and then he went so deathly pale. Within a minute he collapsed.' She breathes heavily on the other end.

'Which hospital are you in? Do you need anything? Food, magazines, a change of clothes? I can swing by the house on my way to the hospital.' I sound almost rational, but I think it's the autopilot kicking in rather than me being composed.

'Just come. Come fast,' she whispers, her voice small like that of a child. 'Just in case,' she adds quickly like we have barely any time left, and then her words undo me.

'OK,' I force calmness into my voice and hang up before I break down on the phone and make things worse. I need to be strong, I tell myself, but as soon as I press end call, my vision starts spinning like I've been stuck on the Gravitron for one ride too long.

I stand on wobbly legs; my bottom has gone numb from sitting on the desk. When I leave the room, I quickly send a message to Catherine and Lydia in a group chat, but my hands shake so badly that there are a lot of typos.

Alex rushes to his feet as soon as he sees me, his eyes under furrowed eyebrows tense. Suddenly, all the guilt sharpens and hones into a single point that feels like the tip of a dagger being inserted between my ribs with excruciating slowness. Weight presses against my shoulders, lead spreading through my limbs and making them unwieldy. The last time I spoke to my dad, I said some truthful, but horrible, things. The fear of losing my dad shakes me so much all that feels insignificant now.

Just as my legs slip under me, Alex grabs me by the waist. 'Let's sit down for a moment.' His face is a few inches from mine, but all I can focus on is my heart pounding so loudly in my ears that it's like I'm standing under a waterfall.

'I'm fine.' Despite my words, I slide down onto the nearest bench.

'When was the last time you ate?' Alex crouches in front of me, his hands protectively on my knees. When he realises that, he drops them to his lap.

I'm trying to rack my brain, but it's too jumbled to be able to process his question.

Alex rises on his feet. 'OK. Stay here. I'll grab your stuff and something for you to eat. I'll give you a lift.' Before I can protest, he's gone. I must zone out because he's back in what feels like no time, my bag and coat in his hand. He passes me a protein bar but carries on holding my stuff.

'Sorry, that's all I had in my locker.' He looks apologetic.

I shove half the bar in my mouth and chew mechanically. 'You don't have to drive me. I can drive myself,' I manage to say between two bites. I feel a little better, my head clearer. Maybe my sugar levels were too low.

'Like hell am I letting you drive like this. We can get your car later. I've already spoken to Jane.'

I nod again uselessly, following him with wooden steps. Who would have known that Alex bossing me around would feel steadying?

My mind is blank while my body is gliding through the corridors and down the main staircase. I feel like I'm on one of those airport moving walkways, my surroundings passing by in a flash. I keep waiting for the tears to come, but instead of tearing up, my eyes feel uncomfortably dry, like there are metal shavings embedded in the tissue of my sockets. I keep blinking to chase the sensation away, but it won't go.

What sort of a person doesn't cry when their dad is in hospital? I must say this out loud because Alex whispers in a soothing tone, 'You're in shock.' The warmth of his hand around my shoulders steadies me.

Alex guides us through the reception where he signs us out. Mary, the blonde receptionist, is craning her nose over her desk as we pass, but Alex shields me from her view. Wordlessly, he leads us to the Mercedes I've been seeing late in the evenings in the car park. He opens the passenger door for me, and then I'm seated in the front. It takes me a few goes to buckle up, but by the time Alex is behind the wheel, I'm strapped in and pretending I'm more composed than I feel.

He manoeuvres smoothly out of the overflowing car park and onto the main road, his demeanour calm and focused. Alex has always been steady in a crisis. Why is it he's always the one to save me?

I keep myself busy to stave off the dangerous thoughts of what awaits me. I scan around the interior of Alex's car. It feels solid and reliable in the same way Alex always used to. It also smells of the expensive, clean smell that I now associate with this Alex. I almost wistfully think of the old days when he smelt of the cigarettes his mum smoked and Lynx.

I watch him, but he's completely focused on the road ahead, unaware of my staring. For long moments we don't say anything. Other people would have felt the need to fill the silence with empty words, but Alex never did. I used to find it equally comforting and unnerving.

Something in me breaks a little. 'My dad cheated on my mother when I was younger. Last week I told him I knew. I said a lot of other things that I'm not proud of. I'm not even sure whether I spoke or shouted them.'

He considers my words. 'When did you find out he cheated on your mum?' he asks without looking at me.

'When I was seventeen,' I rasp. He must connect the events because his hands tighten around the steering wheel.

'That's a long time to carry something like that.' His voice acquires a gravelly quality.

'I thought if I pretended nothing had happened, everything would be fine. But I realise that's not how it works.'

He looks pensive and almost vulnerable for a moment. 'Love is complicated. Just because you don't approve of his life choices and because you're angry at him doesn't mean you've stopped loving him. I'm sure he knows that. Your dad always seemed to me like a very intelligent person.'

I'm surprised he has anything nice to say about my dad after the way he treated Alex when we were teenagers. I think he's not only speaking of my dad, but I have no energy to work out what he means.

The urban landscape slowly changes behind the windows as we hit one of the A roads surrounded by fields and farmhouses.

'What if he doesn't make it and we never have a chance to clear the air?' I hate how weak I sound.

'You don't always get the end you wish for, but that doesn't change the get-going.' He sounds so sad I can't stop looking at him.

'Your mum?' My voice is barely audible above the steady rumble of his car. It starts to rain outside, heavy raindrops pounding against the roof, cocooning us in the white noise of the elements. For long moments, I don't think he will answer my question, but he does.

'She passed away three years ago. Liver failure. All that drinking caught up with her in the end.' He gives me a strange look before he focuses on the road ahead of him again.

'You took good care of her. I remember that.' I say the words that nobody has probably said to him, words that he maybe needed to hear. His lips press together in what I now know is not disapproval but processing some strong emotion. I feel this sudden raw need to understand him.

'Why are you doing this?' The question comes out in an almost unintelligible stream like water rushing through a too-narrow opening. There's too much inside me; my head and chest are overflowing, and there are no channels to release the pressure. Soon enough I will burst like a piñata into tiny little fragments of confetti and scattered thoughts.

'Because you needed not to be alone,' he says matter-of-factly like it's a given. I'm glad there's no trace of pity or satisfaction in his explanation. A part of me wonders whether he was alone when his mum passed away, but I don't ask. I hate the idea.

Alex parks in the visitors' car park, the closest he can get to the inpatients entrance. He opens the door for me, and I lift myself heavily out of the passenger seat and into the breezy air that attacks the layers of my clothing with cold fingers as soon as I'm out.

Hurriedly, we walk through the automatic sliding doors to reception. I've always sensed where Alex's body is in relation to mine, so I can feel his hand hovering behind my back like he's waiting for me to need it at any moment.

My mind bottoms out as soon as we start walking through one of the long clinical corridors after we get sent that way by an older nurse at reception. My back comes in contact with Alex's hand when I come to a halt.

I can't stop the words, 'What if...' but break off before I can finish the question out loud.

'Until you go in, you won't know and not knowing is much worse.' His steady presence settles into my ribcage in a burst of warmth. It soothes the brittle edges of my lungs. A small part of me hates that he's seeing me like this, but a bigger part of me is grateful.

We walk through the entrance to the cardiology ward, big black frightening letters stamped uncompromisingly onto a yellow sign.

'Whatever happens, you'll deal with it,' he says simply. I've missed Alex's pragmatism. He didn't say my dad was going to be OK or it always looked worse than it was. None of the empty phrases that Aaron would fill the space with. I appreciate the words more than anything else that could have been said.

I nod briskly, suddenly feeling that *a thank you* would be inadequate, and yet, I need him to know that I appreciate this, him. He copies the gesture but changes his mind and reaches the space between us with his steady freckled hands and tenderly takes my shoulders. He envelops me in his arms, and without overthinking it, I fit my body flush against him; his heartbeat is my anchor. I breathe him in for a few moments until a throat clears behind his back, and I plunge back to reality. I look over Alex's shoulder and step away quickly. It's my mother.

Alex coughs and says, 'Mrs Collins. I'm sorry for intruding. I'm just dropping Holly off.' My mother stares at him strangely for a few beats but eventually snaps out of it and whispers *thank you*. Her eyes are red-rimmed, and her fingers are gripping her elbows so stiffly I'm worried she'll break the skin with her nails.

He turns to me and adds more formally, the gap between us opening once again, 'Please let the school know if you need anything.' This impersonal Alex is a whiplash to the warm, solid Alex of a minute ago. With those words, he turns around and leaves me alone with my mother.

The faraway beeping machines and rubber shoes sticking to the lino flooring as staff move briskly from one end of the corridor to the other are the only sounds between us.

Does she blame me for what has happened? I'm terrified to move, but then the time unravels, and my mother rushes to me and hugs me so hard my ribs are about to crack despite her not ever being a hugger. I embrace her back, even though I take after her in that respect, and bury my nose in her hair. The smell of hair spray and Chanel are bitter in my nostrils, and yet, I revel in the scent. She feels different in my arms, more fragile. Over her flattened-down hairdo, I spot a male nurse giving us space. He's clearly here to see us but doesn't want to intrude on a private moment.

When we separate, the nurse steps closer to us and informs us kindly, 'Mrs Collins, Dr Sanjiv is ready for you.'

The nurse leads us through the warren-like corridors at an efficient pace. Finally, or too soon, I can't decide which, we end up in the main open-plan ward. It's separated into sections by blue curtains, some drawn shut tight and some drawn partly back. They separate the room like an ice cube tray, cold and impersonal. The smell of disinfectant and rubber is turning my insides. A doctor in her forties is waiting by the farthest bed that is blocked from view by a partially closed curtain. I stiffen. My mother carries on walking and because she has wound her arm through mine, I'm propelled forward by the motion. At the sight of the person in the bed, I flinch.

The man lying in the bed is and is not my dad. His usually unruly grey hair is flattened around his pale face that is barren of his old-fashioned glasses, and his lips are chapped. He doesn't smell like my dad either, of old books and cologne. The sight of him looking diminished and with a machine beeping along with his heart makes me take a proverbial step back. I've been so angry at him for such a long time, and now, at the sight of him so helpless, my anger unravels like a coil of string into nothing. That's when the dam breaks and tears leak down my cheeks. I let them run.

22

The doctor checks my dad's vitals and tells us he was lucky my mother immediately called the ambulance and they managed to get him to the hospital before any permanent damage was done. To our relief, she also informs us that we are to expect a full recovery, even though a change of diet and lifestyle will be needed.

After the doctor has gone, my mother wipes away a stray tear with her pink-shellac nail. She tries to hide it, adding more firmly, 'If you ask me, she was too young to be a doctor. Maybe we should ask for an older doctor that is bound to be…' She leans over my dad's bed to me and finishes with, '…more experienced.'

She's been gripping my dad's hand for the last two minutes. I know she's coping the only way she knows how to, so I let her say her bit even though I don't think antagonising the people who saved my dad's life is the right course of action. At the thought, my mind goes quiet. He could have died today.

'Has he woken up at all since he collapsed?' My eyes flash towards his jaw where stubble has started to dot his usually smooth face. Mother calls it grey whiskers, like a cat's. She hates my dad's stubble with a passion and always bugs him to shave, but when I watch her absentmindedly stroke his cheek, I think it's the last thing on her mind now.

'He was awake when we got him in, but then they gave him

some sedatives and told me he was unlikely to wake up until much later.'

We stay by his bed for an hour or maybe longer. I can't tell because every minute seems to be dragging on, time only separated by the faint beeping of all the machines surrounding us. I've never realised how a hospital is just a jungle of white noise and whispered prayers. Dad's own machine is so loud in my ears it feels almost static. With every beep, it builds this electric current in my body until it's almost painful. Until I can't take it any more.

'It's my fault he had a heart attack.' I drag the confession out. At first, I can't seem to look at my mother, but eventually, I tell myself to be brave and force myself to meet her eyes.

My mother's make-up-free eyes crinkle at the edges as she frowns. She looks suddenly so much older.

'No, it's not. It's because he's eaten a sausage roll every day for lunch for the last ten years and because the only exercise he does is walk to his local newsagents.' Her tone doesn't allow for any arguments.

'The things I said last week,' I start, and I grip the scratchy linen covering my dad's bed for support. I haven't found the courage to touch him yet, scared he might not feel the same and even more scared he might. This is the hardest conversation I've ever had with my mother, but I force myself to carry on. 'I've never wanted you to find out the way you did. I'm sorry.'

'I didn't,' my mother says steadily. She elaborates. 'I mean I didn't find out like that.'

I sit up on the uncomfortable chair because I don't follow.

She takes a long, exhausted breath before she explains, 'Your father confided in me after he finished the affair. I've known for years. I'm sorry that I let you think you had to keep the secret from me for so long so you wouldn't hurt my feelings. I didn't know you knew.' She averts her gaze, obviously embarrassed to discuss her love life with me.

'But.' I pause and start again. 'I don't understand. You forgave him?' My voice is full of disbelief. I let my hands slide off the bed cover and into my lap, fingers lacing tightly.

'Don't get me wrong. I was so angry at him. Your father has made many mistakes in his life, and that particular mistake almost broke us. We weren't happy at that point in our lives, but he's been a great husband and dad most of our marriage. It was the hardest decision I have ever made.'

An uncomfortable feeling starts building in my stomach, and my thoughts are confirmed when she leans in and strokes my hair. 'You were always so dependent on your father when you were little, and even as a young woman you adored him. We never had that, and I didn't want to break that special connection for something that had nothing to do with you. I never had what you did with my father. A big part of me still loved him even after he did what he did. He's got a lot to atone for, so he's not allowed to leave me quite yet. I don't allow it. Why do you think he stands visitors at our weekly roast dinners? He calls it the Suitors' Sunday.' She cackles and the sound surprises me so much I jolt in my seat. I don't think I've ever heard my mother amused.

Despite her usually perfect hair dishevelled and her cheeks sallow, she's never looked so perfect to me. She's the strongest person I've ever known. I know we don't often see eye to eye and will probably argue at least one more time by the end of today, but love rushes through my veins, spreading warmth into every nook and cranny of my chilled body.

'I know that life with me has never been easy. I'm sorry for being so forceful about Aaron. I just wanted you to be happy. I cannot believe that he's turned out to be such a turd,' my mother says crossly. I gurgle-laugh, and my nose starts running; my mother never swears.

She carries on with her confession. 'I was certain I pushed you away. Suddenly, you decided to move out and go to a university across the country. You rarely visit. Of course, it all makes perfect sense now.' Sadness sweeps across her features in a tidal wave.

'I couldn't stand the sight of Dad pretending everything was OK. I had to get out of the house. I'm sorry. It was never your fault.' I admit reluctantly, 'Even though I've always thought that you were embarrassed by me. You always wanted to change things about me.' I never considered how my decisions would affect my mother.

'Don't be daft.' She stands up and moves her chair next to mine with a loud scrape. She squeezes my hands in my lap, her eyes turning shiny. 'I love you greatly, and I'm so proud of everything you've achieved single-handedly in life. Apart from that god-awful studio flat of yours, and I wish you sometimes put more care into what you wear. You look like a Victorian schoolteacher today.' She peers down at my stripy blue-and-white blouse with a bow at the neck and vintage skirt disapprovingly. I'm proud of her description because that's what I was aiming for.

'Mother,' I interject, but amusement colours my voice.

Her eyes turn serious again. 'I've never wanted you to leave. Why do you think I've kept your room the same?' There's a beat of silence between us before she carries on. 'I've always hoped that if I kept your room the same, you'd stay more often. I've even moved my Peloton to your room so I could be surrounded by your things when I'm there. I miss you every day.'

Everything I thought I knew about my mother is wrong. I wrap my arm around her, and she drops her head to my shoulder. For a moment, we're silent.

She whispers into my hair, 'Now. When are you going to tell me who that young man that accompanied you here was?' My eyes roll without volition, and I let go of her.

'Nobody,' I say automatically.

She lifts her head. 'Nobody wouldn't give you such an embrace. I wasn't born yesterday.'

'Alex.' I breathe his name out like a secret.

'I thought I recognised him. I've always thought he was a good boy, taking care of his mum the way he did,' she surprises me by saying. Who is this person who's replaced my mother? I'm about to initiate an interrogation, but she's faster. 'Don't you think I didn't use to keep tabs on people my daughter saw?' She explains, 'Most mothers at your high schools were such gossipers. That boy wasn't dealt much luck, but I'm glad he's turned out right.'

'Mother,' I start.

She *tsks*. 'I know. I'm not meddling. You've got your life to live.'

'It's complicated.'

'Isn't it always?' Who knew my mother would be full of wise proverbs? All hell indeed must have broken loose.

Before I have a chance to react, a female nurse with blonde hair and grown-out brown roots comes over and checks on my dad. She tells us she doesn't expect any changes by the end of today and encourages us to go home, get some rest and come back tomorrow. She also informs my mother, who I can see is getting ready for a tirade, that if anything happens, they'll call.

'Of course, nothing is going to happen until something does. I didn't expect my husband to have a heart attack in the middle of a rerun of an old *Countdown* episode. If I wasn't there, he wouldn't be here, but six feet under. I'm not going anywhere,' my mother says as soon as the poor woman stops talking.

Over her shoulder, I give the nurse an apologetic look and mouth *sorry*. I guess my mother is still my mother. Stubborn as a mule.

When I'm readying to stay with her, she shakes her head vigorously. 'Don't be silly. There's no point in you staying here.' She huffs. 'To only be uncomfortable on these frankly hideous chairs. I think this place needs some sprucing up.'

I'm ready to jump in, but she's quicker.

'But you could pop to the house tomorrow and bring me a few things to cheer things up around here, maybe a chair cushion so these plastic contraptions are a degree more comfortable.' I don't realise I'm shaking my head in disbelief until I get a crick in my neck. Not even a hospital can tame my mother's spirit.

When I'm about to leave, I finally find it in myself to grip my dad's hand. I study my small hand wrapped around his. They're the same shape despite my dad's hand being bigger and hairier.

'Don't be angry with him on my behalf,' my mother pleads.

I only nod because no matter what, we still have a difficult conversation ahead of us. I lean to kiss her cheek, and she squeezes my shoulder as I let go. I leave her among the beeping machines.

When I walk along the corridor back to the reception, I dial Catherine's number. As soon as she picks up, she says, 'Lydia is here with me on the speakerphone.' Her voice is loaded with questions, but neither she nor Lydia says a word, waiting for me to speak.

'He's going to be OK.' I start crying again, but I'm not sure why. Is it relief? Residual anger release? Who knows. But now the dam has been broken, I cannot seem to stop.

'Oh, Hols,' Lydia whispers.

'We love you,' Catherine chimes.

'I wish I was there right now because I would give you one of those god-awful squeeze-the-life-out-of-you kind of hugs that you hate so much,' Lydia announces solemnly, and I cry-laugh. I love my friends so much.

I retell everything that has happened, getting a lift, my dad being stable and finish on my conversation with my mother. They both listen patiently, not interrupting once. That makes me think of Vicky who surely by now would have been on her fourth or fifth interruption. I make a mental note to message her later because I don't feel like I have enough energy for that task right now. It passes fleetingly through my mind that it's not precisely healthy to be mentally fortifying myself to tell a friend my dad is in hospital, but not all friends can be Lydia and Catherine.

'Do you need anything, Hols? I've only had a small glass of wine, so I'm good to give you a lift wherever you need. We can swing by your mum's if she needs anything. I bet she's itching for her make-up bag by now,' Lydia says in a business-like manner. I love her for all her practicality and non-judgment. My mother is my mother after all and my dad having a heart attack is not going to change her.

I hear a person pulling themselves to their feet and gathering their stuff on the other end of the line like they're ready to leave.

'I might need a lift home if you don't mind. I'd take a taxi, but I doubt there's enough money in my bank account to buy a loaf of bread and a tin of baked beans. I can take the bus to school tomorrow and get my car.'

Apart from a few nurses rushing past me in the opposite direction, the corridor is almost empty, my booted feet making squeaky sounds as they peel off the rubber flooring. I see the reception from a distance; a few potted palm trees that I missed are brightening the space that otherwise looks like the inside of a busy train station with all the stairs and blue railings.

I abruptly stop, and an older couple bump into me as they pass. I apologise, but my eyes are trained on the figure just outside the automatic doors. 'Alex.'

'Should I head out?' Lydia asks, the jingle of keys being picked up sounding in the background. Then the line goes silent. 'Come again?'

I hide behind the closest potted plant and nearly poke myself in the eye. 'He's still here,' I say urgently into the phone. I don't know why I'm whispering, but I can't stop myself. A middle-aged man dressed in a hospital-issue dressing gown sitting on the nearest bench gives me a funny look, but I ignore him and continue hiding.

I shouldn't have worried about Alex spotting me because he's pacing up and down the front entrance and talking to someone on the phone. My heart makes a strange leap at the thought of him waiting all this time, like when you jump but realise there isn't any solid ground to land on.

Whoever he's talking to is making him frown. He hangs up and rubs his face, combing through his fiery hair.

'Did Alex give you a lift?' Catherine's voice comes out uneven.

'That school of yours is truly devoted to their staff,' Lydia observes. I detect a trace of amusement in her voice.

'Didn't I say Alex was the one to drive me here?' I ask with confusion.

'No, you only said you *got a lift*,' Lydia offers pointedly.

I tell them about how he delivered the message, and then, after feeding me, gave me a lift.

Silence follows.

'Hello?' I check the line but nothing.

'How long have you been in the hospital?' Catherine finally asks.

I check my watch; it's five past four. 'An hour and a half,' I answer uncertainly.

'He surely was an arsehole ten years ago, but he's turned out OK. It's understandable you're still into him,' Lydia remarks dryly.

'I'm not still into him.' I trail off because I know this is a moot point now. I slide a look in the direction of the guy in the dressing gown. He's now crunching on salt and vinegar crisps while unashamedly eavesdropping on my conversation. I try to move out of his earshot.

Lydia sounds determined. 'Maybe you should stop overthinking it and just give him a second chance. Jump his bones and see what happens next. You'll both feel better after. You two have this suppressed sexual tension vibe and it's been killing me.' I appreciate her straightforwardness but can't fathom why she's so pro-Alex.

Catherine surprises me by saying, 'Whatever you want, Holly. You decide where this goes. Just make sure that you want it for the right reasons and not because of what's happened to your dad.'

I peek from behind the palm tree and catch Alex turning, ready to go. I've never been more uncertain of what to do in my life.

'I asked Jane for a different mentor. Finally, I was done with him.' I'm not convincing anybody here. 'He doesn't know what he wants, and frankly, I have no freaking clue what I want. This is not going to end well.'

Alex starts walking away.

'He's leaving. I don't know what to do.' I panic.

I can just about hear Lydia's haunted voice, a surprisingly good imitation of Gary Oldman, 'I did my waiting! Twelve years of it!' Catherine must give her a look because Lydia grumbles and stops.

I realise I don't want him to leave.

'I have to go,' I say as a goodbye and hang up.

23

Only when I'm rushing after Alex do I realise I have no idea what I'm going to say. I'm momentarily distracted because fresh air hits my face and cuts through my shirt like it's paper-thin. That's when I remember I left my coat by my dad's bed. Shivering, I search the surroundings, but Alex has disappeared. My bag slides off my shoulder and hits the ground, half the contents rolling out onto the wet pavement slabs. 'Oh bollocks,' I mumble, unable to suppress anger over my bad timing and clumsiness.

A familiar figure pulls away from the wall, and I blink rapidly as Alex strides towards me and helps me pick up the stuff that has spilt out of my bag.

I quickly grab the more embarrassing items like my emergency tampon pack and a nasal spray, and Alex passes me my lipstick, charger and a pair of backup tights. This is all done wordlessly without once looking up.

However, when he passes me my phone, which now has a cracked screen, I finally venture to glance up. He's looking all apologetic like it's his fault it's broken.

When we've picked up all the stuff and both stand up, I say, 'He's going to be fine,' at the same time Alex asks, 'How is your dad?'

I carry on because I feel like I owe him more. 'He was lucky my mother called the ambulance straight away. She saved his life.'

'I can't believe you still call her Mother,' he says, disbelief and amusement curving his lips upwards.

'She would probably disown me if I called her anything but Mother.' This time his lips curl in a definite smile.

After a pause, I mumble, 'Thank you for the lift.' I shift from foot to foot. 'And for taking care of me.'

Nodding, he scratches the back of his head, and the muscles in his arm pull the fabric of his shirt taut against his skin. If I didn't know him, I'd say he's nervous. His demeanour is the complete opposite of his usual closed-off manner, like something has shifted inside him since our last encounter. He hesitates before he asks, 'Do you need a lift home?'

'That would be…' I can't quite find the right words but finish with, '…I'd like that.'

Once we're inside his car, he surprises me by saying, 'Does your mum need anything? We can always swing by her house.'

I shake my head. 'I'll stop by tomorrow before I go to see my dad. Do you need me to give you my address or should I direct you?' I start saying when I stop abruptly at the sight of his freckled fingers tapping my address into the satnav.

His cheeks flushing, he grips the wheel hard as he pulls out of the car park. 'I've got a good memory,' he mutters. My stomach does a somersault.

When he pulls up in front of my flat, I shift sideways to face him. His proximity in the small space is intoxicating, and all I want to do is drown myself in him, to forget about my dad and everything else complicated in my life right now. Including what's going on between us.

'Do you want to come upstairs for a cup of tea? After all, that's the least I can do after today.' I try to keep my voice steady but fail.

'You don't have to.' He waves his hand. The engine is still gently rumbling around us, and I'm starting to think that maybe I've read too much into this.

I wet my lips because they feel suddenly dry. 'I want to.' The words are a bare whisper, but at the sound of them, he kills the engine. I tell myself to be brave as I breach the space between us and kiss him. It's a soft kiss, and his lips are so warm I want to stay like that forever, but I make myself pull away. When I do, Alex's expression is unreadable.

'OK,' he croaks.

'The flat is a dump,' I warn him over my shoulder when we walk up the stairs.

He laughs behind me softly. 'I've had my share of dump flats if you recall.'

We stop in front of my door, a bronze *twelve* nailed wonkily to the surface. 'Not like this. I think at some point somebody buried a dead body here. It stinks like decomposing flesh most of the time, and the other day I found a human-shaped stain under the bathroom lino.' I'm stalling because I'm nervous, but the sound of Alex's splutter behind me eases some of it. I unlock the door, and we step inside together.

'As long as you haven't buried any dead bodies here yourself, I'm OK,' he quips. We take our shoes off and leave them by the door.

I give him a mock withering look. 'I'm not that stupid. I'd mince them, make pies and sell them to people I don't like. Make a business out of it.'

'Isn't that pretty much the plot of *Sweeney Todd: The Demon Barber of Fleet Street*?'

'I did wonder why it sounded so familiar.'

He shakes his head in disbelief.

The flat is dark and smells a bit musty as we close the door behind us. Immediately, I abandon my bag on the bed hiding behind an antique partition to our left.

I motion for Alex to sit down on the threadbare double sofa in the middle of the large space. I head towards the kitchen counter tucked in the right corner of the studio.

For a single-room flat, the studio is fairly roomy and allows for a partition wall to divide the space into a lounge and a tiny bedroom. Alex looks down, and at the sight of the familiar rug, his eyes light up with mirth.

I rifle through the cupboards. 'Tea? Coffee? I wouldn't vouch for the quality of either, but it colours the water.' I spin on my heel to realise that he's made his way towards the kitchen.

He's about to lower himself onto one of the stools attached to the breakfast bar. Lifting my hands up in the air, I shout, 'Not that one.' I catch his horrified expression. I force myself to say, much calmer this time, 'Unless you want to break your back. The left one is semi-decent which means there's only a fifty-fifty chance it'll collapse underneath you.'

'I feel so reassured,' he responds uncertainly but sits, nevertheless. 'I don't mind either,' he answers my previous question.

I turn my back on him again, filling the kettle to the brim. It's in desperate need of descaling, but that's only one of the minor shortcomings of this flat. My hands shake a little. I've never been this nervous in my entire life. I head to the fridge because I need something to steady my nerves, and coffee won't do the job.

'Do you mind if I have a glass of wine? I think I need something stronger.' After the day I've had, a shot of vodka would be preferable, but beggars can't be choosers.

'I'll have a small glass if you don't mind. It's been a strange day.' He pales. 'I'm sorry. I didn't mean…' He rubs his face, unsure how to finish the sentence without offending me.

'It's OK.' I reassure him.

The kettle abandoned, I pull out two wine glasses from the overhead cabinet. They're those embossed deep-yellow glasses that were so popular in the eighties. I was really proud of getting them half-price on Etsy last year, but now I wish I had something less *theatrical* to serve the wine in. Not giving it another thought, I place them between me and Alex on the breakfast bar. I pluck the wine from the side. 'I definitely don't vouch for the quality of what's in this bottle. It might be closer to vinegar than wine,' I point out with embarrassment.

He leans over the bar and takes the bottle from my waiting hands, fingers brushing against mine for a fleeting moment. My cheeks flush. With a smooth motion, he unscrews the lid and pours me a generous amount, while only pouring an inch for himself.

He pushes a glass towards me, and the bottom of it scrapes against the speckled surface. 'I think you should have guests more often. You're a killer host.'

I snort into my drink as I take a sip. At least he finds some humour in this.

I take another sip and close my eyes for a moment, calming my nerves. When I open them again, I catch him staring at my lips. When he realises he's been caught, he shifts uncomfortably on the bar stool. He must be getting sore sitting on the death trap.

'Shall we sit on the sofa?' I motion towards the shabby settee that came with the flat.

In unison, we head towards it. I park myself in the right corner, giving him space and time to choose how close he wants to be to me. When he's about to sit in the opposite corner and as far away from me as possible, I warn him, 'Mind the corner. It's a bit collapsed.'

He seats himself in the middle of the sofa. If I wanted to, I could reach out and touch him. The question is not whether I want to, because I'm dying to, but whether I'll find the courage to do that.

He takes a tentative sip of his drink and swallows, his Adam's apple bobbing. 'I'd say it's closer to wine than vinegar. But just about. I wouldn't put it on my salad yet.' I can't stop myself from smirking.

I watch with curiosity as he takes another sip. He catches my perusal and his eyebrow quirks. He abandons the glass on the coffee table. 'What is it?' Interest deepens his voice.

'I didn't think you'd drink,' I confess, not wanting to sour the mood but unable to help myself. I pull my legs underneath me, tucking my skirt under my knees. He follows the movement, but then his focus sharpens on the golden contents of his glass with contemplation.

'After Mum?' I nod. 'I figured that that's exactly the reason why to drink. To learn how to drink without it killing me.' I get a sudden urge to understand what makes this Alex tick. He surprises me by adding, 'The idea of being like her used to terrify me. That's why I didn't drink until my early twenties.'

'Is that why you never finish?' I eye his glass. It's something I noticed at Becky's birthday party. He left every drink he ordered unfinished.

Surprised at my observation, he nods almost imperceptibly.

My glass joins his on the table. 'Addiction is a mental disorder. It's not a choice. You don't suddenly wake up and turn into an addict.' The weight of his gaze nails me to the sofa like a butterfly pinned to the spreading board.

'Logically, I know that, and I know she tried to get better, but she couldn't.'

The sadness that radiates off his body shakes me to the core, and not for the first time I hope that Jane was there for him when his mum passed away. I hate the idea of him carrying it alone. Nobody has ever cared for Alex, and I realise with fear that I want to be the one to care for him. I want to be the person he relies on, the person he comes to when he's feeling sad or angry.

He brings me back to reality. 'What are you going to do about your dad?'

A desperate need to unload my thoughts, even though they are crude and a little naïve, takes over my logic. 'I'm relieved that he's OK.' I hesitate, swallowing nervously. 'But I don't know whether I can just forgive and forget.' My voice is as weak as a thread about to snap. 'But I want to so much. I want to go back to what we had before I found out. I miss it. I miss us.' I don't think I'm talking about my dad any more.

Alex shifts in his seat and ends up so close I can smell the woody, and now familiar, smell of him. Goosebumps creep up my arms. The air changes between us and becomes charged. If I touched him now, he'd send an electric shock through my body. His hand rests in the space between us, and I agonise over the few centimetres that separate our bodies.

This is far from what I intended. All I thought I would get was an easy conversation followed by passionate sex. I didn't expect to steer into dark, murky waters, and I didn't expect to need it this much.

His chest under his shirt expands with rapid breaths. 'Before we left school, Jane told me you asked her to assign you a different mentor.'

'I don't think I can carry on like this.' There's no space for lies between us now. 'I thought it would be for the best to go our separate ways.'

He closes his eyes briefly before he says with resolution, 'I lied to you the other night.' His expression changes from hooded to open and vulnerable. I frown. 'When I said I didn't know what I wanted.' Everything goes completely still.

'I want you.' My mind scrambles, but he's not finished. 'Any way I can get you. I know this is not the right time, with your dad and…' He trails off. His confession unlocks me.

I only hesitate for a few seconds before I bring my hands to his cheeks. Holding him steady, I whisper, 'I want you, too.'

I lift to my knees, and without overthinking it, I straddle him. Immediately, his hands roam up my back, pulling my hips forward. Every contact of our bodies sends shivers to my core. His thighs feel powerful underneath me, and I shift to find a comfortable position which makes us flush against each other in all the places that matter. Heat radiates off his body; he's a furnace, and I want to warm myself against him.

He smells of wine and mint, and the combination is heady. His eyes glaze over with desire as he finds purchase on my thighs. My skirt hitches up over my knees, exposing white expanses of bare skin. When his fingertips connect with my bare flesh, his grip tightens. He leans into me at the same time I arch against him, and then we're kissing. The kiss immediately deepens. I anchor my hands against his broad shoulders, and he grips my bum under my skirt. I shift against him to get better access, and that's when I feel him hardening. He groans, and a sense of thrill travels the length of my body. It's intoxicating to know that we still do this to each other. But this time, there will be no playing around. I need him now.

He pulls at the bow at my neck, and it unravels with the flick of his expert fingers. I proceed to unbutton my blouse as he does the same to his shirt, his hands swift and impatient. Finally, we're on the same wavelength and want the same thing.

He grinds against me as he disposes of his shirt. We're both out of breath by the time we're topless, but it's heavenly to feel his skin against mine. His chest is big and powerful. A light smattering of golden freckles covers his shoulders and upper body, the rest of him is the palest white.

He buries his head against my collarbone and kisses the space between the bone and shoulder. I shiver when he lowers one of my bra straps, nipping the exposed skin underneath. He repeats it with the other strap. 'I've dreamed of doing this so many times.' His tone is reverent.

'I've dreamed of you doing this so many times,' I admit in a hushed tone, echoing his words. He dips his fingers inside my bra, stroking my breast. I tip my head back as a sensation bolts through me like lightning. He starts undoing the clip of my bra, but before he manages to unhook it, he sits up and yelps.

He hefts me up in his arms, making me squeal, and moves us sideways to discover a spring popping through the threadbare fabric of the sofa where he was sitting. I didn't even know the sofa had springs inside.

He must think me a total loser for living in this dump, but instead of saying anything of that nature, he starts laughing so hard his chest rumbles against mine. It gets me laughing as well, and I start shaking with violent fits of it. We look at each other for a moment and that sends us into another bout of laughter. I can see the humour in this.

'This place is not safe for habitation,' he offers when we finally stop.

'You haven't seen the bathroom,' I respond coquettishly.

He tightens his grip on my waist. 'Oh, the infamous bathroom where dead bodies have been known to have been buried.' I love how playful he is. He feels different, like a door has been opened and I'm standing at the threshold ready to walk in and see all the wonders that are there to offer. Just looking at him, all flushed and eyes shiny, I want this moment to last forever.

'A dead body, singular. I'll have you know this is a respectable place. We don't cater for serial killers. Not enough room,' I announce sardonically, and it sends him into another fit of laughter.

He leans into me, and then there's no laughing.

'Bedroom?' I suggest between kisses, and he nods frantically. I'm about to stand up when he grips my thighs and pulls himself to his feet with me. I wrap my legs around his waist and let him carry me towards the bed.

When we reach the destination, he swipes the bag I abandoned on the covers and it clatters to the floor, a few items scattering about the lino. Again. He drops me on the bed and then immediately stretches over me. The weight of him against my slight frame is exhilarating. We're an unfinished dot-to-dot puzzle; I savour every place we connect, and I'm thrilled about every place we don't yet. I have never wanted anything more than this right now. Him. Us.

My skirt gets discarded and then I'm underneath him only in my underwear. He's still wearing his work trousers and a kinky part of me is thinking of leaving them on, but then the idea is chased away by another more urgent and primal thought of having Alex completely naked above me.

He grinds against me, and I can't stop the moan from escaping my mouth. This is really happening. Now. Finally. I reach down to unzip his trousers. This is an unknown territory because as much as he's touched me before, I've never touched him like this.

After I unzip his trousers, I reach into his boxers. But a moment later, his hand shoots from nowhere and stops me mid-movement. His breathing is ragged above me, and he looks agitated. Closing his eyes, he swallows hard. His reaction surprises me so much I freeze.

'Have I done something wrong?' I whisper, searching his face a bare inch above me. His expression shuts down like he's retreated into himself again, the door closing. When he opens his eyes again, they're distant.

My phone starts buzzing on the floor and breaks whatever was left of the electric atmosphere between us.

He pushes off me and sits up, turning away from me and in the direction of the phone. It keeps buzzing and whoever's calling is persistent. Alex's back stiffens. I lean over his shoulder to find out who's calling and wince. On the cracked screen, it reads *Vicky*.

'I can't do this. I thought I could do this, but I can't.' Alex mutters like he's speaking to himself. 'I need to go. This was a mistake.' He starts hastily collecting his clothes like he can't wait to be out of here. It makes me feel cheap and unwanted. It's such a sudden change my head is spinning.

'What?' I quickly grab the dressing gown that's hanging on the chair by the bed and follow him into the lounge. I pluck the phone from the floor, but Vicky hung up. Not that I was ready to pick up. I abandon it on the breakfast bar.

He puts his own phone into the pocket of his trousers and when he finally turns around, his face is made of steel. 'I have to go,' he repeats in an expressionless tone. I hate it.

'Stop being like this. Is this some twisted game of yours?' I say louder than I expected, but I can't stop myself. I don't do drama. I don't shout, but everything is breaking inside me. Again. He doesn't say anything, which enrages me further.

I jab his chest with my finger, and he takes a step back. 'You don't get to pretend it's all my fault this time. I'm done with you breaking me.' His expression turns confused. 'I'm done with you turning me on and off like a switch. To see what I'll do. Do you like these power games? Is that what turns you on? You haven't changed that much after all. But I'm done.' This time I know it's true; there's no more chances. I step away, and it's his turn to invade my space this time.

His lips are a bare centimetre from mine, and yet, we are as far from kissing as we've ever been. 'You don't know what you're talking about.' His knuckles gripping his coat turn white.

'I don't? I think you secretly like this. Making me crawl to you so you get the upper hand. That's what it was ten years ago, wasn't it?'

Before he responds, his eyes fly towards my buzzing phone. This time, John's name flashes on the display. I suppress an eye-roll; this is the worst timing possible. The news of my dad must have reached him. Alex turns grey, and he stumbles like the phone has burnt him.

'You're one to talk. Looking so innocent in your buttoned-up dresses and patent shoes, Miss Righteous. Despite your pretence, you are no better than others. All you do is play with other people's feelings, and when you get bored of them, you discard them like they are no better than single-use plastic.' He looks at me with so much scorn it makes me flinch. 'That's what you did then and that's what you still do. I can't ever trust you. After all, I'm just a *worthless waste of space*, aren't I? How long would it take you this time to get bored of me?'

He grabs his car keys. I'm so shocked by his accusations, I have no comeback. I'm not sure what's going on here, but I feel like I'm missing some vital piece of information.

He reaches the door, but before he opens it, he spins around. 'Are you sleeping with him?' Utter confusion must show on my face because he adds grudgingly, 'John. Are you sleeping with him?' He's back to the person he was when I saw him for the first time after ten years. I hate that guy.

I don't deign to answer his question. 'Leave.' His lips pursed, and he waits like he thinks I'm actually going to answer. 'Should I draw you a plan for how to get to the door? I know you like to be organised.'

He blinks wildly like he's just woken up from a daze. 'You never gave me a chance.'

At least he has the decency to close the door soundlessly behind him. Once he's gone, deafening silence presses against my ears almost painfully. I slump to the floor. Tears start running down my cheek for the second time today. I pull my knees to my chin and wrap my arms around my legs as I let go.

With unequivocal certainty, I know that my heart has just been broken. I know this because my chest feels like it's made entirely of glass shards. When I breathe, they are cutting into my organs, ripping me apart from the inside out. Every breath and every move suddenly feel laborious.

I finish the bottle of wine in less than twenty minutes and email Jane that I won't be at work tomorrow or the day after. I turn my phone off and hide under the duvet for a while, but all I can smell is Alex. I strip the bedding. After, I scrub the whole place, trying to get rid of Alex's scent, but after two hours, it still lingers in my nostrils, and I wonder for the first time whether it's me and not the flat.

I'll never be rid of Alex because he's woven into the very fabric of me, nestling in every cell of my being.

24

I'm lying on Vicky's single bed. It's covered in the most hideous, fuchsia-patterned bed cover and everything smells of potpourri and rose oil. Her mother has walked in three times already, at first castigating Vicky for the state of her room that seems spotless to me, then for Vicky's messy hair which is to be expected at eight o'clock in the morning, and then for her unfinished English assignment that Vicky left lying on the coffee table. Despite her mum's disapproval of Vicky, she's been nothing but welcoming and sweet to me as always. Maybe I should start appreciating my mother more because she's never talked to me the way Vicky's mum talks to her, especially now that I know my dad is a womaniser.

When her mum finally leaves the room to get ready for work, I rub my eyes and grab a tissue from a box that has been conveniently placed next to me.

As soon as I entered Vicky's room earlier, I told her about my dad. I shared my fears about Alex turning out to be like my dad. I even admitted Alex has been a little strange the last few weeks and cancelled a few of our plans.

Dressed in baby blue pyjamas, Vicky's sitting on the only chair in the room, worrying at her lip. She's been doing that for the last few minutes while listening to her mum moving around the house. She rakes through her dishevelled blonde hair for the third time. Her make-up-free face turns serious.

In the silence that settles between us, the front door opens and closes, followed by the sound of a car leaving the driveway. Vicky's shoulders drop, and she leans back in her seat.

'End it,' she says with such resolution I think I must have not heard her right.

'What do you mean?' I sit up on the bed.

She looks around the room like she doesn't want to face me. When she finally gazes at me, her eyes are watery, and her hands once again end up in her hair in a feeble attempt to smooth it. 'I didn't have the strength to tell you, but Alex has been chasing Sara. I don't think anything has actually happened, but everybody knows he's got it bad for her. He's just gotten bored. That's what guys do.'

I think of all the times he's talked to Sara in the last month. He even offered to help her with her science homework the other day. How stupid have I been?

'What? Why are you saying this now?' A small part of me doesn't want to believe it, but Vicky wouldn't lie. I've been such an idiot. How many people know?

'I didn't want to tell you because I hoped I got him wrong, but the other day when I went to Sam's party, he was all over her.' She stands up and sits by the bed, squeezing my hand supportively. 'Just end it before he does and be done with him. He doesn't deserve you. He's going to Meg's tomorrow night, so why don't you talk to him then?' I recall that on the day of Sam's party, he cancelled our plans to go to the cinema. We had tickets and all. Despair hooks into my insides.

Vicky's right. Even if he hasn't cheated yet, he might. I don't ever want to be like my mother. Everybody talking about me behind my back. 'I can't confront him. Not at the party and not at school.'

My whole chest is hurting like someone has ripped my ribcage open and scraped my heart out. How can one hurt so much from something that isn't physical?

'Text him.' She pushes my phone towards me, and I take it uncertainly.

My fingers quiver as I type, delete and retype the message for what feels like an hour. Eventually, I settle on, *I can't do this. This isn't working. Let's not see each other any more.*

A few seconds later, my phone starts ringing.

'He's calling.' Even to my own ears, I sound panicky. The hand holding the phone is shaking.

'You don't have to pick up.' I hate how calm Vicky sounds, but she's always been the calmer and more confident one of the two of us.

The phone goes silent, and then another call splits the quietness that has settled over the room.

When I don't pick up, he messages back, *What do you mean? Has something happened? Talk to me.* He carries on messaging. *I thought things were good. I thought we were good.*

When I don't respond, he starts calling again.

Vicky *grrrs*. 'The audacity. Come on. Give me your phone.' She grabs it before I'm ready to give it to her. I stare into nowhere, leaving her to take control because I'm a coward.

She fires away a few messages after which my phone stays deadly silent. I don't dare to read them, but Vicky deletes them alongside deleting Alex's number. I know it's for the best because I know I'd agonise over whether to message him.

The next day I torture myself over my decision. I keep pacing in my room, feeling indecisive. I call Catherine who doesn't know anything about Sara and Alex and even thinks it's very unlikely. She reassures me that he's smitten with me. I start wondering whether maybe I shouldn't have split up with him. Whether Vicky has gotten him wrong. Maybe I should have given him a chance to tell me what was going on instead of rushing into ending things. I feel incredibly fickle and shame flares in my stomach. How could I have been swayed by Vicky so easily? She's never liked him, so of course she's biased. I should have thought it through.

A split-second decision makes me get changed into the first thing I find in the wardrobe, a spaghetti-strapped red dress with black buttons down the front. Because it feels too revealing, I wear a white T-shirt underneath it. I don't text Vicky that I'm heading to the party because she's notoriously bad at responding when she's out. I check the time, and it's just past ten, which means that half the people will be drunk by now and the other half paired up. On my way, I message Catherine who texts back, *Go get him, tiger*, which makes me almost smile. Almost.

Meg lives only twenty minutes from me, so I decide to walk. When I'm near, dread knots my insides. What if he won't even listen? From a distance, I see that the house has all its lights on, and muffled music is coming in steady beats.

Inside, the spacious lounge is full of people. The two beige corduroy sofas are occupied by four couples snogging. A few guys I recognise from school are sitting by the coffee table playing the Circle of Death. Several half-empty bottles are scattered around the centre of the table.

Everywhere is loud and smells of cheap perfume, booze and cigarettes. I'm already regretting that I've come. I can't imagine finding Alex in this crowd.

I look around, eyes narrowing as I search, but I can't see either Sara or Alex. My nerves are jangling. I quickly text Catherine to let her know I arrived OK.

She texts back, *I hope it goes well. Let me know if you need to sleep at mine tonight. X*

I roam through the house, and after I've gone through the kitchen and checked the empty garden, I head upstairs. The first bedroom is occupied by two couples in various stages of undressing, so I quickly click the door closed before they notice me. At this point, my anxiety levels have doubled. I cannot stand the idea of Alex touching another person.

My heart pounds so fast in my ears it takes over the steady beat of the music downstairs. The second bedroom door opens, and I exhale with relief. Three girls, including Sara, are smoking weed on the large bed. When she spots me, she waves. The room stinks so badly I quickly shut the door with an embarrassed sorry. My heartbeat slows down to an almost normal speed. Everything is going to be OK, I tell myself.

When I approach the third bedroom, I can hear the muffled noises of two people arguing from the other side of the door. The voices belong to a boy and a girl and straight away I recognise Alex's deep voice but don't recognise the other. Everything inside me stills when they stop talking. Suddenly, I want to be anywhere but here. I half-turn, ready to go home, but then I inhale, and my hand ends up on the doorknob. I hover for a moment, unsure what I might find on the other side.

Eventually, I find the courage to turn the knob. At the sight inside, my stomach churns like I've ingested acid. I'm going to be sick. Alex is sitting in an old-fashioned armchair, but there's a person on top of him. His hand resting on the armrest has the girl's hand wrapped around the wrist like a tourniquet. Her other hand is down his trousers. He's gripping her shoulder with such urgency that I think I'll vomit right there. The girl's short blue dress has hitched up to reveal her perfect bum. Somewhere in my brain, a thought occurs. Vicky got that exact dress for her birthday last week. This girl is wearing her dress. When the two facts connect in my brain, I close the door and run.

I grab the first bottle I see downstairs. I think it's vodka. I glug half of the remaining contents down and take the rest to the closest toilet where I force it down my throat. I gag as I swallow, but I don't stop because all I want to do now is to forget, to bleach my eyes and glue my heart back together. My head is whirring, and my vision is starting to spin. What now? Should I call Catherine? She would pick me up.

I stare at myself in the mirror and my stupid dress. I look like a child. I take off the T-shirt underneath it and undo the top two buttons. My black bra peeks just between the folds of the now-open fabric, but I don't care. The stupidest decision is brewing in my head, but I'm hurt and drunk.

I re-enter the party and join the table in the lounge with an *uff*. I have to pull on my dress because it climbs up my legs. 'Can I play?' My voice wobbles with alcohol and devastation.

'Hell yeah. Come sit with me,' one of the boys with brown hair says eagerly after his gaze lowers to my cleavage. I learn his name is Tom, and we have physics together, not that I care.

After a few rounds, I feel so drunk I can barely keep my eyes open. But even in my state, I spot Alex weaving through the crowd, a phone to his ear. Immediately, my phone starts ringing in my bag with the familiar tones of Florence and the Machine's *Drumming Song*. He follows the direction of the tune. Immediately, he scans my dress, his eyes hitching up the two open buttons. His face turns into a confused scowl.

Without hesitation, I grab Tom by the shirt and kiss him on the lips with all the intensity of my anger and betrayal. He doesn't expect it but doesn't resist either. There are hoots of approval from around the table, and when I pull away, half the room is cheering. Turning as white as a sheet, Alex hangs up and puts his phone in his pocket. His expression turns from addled hurt to impenetrable cold. Tom's hand rests on my bare knee, and I let him leave it there, even though everything inside me is screaming to jerk away. As soon as Alex is gone, I push Tom away and lock myself in the bathroom. Crying, I dial Catherine's number.

'Can I stay at yours tonight?'
'What's happened?'
'I've done something awful.'

*

I still remember how the next day Vicky told me that she went to speak to Alex about me and argued with him. But instead of listening to her reason, he told her he liked her all along. Then he suddenly started kissing her, and she was so shocked, she only pulled away too late. When she told him no, he just shrugged and spent the rest of the evening snogging Sara. I didn't believe her until the next day when I saw him with Sara, whispering and laughing together by the lockers. He didn't give me a second look. That was that; we were done. A few months later, we graduated, and I was convinced I'd never see him again.

I'm laden with decade-old guilt. It presses against my chest and threatens to suffocate me. Thoughts chase each other in my head until it's a jumble of old and new memories of Alex. For the first time, I feel like significant pieces of the story are missing.

I look at my phone again and decide to deal with the lesser evil of the two unread messages. John.

hey i've heard you had to leave in a hurry today. i hope your ok. If you want to talk i'm here x

I'm done with John and the rest of the male population. His message only confirms what I already know about him and myself. I will not settle for a two-faced man with ambiguous motives and who doesn't know the difference between *you're* and *your*.

I'm fine. Thanks for the offer, but you are the last person on earth I'd want to talk to right now, to be honest. Please leave me alone.

After the message is delivered, I block his number.

Next, I decide to deal with Vicky. I'm surprised she picks up on the first ring.

'Hi, Vicky.'

'Oh my god. Holly. I heard about your dad. Is he OK?' She sounds genuinely worried, and I tense up for some reason.

'He's going to be fine. How have you heard?' I feel so exhausted, I lie back on the bed, banging my head against the headboard. Wincing, I massage the back of my scalp.

'Your mum texted mine. I'm glad to hear your dad is OK. You sound awful, like you need some cheering up. Why don't we go out and try to do that? I know just the right place.'

I tell her it's the last thing on my mind. It shows how much she knows or understands me.

'OK. Just let me know if you need to get out of the flat. I'm at your beck and call.' She laughs quietly. She's about to hang up.

'Vicky?' My voice is croaky, and I shift the phone from my left hand to my right. I stare blankly at the ceiling for long moments, unsure what I want to say.

'Yeah?' She hesitates at my strange tone.

'Do you remember when you told me Alex was after Sara?' I'm not sure what I'm trying to ask or what I want to hear back. 'How did you know? I mean, who told you? Did Sara speak to you about Alex showing interest?'

For a long time, she's silent. 'Everyone knew. It was common knowledge. Why are you rehashing old history? What has Alex done?' she says with unexpected bravado.

I force a neutral tone into my voice. 'No. It's nothing. It's just something that has popped into my head. It's stupid.'

'Well, that school of yours doesn't sound like the best place for you if it makes you relive ancient memories and reopen old wounds.'

We chat some more, but my mind keeps flitting back to the past. Not long after that, we hang up, and for the first time, I have a feeling that Vicky is not being entirely honest.

The next day, I get a surprising call from Mother that Dad is awake and is coming home, so I shouldn't *bother to go to the hospital*, quoting my mother. She tells me that he's doing well, and it would be better if I came over to their house because it would be more comfortable for my dad.

On Saturday, I pick up my car from work and head to my parents' house. There's no room in my body for any more dread. I'm so tense my shoulders are permanently locked in a hunched position over the steering wheel. I park on the road because both my parents' cars are parked in front of the house.

My mother opens the door after the first knock clad in a salmon-pink cocktail dress that looks like it was taken from a '50s edition of *Woman & Home* magazine.

'Close the door behind you, darling, will you?' she says by way of hello. Business as usual. I do as I'm told and shuffle along the way in my corduroy dungaree dress and heavy boots. I'm reviving the '90s goth style today. I'm counting down the seconds until my mother comments on my look.

However, she surprises me by abruptly pivoting on her heel and squeezing the life out of me. 'I'm glad you've come,' she whispers softly before she pulls away.

Then, as to be expected, she scans my outfit, pausing at my slightly outgrown bob. I desperately need to book a hairdresser, but it's currently last on my list of problems.

'I wish you hadn't cut your hair.' She strokes one of my locks with her manicured hand. 'You look like a fifteen-year-old boy wearing a wig.' I frown. All is right in the world. 'I meant to say that you were very pretty with your long hair,' she adds hurriedly. I guess she's trying the only way she knows how.

She confirms my suspicions. 'I know we agreed I would stop interfering with your life and – what did you call it – *judging your life choices*, but couldn't you at least take those monstrosities off your feet? We aren't some vagabonds or anarchists.'

'They're vintage Martens. They cost almost two hundred pounds,' I say, offended.

'I don't care who Vintage Martens is. They are ugly, and you should leave them by the doormat like normal people.' She crosses her arms, numerous silver bracelets gleaming around her wrist with the movement.

I look pointedly at her feet which are strapped in silver sandals like she's going on *Strictly Come Dancing* after lunch.

'These are my indoor sandals. I thought I'd dress for the occasion,' she responds impatiently. Only my mother.

We walk to the kitchen, and through the conservatory window panel, I spy my dad's greying hair peeking over the top of his favourite lounger chair. The view is so familiar, my hands start sweating, and I rub them against my dress.

A sombre expression passes across my mother's usually insouciant features. 'Go speak to your father.' She squeezes my elbow in reassurance, making my throat tight with emotion. 'I'll wait until you come back inside. Do what feels right.' I nod, ready to say more on the topic, but she's back to her old self in no time. 'Make sure you use the outside shoes and take them off on the mat. I've just hoovered.'

The air outside is chilly but fresh and refocuses my mind a little. At my approaching steps, my father pokes his head out. His expression shatters when he sees it's me. Wordlessly, he motions for me to sit next to him on the other lounger. Mother must have rummaged in the loft to find it because I haven't seen it in years. It reminds me of the times when we used to sit here together, my dad with his newspapers and me with a paperback. I should hug him, but now he's in front of me I can't decide whether I'm more relieved or angry. A headache starts pressing insistently against my temples.

We sit in silence, staring at the overgrown laurel hedge that pens the back of the garden. Wrapped in, what-was-no-doubt-my-mother's-idea, a blanket like a mummy, he looks weary. His cheeks are a little sunken, but he's wearing his customary unfashionable glasses. He's more himself again. Without volition, tears start running down my cheeks, and I swipe at them angrily.

'I should arrange for the hedge to be cut. It's getting out of hand. It will swallow us whole one day,' he finally says. 'I'm so sorry, Holly,' he laments with misery when he catches my tears. 'I've failed you.' He reaches into the space between the chairs, and I extend my hand with uncertainty and let him take it. Immediately, he leans over and kisses it. Then he pats it with his other hand and doesn't let go, making me feel like he's holding a special treasure that might escape if he only left a tiny gap between his hands. 'I've made a mess of everything, haven't I?'

I'm finding it hard to speak at first. 'I've been so angry at you.' He's about to carry on, but I jump in before he says his piece because I need him to understand. 'But when you had a heart attack, all I could think about was how I've never given you a chance to make it up to me.' Alex's words echo in my head. I realise too late that I've never given Alex a chance to explain or to make things right either. Neither have I ever explained myself.

'You were right to be angry. I did something unspeakable, and I hurt your mother.' He gazes sorrowfully towards the kitchen. 'I wasn't happy, and instead of speaking to your mother about it, I broke her trust. She forgave me, and I admire her for it immensely. I never realised how my decisions and my mistakes would affect you. I should have been your role model. Instead, my bad choices influenced some big decisions in your life. That should have never happened. I will never forgive myself for that.' He starts crying quietly, his big shoulders shaking.

'Dad,' I croak. I've never seen my dad cry, and it rattles me. He's always so stoic.

He takes a fabric handkerchief from his waistcoat pocket and blows his nose loudly with his free hand. 'I will try to prove to you and your mother for the rest of my life that my mistake isn't who I am.' I nod. 'As for Aaron,' he starts, sounding a little steadier.

I squeeze his hand reassuringly. 'I don't want to talk about Aaron. He's history.' This time it's his turn to nod.

We sit there in silence until the tip of my nose feels numb with cold. I've never realised how uncomfortable the loungers were. I guess we often see memories before a rift through rose-tinted glasses.

'Shall we go inside and get some tea and biscuits?' I offer, rising to my feet.

'I thought you'd never ask.' Together we head inside.

In the time Dad and I were talking, my mother has created a feast. On various plates placed on any available surfaces are sandwiches, crackers, hummus, carrot and cucumber sticks. A pot of tea, a milk jug and three cups with saucers rest in the middle of the table, ready for us. I notice there are no sausage rolls or biscuits and the sandwiches are made of brown bread with cream cheese filling instead of butter. I think I also spot some micro herbs in them. I gulp heavily, my appetite gone.

'Come on, you two. Sit down and eat,' she commands like the general she is. She plates two sandwiches for my dad and some hummus with a few carrot sticks. He eyes it suspiciously but starts eating straight away.

I sit on the opposite sofa from my dad while my mother is fussing over both of us, her favourite activity, only narrowly followed by gossiping. At first, I pick at the sandwich my mother plated for me, but when I take a proper bite, I *hmm*. It's my favourite sandwich, BLT. She winks at me. At least one person is still allowed to eat bacon in this house.

After every last morsel of food is ingested and we're sitting and watching *Murder, She Wrote*, my mother casually asks, 'When are you heading back?'

'I'd like to stay overnight. If you don't mind.' I don't know why I feel so nervous.

'That would be lovely, darling.' My mother beams at me.

25

On Sunday, I agree to meet with Lydia and Catherine at Lydia's. I remember that Lydia had some previous plans, but when I ask her about them on WhatsApp, she becomes evasive. I guess everyone has the right to have some secrets.

Lydia's flat is only a five-minute walk from the town centre, so I decide to park in the multistorey car park just off the high street and head to hers, my bag loaded with chocolate Viennese biscuits and bacon rasher crisps.

I arrive before Catherine, and the first thing Lydia does when she opens the door is deliver on her promise of squeezing me alive. I grip her back with so much force my arms go numb after a while, but I'm not ready to let go.

When we separate, I'm crying. Again.

'Hols,' she says softly, her sharp eyebrows knitting in the middle.

I wave my hand in dismissal. 'Don't mind the waterworks. I can't seem to turn it off now I've started. My tear ducts are faulty. I want a refund.'

'You're allowed to have a bit of a cryfest after all the shit you've been through.' She pulls me into her uber-modern and minimalistic flat. Everywhere I look, there's slate-grey furniture, geometrical tiles and marble. It's like Lydia herself, sharp and edgy.

She makes me a cup of coffee, and sitting down on her

Chesterfield-styled grey leather sofa, I pull the biscuits out of the bag.

'I strongly approve,' Lydia mumbles, stuffing her face with a Viennese finger dipped in milk chocolate.

A moment later, Catherine arrives, wavy hair pulled back with a red clip. She looks rested and has even put on some make-up. 'I'm sorry I'm late. The traffic was awful. Gabby is with Richard, but I promised to be on the phone if anything happened. He spent the last two days with Gabby to give me some me time,' she says mildly, but I can see the love hearts popping in her eyes; Richard is a good one. She drops her multiple bags by the coffee table. Immediately, she plants herself on the sofa next to me and smothers me in a hug. This hug is soft and fluffy. I bury my face into her teddy bear fleece, trying not to spill any tears on it.

When we're done, she swiftly unpacks her bags that contain various snacky bits. Prawn cocktail crisps, sesame bread sticks, lemon-stuffed olives and extra-large marshmallows. Basically, all my favourite foods. Then she takes off her fleece with the words, 'I'm ready.'

I look from Lydia's chic red jersey to Catherine's navy-dotted blouse. Then my gaze drops to my stained black leggings and an old sweatshirt with a hole in one of the sleeves. I'm not impressed with myself. 'I don't think I got the memo about the dress code,' I complain, wiping my nose on the sleeve to add insult to the injury that is my sweatshirt.

'*Uff.* The owl must have gone to the neighbours' again,' Lydia laments dramatically which makes me cackle.

I pat the sofa next to me and she installs herself on my left side, putting her feet up on the glass coffee table now offering various spreads. Catherine flops to my right, and it would be almost perfect if I weren't this miserable.

'If you don't want to talk, that's fine.' Catherine threads her arm through mine.

'We could watch a movie instead,' Lydia offers and turns the sixty-five-inch TV on.

I called them yesterday from my parents' house, so they're kept abreast on the developments with my dad, but I didn't mention Alex once. They both know something happened on Friday, so I love them even more for not prying and giving me time to sort my thoughts.

We eat unhealthy food and watch daytime TV for the whole morning. After a lunch of pizza and marshmallows, we end up watching *Bridget Jones*. I get a bit teary and bury my face in the sweatshirt, but I must not hide it well because Lydia squeezes my arm resting on her lap, and Catherine snuggles closer.

When Mark Darcy finally says to Bridget he likes her just the way she is, I start full-on sobbing.

'I think I'm turning unhealthily egocentric. This movie feels like the story of my life.' I laugh through my tears.

Lydia turns the volume down and sits up, pushing her legs underneath her. 'Let's see. A cheating boyfriend, a cold-on-the-outside but enigmatic sexy love interest. A ridiculous-yet-loving mother. I would sue Helen Fielding if I were you.'

'She didn't get you right though. You're nothing like Bridget.' Catherine crunches a bacon rasher crisp, contemplating.

'I don't know. Holly's fairly accident-prone, and bad luck seems to stick to her like glue,' Lydia interjects.

'Which friend would I be?' Catherine plucks another crisp from the bowl in front of her.

'I'm totally Shazzer,' Lydia announces proudly.

'Totally,' both Catherine and I say at the same time. I quickly say, 'Jinx,' before she has a chance to say it first. Catherine frowns because she's a sore loser. We've reverted to teenagers.

'You'd be Jude,' Lydia ponders out loud, and Catherine throws the nearest cushion at Lydia's head. Lydia snorts.

'Except Mark Darcy turns out to be the right guy in the end.' I sour the mood.

Lydia picks up the cushion and hugs it to herself. It feels like someone has pressed pause in the room.

I inhale and tell them everything that happened. After an embarrassed pause, I also tell them how Alex froze when things got heated. I finish with Vicky calling and Alex getting cold feet.

Lydia is frowning while Catherine is outright confused.

I shake it off. 'I'm OK. I'm done with him. For real this time. He enjoys keeping me hanging, and I'm done being his entertainment, his backup plan or whatever I've been to him. No more Alex and Holly. Holly and Alex.'

Catherine looks at me like I'm a simpleton.

'Don't give me that look,' I warn her and grab a cushion of my own for emotional support. My fingers frantically start plucking at the silk tassels sewn to the corners like I'm a harpist performing at a speed metal concert.

'It just doesn't add up,' Catherine mumbles.

'I agree for once.' Lydia pushes off the sofa and brings the last bag of crisps from the counter to the table. When she sits, she frowns. 'I definitely don't think he's not *not* interested in you if you know what I mean. A person who's gotten over you doesn't look at you the way he did at the Thai restaurant. That boy was trying to pretend to keep it cool while he had the hots for you.'

I'm waiting for Catherine to argue and talk about dignity and breaking one's trust, but instead, she shrugs. 'I don't think that everything is as black and white as we think.' Her tone is almost apologetic. Her eyes flash towards Lydia, and then she starts biting her nails. What's going on here?

'What are you trying to say? That Vicky lied? Or that nothing happened, and I just misunderstood?' My voice rises, and I have to temper it to keep it from rising again. When loose threads start to come out of the tassel between my fingers, I still them. 'I found her on top of him. He didn't look like he minded it.'

'And the first person he calls after his supposed tryst is you. That's weird.' Lydia tries to apply logic to something that doesn't have any. 'Do people still use the word *tryst*?' She ponders out loud.

'Guilty conscience? Or it gives him a kick to play around with people's feelings, making me sound like the villain here,' I offer and start systematically taking apart another tassel. I will have to buy Lydia a new cushion after this conversation is done if we carry on in the same vein.

'You already split up with him. There was no need for a guilty conscience, and I don't agree he was a player. There's no evidence apart from what Vicky is saying,' Catherine reminds me gently. 'Also…' She averts her eyes like she wants to avoid eye contact. 'He sounded sort of hurt when he hurled all those accusations your way. Take it from his perspective, he's been labouring under the delusion that you broke up with him ten years ago because you got bored, and then you made up with someone less than twenty-four hours after.' Her face is flushed, and she's still refusing to look at me.

'I don't know why he did what he did, and it doesn't matter because it was ten years ago. Ever since he showed up back in my life, he's made things nothing but complicated. He's been kind and understanding, and yes, even friendly at times, but that doesn't even out the times he's been outright hostile, scornful, unfair and hurtful. I can't keep up with his hot and cold ways. It hurts too much,' I growl desperately. 'Why are you both standing up for him?' I'm not angry, I just feel defeated. They look at each other with a strange expression.

'What's going on?' Standing up, I leave the almost tassel-less cushion on the sofa.

'You know I love you, and I would never hurt you,' Lydia starts carefully. Whatever this is, it's nothing good.

The lounge is so tense I could cut the air with a knife. I jerk when Catherine's phone starts buzzing. She plucks it from among the cushions and apologetically mumbles, 'It's Richard,' before she picks up and walks in the direction of Lydia's bedroom.

The lounge is silent.

'There's something I need to speak to you about. I've wanted to bring it up before, but I've never found the right time.' Lydia rubs her hands together, and her face turns pink. She's obviously distressed over something to do with me.

'You can tell me anything.' I try to sound reassuring, but uncertainty creeps into my voice, nevertheless.

The doorbell buzzes and cleaves the tense atmosphere.

'Have we ordered any more pizza?' Lydia wonders out loud but strides towards the door. She sounds almost relieved to abandon our unfinished conversation.

When she opens the front door, she sounds surprised and apologetic. I conclude she knows whoever is on the other side of the door. It doesn't take me long to recognise the other person. I march stiffly to the door, thinking this day cannot get any more confusing.

'I'm sorry I haven't checked my messages. Is now not a good time? Should I leave?' Jane is looking genuinely perplexed. Her hair gleams under the artificial light of the hallway, a few purplish strands I've never noticed standing out in her otherwise dark hair. She is as smart as ever despite wearing a pair of black jeans and a burgundy pullover. When she spots me over Lydia's shoulder, she flinches imperceptibly. It takes her only a second to assess my outfit and messy hair to read the situation.

I connect the dots surprisingly quickly too. Now it makes perfect sense why Lydia was so nervous; she was worried about my reaction. Guilt squeezes my chest, and for a moment, I struggle to breathe.

'Do you want to come in?' Lydia invites Jane in.

Silent communication passes between them, but I avert my eyes before I can decipher it, feeling embarrassed. When I look back, Jane is still hesitant, which is unusual for her. With the same level of certainty that I know Taylor Swift is the best country and folk singer of this century, I know that Alex has spoken to her.

'Please.' Lydia's voice comes out sort of desperate. My eyes flash to her in surprise. Probably as shocked as me, Jane nods and comes in. She places her shoes in the cleverly hidden shoe cupboard which straight away confirms she's been here before.

Catherine walks out of Lydia's bedroom with the phone in her hand. She blinks a few times at the sight of Jane. 'Hi,' she says slowly, unsure of the atmosphere. She turns to me. 'Holly, I'm sorry. I'll have to shoot off. Gabby fell and scratched her knee. She's inconsolable.'

'That's alright,' I say numbly. I think I'm shell-shocked.

Catherine quickly hugs me and Lydia, eyeing Jane as she goes. Then the three of us are alone.

Lydia excuses herself to make us fresh coffee, so I end up sitting with Jane on the sofa.

'How's your dad?' Jane starts, offering an olive branch of sorts even though she's not the one who's at odds with me. If this didn't confirm that Jane was a decent person, her deciding to date Lydia would.

'He's going to be fine. He's back home.' I bet she knows this already.

'I'm glad to hear that.' She sounds genuine despite the stilted air between us.

'So how long have you been seeing each other?' I ask carefully. Even though she's not my boss right now, she's a woman my best friend has been dating. I feel awful about how consumed I've been with my problems to not know this fact.

'Since we met at the restaurant. After you left, we got talking,' Jane offers, and a sweet smile pulls on her lips.

'I'm glad she's seeing somebody nice for once,' I admit, because no matter how I feel about Alex, Jane is great.

'Holly.' She opens her mouth and then snaps it shut like something is preventing her from speaking freely.

Lydia plonks three cups of coffee on the glass surface. 'So, have you told her?' she asks without preamble.

'Lydia,' Jane interjects.

I'm an elastic band stretched so far, I'm about to snap. My gaze keeps switching between her and Jane, waiting to see who's going to tell me what's going on here.

'It's not my place,' Jane protests and pretends to sip her coffee, even though I know for a fact it's scalding hot because I've just burnt my tongue on it.

'Not getting involved at this point is not helping. You told me yesterday on the phone that Alex is a mess.' At the mention of Alex, I blink.

'If you don't say anything, I will,' Lydia threatens and Jane exhales.

She abandons her coffee and faces me fully. 'I have a hunch you're a nice person, Holly.'

'Of course she is.' Lydia jumps in, and Jane shushes her. 'I'm usually right about these things. It's not my business to butt into what happened, or what you think happened, between you two ten years ago. Just know that Alex is a good guy. One of the best, and if I was interested in men, which I'm not' – at this point she flashes an enamoured gaze towards Lydia – 'I'd be all over him. He's just not the best at communicating his intentions, but his actions speak for themselves.'

'What did you mean by what I think happened ten years ago? What has that got to do with this? He made it clear that he didn't want me, and that we were a mistake.' If I wasn't so bewildered, I'd be mortified right now at spilling the most embarrassing parts of my private life to my boss.

'Is that what he said?' Jane scoffs. 'That's just typical Alex. He always runs away from his feelings. He's besotted with you.' She mutters, *he's going to kill me for this later.*

'What happened ten years ago, Jane?' I insist. A strange feeling starts bubbling in my chest.

'He wasn't a willing participant.' Jane's tone is regretful.

'What?' My breath hitches.

'That friend of yours, Vicky, she chased him, messaged him and called him. She wouldn't stop. I understand that on that night she threw herself at him and didn't care much about Alex saying no,' Jane explains, and Lydia makes a disgruntled sound.

It feels like someone has thrust my head in a beam clamp and is slowly tightening the screw. 'What?' I repeat, my voice a faint echo.

'I've already said too much. I should go, but you should speak to Alex.' She looks apologetically at the stupefied Lydia. Judging by my best friend's expression, she didn't know the full extent of things.

They both head to the door, leaving me to my rampaging thoughts. Alex did nothing wrong. At the idea of Vicky launching herself at him, I feel queasy. He wanted to tell me, and I let him down. He called me straight after, and the first thing I did was kiss some guy to make him jealous. I've never deserved Alex.

'Fuck. I'll fucking punch that sleaze in the windpipe if I ever see her again,' Lydia shouts when she comes back and sits heavily next to me on the sofa.

I'm unable to stay sitting so I stand up and start pacing. Long moments pass, but my head is no clearer.

'You're worrying me. Say something,' Lydia urges from behind me.

I stop pacing, desperation making my words uneven. 'What do I do now? I've screwed up everything. I've hurt him. I haven't trusted him when he needed me to. When he wanted to tell me and called me, I kissed some random guy. No surprise he feels now like he can't trust me. I'm not a very trustworthy person in his eyes. I'm such an awful person.'

'Hey.' Lydia grips my shoulders, and the gesture grounds me. 'Stop there. You've made some bad decisions based on misinformation. You're not a bad person and you deserve to be happy. Fuck me, this is your epic love.'

I start crying. 'I said some horrible things to him on Friday.'

'Yes, you did, but so did he. I bet he's feeling terrible. You're like some cheesy, star-crossed lovers, kept apart by misunderstanding and poor communication. I can justify the bad communication ten years ago when you were teenagers, but now you have no excuse. Go and talk to him. Spell it out to him how you feel because he obviously needs it. Men always do.'

'Can you get me Alex's address?' I only hesitate for a moment, hands shaking with adrenalin.

'Already on it.' Lydia scrolls down her phone.

I inspect my outfit with disgust. 'I look like a slob. I can't wear this.'

'Is this the moment in the movie when the best friend does a total makeover of the main character? Should I put the *Pretty Woman* soundtrack on?' She winks at me. I don't understand how she can find any humour in this situation, but her answer makes me feel a little lighter.

'No, I'd just like to borrow something that doesn't have yogurt or pizza topping on it,' I respond sardonically.

'On it.' Lydia heads towards the bedroom and comes back with a maroon dress, too slinky and totally not me.

'Lydia,' I warn her.

She guffaws. 'Sorry, that was a joke. It's like *She's All That* all over again. I've got some jeans and a jumper in the cupboard.' She heads back to the bedroom.

'I'm glad my life is a source of amusement to you,' I shout after her.

After I get changed into a pair of blue jeans and a navy jumper that is way too posh for me, I'm ready to go. Or at least as ready as I'll ever be.

'So, you and Jane?' I start with caution, standing awkwardly by the door. I'm a terrible friend.

Lydia's cheeks flush, which is very unusual. 'I really like her.'

I give her a bone-crushing hug. 'I'm sorry I made you feel like you couldn't tell me.'

'You didn't. I wasn't ready to admit it to myself that I liked her. It's got nothing to do with you.' When she sees my worried expression, she adds, 'I promise. Now, go and get Alex.'

I kiss Lydia goodbye.

The traffic to Alex's is bad. I get stuck for fifteen minutes solid, my fingers tapping the wheel impatiently.

My phone starts buzzing, and because it's in the holder right in front of me, Vicky's name jumps at me, and I almost swerve. I pull in as soon as I get a chance. She messages, *Please meet me in St Paul's Park. It's urgent.*

Everything inside me tenses as I do a U-turn and head towards a place that holds so many teenage memories.

26

The car park is abandoned save for my car and what I recognise as Vicky's silver BMW. The grey clouds are gathering above my head when I park the car as far away as possible from Vicky's and head towards the main path slithering among the trees. I spot Vicky from a distance, not far from a gazebo we used to drink in as teenagers. Dressed in a tailored black dress, swanky cream coat and red heels, she stands out among the ancient oaks like a sore thumb.

When I'm close enough to hear her heels grinding against the gravel and decomposing leaves, I inhale.

'Is it true?' I shout because I'm ready to be loud.

Her back stiffens at the volume of my voice. It takes her a few beats to spin to face me. When she does, she's a rabbit caught in the headlights.

It starts to rain, and water and wind start lashing against my body. I damn the decision to leave my coat in the car. I've never felt like the weather has mirrored my mood like now. I'm soaked within seconds.

'Is it true?' I repeat over the booming whoosh of the water, taking resolute steps towards her.

She doesn't speak and just stands there helplessly. She looks like a stranger. White-hot rage blinds me, and before I compose myself, my fist connects with her jaw. Sharp pain lances through my knuckles, and I shake my hand to chase it away.

Vicky stumbles back with the force of the blow and grabs her jaw which immediately starts swelling. I have never punched another person, and I don't think I've done it right because my knuckles hurt like hell.

My lip wobbles, but I brace myself. 'How could you? You were my friend.'

'I'm not proud of myself. For what it's worth, I'd take it back if I could.' There's no redemption for her. Not now, not ever.

'Do you know what you've done? You've ruined us. You've ruined our lives.' I'm not sure who this *us* is that I'm referring to, but I realise it's all of us. Alex, me, and even Vicky. None of us has been spared the consequences of her actions.

'I was in love with him, you know. Long before you even noticed him,' she confesses miserably, her words a bare whisper over the storm. 'He never noticed me even though I made it clear I liked him. And then he only had eyes for you. Do you know how that feels?' She wraps the coat around her body protectively, but the wind laces through the layers of her clothing like a knife through half-melted butter. She looks suddenly smaller, less glamorous.

'What? One person out of the whole universe rejecting you? Boohoo. That must have been tough.' My words are harsh, but I'm done being cowered by her personality. I like myself the way I am and that's enough.

'You never knew what it was like for me at home. My dad was emotionally abusive, and Mum always expected me to be perfect because, in my dad's eyes, she could never be. One misstep and it was marked against me forever. I always paid for it.' A sick feeling builds up in my body at her confession. 'They've always doted on you. You were perfect. I was too loud and not studious enough. But Holly was perfection. Holly did this and that. That's all I had to listen to when I was a teenager. And then the only boy I ever liked wanted you.' She sounds so miserable and so unlike herself I hug my arms around my freezing body for comfort.

She always made me feel she had a perfect life. She's always been pretty and bright and funny. Everyone always loved her. Or did they?

'Even now my parents are like, "Look at Holly. She's a fucking teacher." I'm so sick of being second. Why do you think I had to get out as soon as I could?' Her voice breaks, water sluicing down her coat and to her bare legs that are covered in mud splatters. She resembles a drowned rat, her blonde hair plastered to her long, graceful neck. 'Back then, I didn't think. I wanted him, and I would have done anything to get him. I chased him even when you got together. I messaged him some awful things to make him feel the way he made me feel, but I still made the messages sound like he was the one following me. I knew he was trapped; he couldn't tell you or show you. I made sure of that. I was beyond reason because I was hurting.' Her voice is all over the place like a badly tuned instrument.

'Then you launched yourself at him at Meg's party? What did he do? The truth this time.'

'I kissed him, and he said no. But I convinced myself that he was playing hard to get so I pushed him into an armchair and threw myself at him. He froze and stupidly I took it as a yes. When he eventually pushed me away, he sent me to hell. I threatened that I would tell you that he forced me if he told you about it.' She looks everywhere but at me. When she does, mascara is running down her face in rivulets, and I'm not sure whether it's her tears or rain. 'I was embarrassed and desperate, and I didn't want to lose you. I knew I made a mistake, and I didn't want you to find out. You were all I had left.'

'I'm truly sorry that you suffered as a child, but it doesn't justify the decisions you've made. You're a shark, Vicky. You carve your way through people, leaving only debris behind. Nobody can make you feel better but yourself. We're done.'

'I went to apologise to him,' she whispers weakly. 'I found him on Facebook weeks ago when you told me he worked at your school. I finally contacted him today to apologise. I told him what I'd done. I told him you were innocent in all of that.'

'You can't fix something that broke ten years ago.'

She nods like she expected me to say exactly that.

'You should have told me that things were tough at home. I would have listened; I would have been there.' My tone is desperate because my heart is breaking all over again, but this time over a friend I've just lost. I wonder at my heart's capacity to break over and over again, and yet, be able to pump blood around my body and keep me alive.

'You looked up to me so much. I didn't want you to pity me.'

'How has that worked out for you?' I don't expect an answer. 'And please don't question my intelligence by pretending you did things out of not wanting my pity. You liked that I worshipped you, but I'm done feeling belittled by you. Goodbye, Vicky.' I turn my back to her and head back to the car park. When I get in the car, she's still standing there in the rain. I've never seen a lonelier sight. I pull myself together and put the car in gear.

When I finally get to Alex's flat, it's twenty past three. I'm soaked to the bone, and my hand is on fire, my knuckles starting to bruise. I park a street away and walk towards his flat. The area seems nice. Tall pine trees shield the view of the busy road, and everywhere I look, there are red-brick houses converted to flats. Alex's flat is in one of the older buildings with big bay windows and perfectly manicured hedges around the communal garden. He deserves to live somewhere as peaceful as here.

A couple pushes through the main entrance, and I squeeze in after them, shaking water onto the thick carpet like a dog. Lydia's jumper is soaked through, and the jeans haven't fared much better. There goes looking respectable.

Fuelled on adrenalin, I run up the stairs in one go. I come to a halt in front of a door with an eighteen on it. I can't catch my breath, but it has nothing to do with me running and everything to do with the fact that I have no idea what I'm going to say to him. At this point, I'd be happy with some ice for my hand and a cup of coffee.

I brace myself and press the bell anyway.

27

There's shuffling on the other side of the door, and when it opens, Alex is standing in the doorway, completely nonplussed. His hair is a tangle of amber waves around his freckled face, his green eyes containing multitudes of emotions. He's wearing an old T-shirt with *Ramones* on it, his long, freckled arms braced against the door in tension. He's more like the old Alex than ever.

He scans my drowned state and homes in on my injured hand that I'm trying to hide behind me.

For a moment that feels like an eternity, I'm convinced he'll close the door on me. When he steps to the side to let me through, my knees almost buckle with relief. 'Let's ice it before it swells up.' His voice is business-like, but his stiff body and the dark circles under his eyes tell me he's anything but calm.

Alex's flat is everything that mine is not. It's spacious, light and immaculately clean. Everywhere I look there are thick carpets, comfy cushions and there's even a knitted throw over the cream sofa. It's like I've walked into a Scandinavian living catalogue. I'm worried that my socks will leave wet footprints on the lush beige carpet, so I hover by the closed door, staring longingly at the sofa.

He looks down at my feet over his shoulder, understanding my predicament. 'Don't worry about it. Sit down. I'll bring some ice.'

I pad towards the sofa and when I sink into it, my eyes close without volition. When Alex is gone, I cradle my hand in my arm like a baby. The knuckles have turned pink and red, and the area around them is puffy.

He comes back with a bag of peas hastily wrapped in a tea cloth in one hand and a towel and a pile of clothes in the other.

He immediately kneels by me and starts helping me out of the soaked jumper, disposing of it on the coffee table. He lifts my foot and then peels the sock off. Then he proceeds to the other. He's very systematic like this is something he's done hundreds of times before. Then he pushes to his knees and rubs the towel in my wet hair, obscuring my vision for a few moments. I try to empty my jumbled mind and just savour the feeling of his hands in my hair, but I cannot deny the fact that after everything that has happened, he's still here, taking care of me. Stripped of all my defences, I choke on all the emotions pushing up my throat at the same time.

When he's towelled my hair, he takes the wet pile to the kitchen.

'I've found you some fresh clothes if you wanted to change. I'll dry the rest of your clothes when you take them off,' he offers, sounding oddly hoarse.

Wordlessly, he shows me to the bathroom. I quickly remove all my clothes except for my knickers because the idea of Alex drying my underwear is unsettling and pass it to him through the gap in the door. A moment later, the tumble dryer starts whirring in the distance.

I lock the door behind me and have a good silent cry. Once semi-composed, I pull on his jogger shorts and an old blue T-shirt with the London skyline and the words *London Marathon* on it. It smells of Alex, and I stand there with the T-shirt glued to my nose for long minutes, just inhaling and memorising his smell.

I stare in the mirror. It's an old antique piece with carved fish and sea creatures around the wooden frame. I love it. The image in the mirror isn't that great. My short hair lies floppily around my face. I look tired, my lips are almost blue, and the tip of my nose is pink from the cold. Plus, Alex's clothes are ridiculous on me. They're too big around my shoulders and waist, but I've never worn anything this comfortable.

Eventually, I come out and find a steaming cup of coffee waiting for me on the table, and a stiff-looking Alex sitting on the only armchair in the room. I sit on the sofa opposite him and cradle the coffee in my hands.

He reaches over the space between us, holding the bag of peas out to me until I take it.

For long moments, we're just sipping our coffees. I'm so tongue-tied I don't think I could speak even if I wanted to.

'What are you doing here, Holly?' he asks carefully.

I abandon my cup and the bag of frozen vegetables, locking my eyes with his. All I want to do is to memorise every centimetre of him. All I see is this kind, beautiful and selfless man. I see his strengths and his flaws laid out in front of me because neither of us is perfect, but I don't want perfect.

'The day before I walked in on you and Vicky, I saw my dad cheat on my mum. After I broke up with you, I went to Meg's party to make things right. There's no excuse for what I did after I saw you and Vicky. For what it's worth, I wanted you to understand why I did what I did. I guess I'm here to say sorry.' I'm a coward. I promised myself I'd stop coming up with partial truths where Alex is involved.

Picking up the peas off the table, he stands up and sits next to me on the sofa. I forget to breathe as he takes my hand gently between his.

'It looks worse than it is,' I say, but when he presses the bag to my knuckles, I hiss. 'Actually, it might be as bad as it looks. I might need to make a short stop at the hospital on my way back home,' I babble.

'I hated you so much.' Alex finally speaks but doesn't let go of my hand. His eyes are now trained on my battered knuckles, his shoulders lift and fall with deep breaths.

'I didn't know that you saw us that day, and I didn't know about your dad,' he says heavily. 'After, all I wanted to do was to tell you, but then I saw you with that boy.' He drops my hand and pinches the bridge of his nose for a moment like this conversation is causing him pain. 'It confirmed all the things that Vicky made me believe about myself. That I was unimportant and worthless, and you could do so much better. I knew logically that you didn't do anything wrong because you broke up with me the day before but… God, I hated you for it for years, and then you came back into my life.' He's silent for a full minute. The bag of peas slips from my hand onto the carpet. 'I told myself you were a different person, and it wasn't fair to compare you to the person you used to be. I convinced myself that I would be fair and impartial, but I know I was the opposite and made things hard for you. I'm the one who should be apologising.' He slumps against the back of the sofa, dispirited.

I crave his touch, but I feel that's the last thing he wants right now. 'Alex, what I did ten years ago was awful. The only reason I broke up with you was that I worried you were seeing someone else because Vicky made me believe it. You were so distant at times.'

He studies me, and I try not to fidget under his gaze. 'I kept you at arm's length on purpose. I was terrified that you would realise what a screw-up I was. I put you on a pedestal. You were so perfect and *clean*.'

I can't help myself and utter, 'Thank you. I've always prided myself on my personal hygiene.'

His eyebrow arches. 'That's not what I meant, but maybe it is…' He breaks off. 'I meant your life felt uncomplicated and perfect compared to mine. You never had to go to a lesson twenty minutes early so you could snatch a back seat so nobody could smell your smoky clothes. You never had to hide a bottle of vodka from your mum and stash it in your schoolbag because that was the only place she wouldn't look. You never had to pretend it was your bottle so the teacher who found it didn't call social services on your mum. I didn't want to tarnish your life like that.'

I feel suddenly bone-tired. 'Nobody's life is perfect. Everyone's flawed. It's not fair to put somebody in that position. It's not an easy place to be and far to fall if they disappoint you.' I shuffle in my seat but don't make a move to touch him.

'I know that now. Trust me,' he says with bitterness, and his focus shifts to his hands gripping the armrest. 'If I had been more open, maybe you would have told me about your dad and things would have turned out differently.' He sounds self-deprecating. 'I should have been honest, and I should have told you things about myself. My mum wasn't always an alcoholic, you know.'

His voice takes on a strange vulnerable quality. 'She used to be a decent mum until my dad died when I was ten. Then the drinking started, and she couldn't hold down a job for more than a month. We had to move out, and then we moved to that atrocious flat.' His tone turns bitter. 'Quickly, I became a carer. I did all the shopping and cleaning. I made sure that the bills got paid. I even got a part-time job at Tesco. I had no time or desire to think about girls.' He pauses. 'I knew that Vicky was always on the outskirts, but I never liked her. Then I noticed you, and I was undone. I was a mess, and so when you noticed me and even liked me back, I couldn't understand why. When we started dating, I tried to keep it together and look like I was cool. I pretended I wasn't a screw-up. But Vicky never stopped following me. She became persistent, turning up at places I went to, messaging me and calling me late at night. She told me I was nothing, that I was worthless, and that eventually you'd get bored of me. My worst nightmares were confirmed when you messaged me that things weren't working out.' He averts his gaze in shame.

'I spoke to Vicky. I know what happened at the party,' I admit.

He nods towards my knuckles. 'Spoke to her? Is that what you call it?' For the first time, there's a ghost of a smile on his lips, but it disappears in a flash. 'She came to apologise earlier. It's turned out we're all screwed up one way or another.' He laughs humourlessly. 'To her credit, she didn't realise I wasn't a consenting party until I pushed her away. But it didn't stop her from threatening me after and warning me if I ever told you she'd deny it and say that I forced her.' My stomach twists in disgust.

I will myself to be brave.

'I never thought you were worthless. You're the best thing that has happened to me.'

'You say that even after the way I have behaved to you these last few months?' Disbelief fills his eyes. 'I knew that you got a job at the school. Jane spoke to me straight after she decided to employ you. I convinced myself I was OK and that you didn't mean anything to me any more.' He clears his throat loudly. 'That is until you walked into the classroom following John, and I knew that I wasn't OK.'

'At least you were better prepared than I was. Imagine my shock seeing you there and then finding out you were also my mentor.'

'I asked to be your mentor,' he rushes out, stunning me.

'Why?' I hold my breath.

He moves in his seat but doesn't breach the distance between us. 'I'm not sure. I convinced myself that I needed to keep an eye on you. I was so resentful and thought you were a spoilt brat, and then I heard you on the phone with Catherine talking about your life. I felt miserable about the way I spoke to you but not miserable enough to stop being unfair to you.

'I was convinced you were sleeping with John,' he confesses, his cheeks colouring in mortification.

I can't stand the distance between us and hesitantly take one of his hands in mine, hissing at the pain that shoots through my knuckles.

A moment later he rears back, and my hand slips from his with the movement, breaking the precious contact. Dread takes over. Maybe I haven't read the situation right. I feel sore on the inside, like all my organs are bruised.

'Was any of it real between us? Or were you just trying to prove something to yourself?' I must know. His face is tilted away, and I take that for an answer. I ready myself to go.

'Holly,' he rasps and grabs my cheeks with heart-shattering gentleness, his hands warm against my chilled skin. I lean into the touch like a sunflower to the sun. 'I'm a mess. I have control issues and I'm a miserable person to be around.'

'That's not what I asked you,' I whisper, unable to focus with him this close. 'I find it hard to trust people, and I can be withdrawn at times. Who doesn't have issues, Alex?' He's about to pull away, but I clamp my hands over his to keep him in place. 'Let's not misunderstand each other again. I've never been interested in John because I've never wanted anyone but you, despite my best efforts at times.' My breathing is harsh, but I push through. 'You said you wanted me. Does that still stand?'

He nods slowly, and if I were standing, my knees would have buckled underneath me in relief.

'Ever since you walked back into my life, I have felt angry and resentful, but I have never stopped loving you, Holly. I loved you even when I hated you.'

'As confessions go, this one is an awful one.' I'm choked with tears and laughter.

'I've always been better at actions than words,' he quips, and I have to agree with him on this one.

He bends his head towards me and pauses. Tentatively, he

meets my lips and fireworks go off in my belly. He pulls me closer, and I end up sitting in his lap, his arms circling around my waist and back. I wrap my arms around his shoulders and neck. I hiss as pain shoots through my hand, and he pulls away, his eyes so close to mine, I feel like I'm drowning in their green pits.

'What exactly happened to your hand?' His lips are an inch away, and I want to kiss them again, and so I do because I can now. I never want to stop kissing them.

'I punched Vicky in the face,' I confess in between kisses.

'Oh,' is all he says and kisses me again, immediately deepening the kiss until we're both breathless.

When we pull away, he confesses, 'I like you wearing my clothes.'

'Wouldn't you rather I didn't wear any clothes?' I ask and immediately feel embarrassed because I didn't mean to say that out loud. He laughs, his chest rumbling against mine. A shadow passes across his features, and I stroke his arm. 'We can go slow. We've got time; I'm not going anywhere. In fact, the only way you can get rid of me at this point is a restraining order.' I try to lighten the atmosphere.

'Holly,' he says hoarsely and stands with me in his arms, one hand under my knees and the other behind my back. I make a strange *whoop* sound of surprise as he carries me to what I assume is his bedroom. 'I've waited ten years for this. Trust me, I don't want to go slow.'

I make a relieved sound. 'I'm glad to hear that.'

His bedroom is like the rest of his flat, light and cosy. When he deposits me gently on the bed, I stretch like a cat because it's the softest bed I've ever been on. He just watches me with amusement.

I spread my arms wide, my fingers skimming across the smooth silk of the bedding. 'What? You've seen my flat. Your place is amazing, I want to stay in this bed forever.'

'That can be arranged. I'll speak to Jane on Monday.' He smirks, and I can't stop the laugh from forcing itself out.

He pulls his T-shirt over his head and my breath gets stuck in my lungs at the wide expanse of his freckled skin. He self-consciously climbs on the bed and stretches over me. The weight of his body settles against my frame, and I anchor my hands on his hips.

He kisses me again, his hands exploring my body through the T-shirt. At first, the curve of my shoulder, then the indent in my hip, and finally, the roundness of my breasts. Before long, I'm panting shamelessly.

'Not that I don't like you in my T-shirt but is it OK if I take it off?' he asks in between kisses. I nod and anticipation and nervousness tighten my stomach because I'm not wearing a bra underneath it. What if he's disappointed? What if I don't look the way he imagined me all these years?

He slowly peels off the T-shirt like he can sense my nervousness, and when I end up naked to the waist underneath him, he presses his lips together like he's trying to compose himself. Immediately, he kisses my left breast and then moves to the right. His lips are warm and my sensitive skin puckers as he explores every centimetre of it. When he nips me, I shiver and arch against him. He moves to my collarbone while his hands replace his mouth. I can't stop writhing underneath him because it's too much, and yet, not enough.

He takes his jeans off, and my shorts follow. Then he slides my underwear off, and I'm completely naked underneath him, but he's still wearing boxers. Reverently, I explore his back and his powerful thighs, but I need more. I pause at the band of his boxers.

I don't want to get it wrong this time. I'm scared to hurt him.

Unaware of my fear, he pulls me closer while his hand draws torturously slow circles between my legs. I can feel every part of him against me. I know he wants me, but I'm scared if I go too fast, he'll freak out.

'What can I do? I don't want to do things wrong,' I whisper, my hand still hovering at the elastic band of his boxers.

'I want you to touch me. I trust you,' he whispers back, and so after some hesitation, I pull his boxers down. Then we're completely naked, and it's everything I always thought it would be and more.

He pauses as I reach between our bodies. The feel of him almost undoes me. His gaze is serious and dark. But he doesn't look hesitant, and all I see is want and love.

'I love you,' I rasp, and he kisses me fiercely. He whispers *I love you* into my ear, my hair and into my skin so many times it makes me dizzy. I don't think I'll ever tire of hearing it.

We touch and stroke, and it's so perfect, I think it can't get any more perfect, but it does. He reaches into the bedside table and takes a condom out of it. We go slowly at first and then fast when we lose control, moving together like we've done this a hundred times. Our bodies are in sync, our limbs entwined. Eventually, tension builds in my body, but this time I'm not scared to let go. When I do, it's the best feeling in the world.

After, we lie in bed, panting and content. My body is languid and warm everywhere Alex is touching it. He wraps his arms around me and pulls me even closer.

Still breathless, Alex says into my ear, 'It was definitely worth the wait.' He rolls on top of me and gazes at me with a mock-serious expression. 'Maybe we should wait another ten years.'

I push against his chest playfully, but he tightens his arms around me. There's nowhere else I'd rather be now. 'Sorry, I can't let you go. You're stuck with me,' he says as he leans down and gently kisses me.

But I'm OK with that. After all, we have ten years of catching up to do.